HOLIDAY HA HA HA!

HOLIDAY HA HA HA!

Super silly stories by...

David Solomons! Joanna Nadin!
Candy Harper! Jonathan Meres!
Steven Butler! Jeremy Strong!
Steve Cole! William Sutcliffe!

Simon & Schuster

First published in Great Britain in 2016 by Simon & Schuster UK Ltd
A CBS COMPANY

1 3 5 7 9 10 8 6 4 2

Simon & Schuster UK Ltd
1st Floor
222 Gray's Inn Road
London WC1X 8HB

www.simonandschuster.co.uk

Simon & Schuster Australia, Sydney
Simon & Schuster India, New Delhi

A CIP catalogue record for this book
is available from the British Library.

PB ISBN 978-1-4711-4622-0
eBook ISBN 978-1-4711-4623-7

Contents

BETTER THAN PEANUT BUTTER

CANDY HARPER

MONDAY

It was the first day of the holidays. Some kids love doing crazy new things in the summer. My best friend, Josh, was going to learn to windsurf, and my next-door neighbour, Rhys, was going to stay in a yurt halfway up a mountain. But I wasn't interested in that stuff; I had no plans to do anything new this holiday and I was really pleased about that. Instead, I would spend my time doing all the things that I already knew I liked, starting with eating peanut butter sandwiches while watching every episode of my top TV programme, *Silver and Gold*, featuring ace detective Sam Silver and his sniffer dog Goldie. Absolutely no dangerous sports or visiting any strange new places with weird food for me. Just relaxing with all my favourite familiar things.

At least that's what I'd thought.

3

'You'd better get packing, Daniel,' my mum said, as she barged into my room. 'We've got to leave early tomorrow morning.'

'Where are we going?' I asked.

Mum started pulling clothes out of my wardrobe and piling them on my bed.

'Don't pull that surprised face at me. I told you about this weeks ago. Tomorrow, your dad and I are going to France to your cousin Louise's wedding and you and Simone are going to stay with Great Granny on her farm for the week. Now pack your bag.'

Mum stomped out of the room. Unbelievable! Why was *she* so grumpy? I was the one being sent away. Right at the beginning of the holidays, too. I would miss Josh's birthday and his swimming party. Also, David Chaplin, the most annoying boy in the school, had challenged me to a battle on my favourite computer game, *Vampire Vengeance*, in ten days' time and I really needed to practise. This was the worst possible time for me to go away. Why hadn't Mum warned me properly? I sort of remembered her saying something about a wedding, but I'd thought it was weeks away. Why would anyone spoil the start of the holidays by visiting people?

I flopped back on my bed. I'd never been to the farm and I hadn't seen Great Granny since I was a baby. My mum is always saying that I should try new things because I might be pleasantly surprised, but I don't like going to new places, and I especially don't like eating at other people's houses;

they eat weird vegetables instead of nice things, like peanut butter sandwiches. It didn't matter what Mum said, I already knew what this holiday would be like: the food would be disgusting, the farm would be stinky and boring and so would Great Granny.

I packed my stupid bag, (just to be on the safe side I put in a jar of peanut butter), and then I spent the rest of the afternoon eating and trying to work out how to get out of going. After three packets of crisps and seven biscuits, I decided the best idea would be to go on a hunger strike. No munching for me. Not a thing. I used all my willpower and I stuck to my strike.

Then my sister Simone yelled up the stairs, 'DINNER TIME, MONKEY FACE!'

The smell of the shepherd's pie was too tempting. I thought maybe I'd go on hunger strike after I'd had pudding.

At the table Mum said, 'Daniel, you won't need all those computer games you've packed, so I've taken them out of your bag.'

I dropped my fork. This was terrible. 'I do need them!' I said. 'I've got to play *Vampire Vengeance* every day.'

It was bad enough when I thought that my practising might get interrupted by Great Granny, but if I couldn't play at all, there was no way I'd be able to beat David. 'I have to take them with me,' I said.

Mum ignored me. She's a bit rude like that.

'Why can't I take them?' I asked.

5

Mum sighed. 'It's only for a week. You've got the rest of the holidays to stare at a computer screen. Besides, you need the room in your bag for really essential things.'

'What essential things? There's nothing more essential than computer games. What could I possibly need more?'

'Clean pants,' Mum said.

Simone laughed. 'He'd rather keep his games and have a smelly behind!'

I threw a pea at her. 'I could take pants *and* computer games. How much room can pants take up?'

'Yours could fill a suitcase,' Simone said. 'They have to be big to cover your ginormous bum.'

'That's enough, Simone,' Dad said. 'Daniel, there's no point in taking those games, Great Granny doesn't have a computer.'

I nearly spat out my shepherd's pie. 'How can anyone not have a computer?'

'Great Granny hasn't,' Dad said.

'But how does she live? How does she do her shopping?'

'Some people still like to do their shopping in shops,' Mum said.

'How does she send emails? Or play games? Or look up stuff about animals? Or find out what's on telly? Or … or have any fun at all?'

'Calm down,' Dad said. 'Life without a computer can be quite jolly. You'll find out how much fun you can have on a farm.'

My parents are always trying to persuade me to do things that they say will be 'fun' or 'jolly' or 'a good experience' but it usually involves eating something disgusting or going somewhere new where I don't know anyone. I like things to be the same. I like knowing exactly what I'm going to do and what it will be like.

'I don't want to do anything "jolly" and you can't make me,' I said.

Dad didn't say anything, but he raised his eyebrows. This is Dad sign language for 'we'll see about that'. I was losing the battle. 'I'm not going,' I tried again.

'You are,' Mum said. She's a bit childish as well as rude.

I thought that if I was going to lose then I ought to get something out of it. 'I'll go if you give me a dog,' I said.

Mum tutted.

'You're the one who says I should try new things.'

'I meant drama club, and clean finger nails and broccoli.'

'I thought you said that good behaviour was always rewarded.'

Mum looked at Dad.

Dad said, 'It is, but it doesn't work like that. You can't make deals. You'll be rewarded when you're not expecting it.'

'All right, I'll act really surprised when you bring the dog in.'

'You are *not* getting a dog.'

'Just think about it for a minute. If you gave me an animal

7

whenever you wanted me to do something, imagine how well behaved I'd be! It doesn't have to be a dog every time. Small jobs could be a guinea pig or a rabbit, maybe a mouse for cleaning my teeth.'

Mum shook her head. 'I'm not talking about this any more. You're going to the farm and that's final. You know, there might even be a dog there.'

I did like the idea of a dog. But it didn't make up for the fact that they were leaving me with an old lady I couldn't remember, who would probably make me do things I didn't like.

Mum thought she'd found a way to get me interested.

'There'll be lots of other animals for you to play with too.'

'But I don't want weird animals with horns and feathers and stuff. I just want a pet. I don't like the kind of animals that smell bad and make funny noises.'

'Neither do I,' Simone said. 'But Mum still makes me spend time with you.'

'If you bought me a dog then I would promise not to wallop Simone when she says horrible things,' I said.

'I'm not buying you a pet because you're not ready for the responsibility,' Mum said. 'I can't trust you to remember your PE kit, let alone to feed an animal. And who is going to walk a dog? I can never get you out of the house even on a sunny day.'

'That's because all the good stuff is indoors. If you'd buy

me an iPad I could watch episodes of *Silver and Gold* and walk the dog at the same time.'

'You've watched that dumb series a million times,' Simone said.

'But I'd be watching it and getting some exercise.'

'That's not the point,' Mum said.

'Don't start trying to explain the point to him,' Dad said to Mum. 'Daniel never gets the point unless you take the point and poke him in the eye with it.'

I thought that was a bit unfair. Just because I don't always understand what people are going on about. This was exactly the reason they shouldn't be sending me off to stay with a stranger.

'We haven't got time for any more explaining,' Dad said to Mum. 'You need to pack. Last time you packed it took longer than the holiday itself.'

So Mum went upstairs and Dad said, 'Right, Daniel, it's your turn to clear the table.'

'What will you give me for it?' I asked.

'Nothing,' Dad said. 'Just get on with it.'

'Oh, come on, it's got to be worth at least a goldfish.'

'You can have this,' he said.

And he threw a pea at me.

After I'd washed up, I went to my room and stared at the case for *Vampire Vengeance* on my desk. If David Chaplin beat me, I would never hear the end of it. I wished Mum and Dad could understand that all I wanted was to be left alone to play it, instead of being stranded in the middle of the countryside, where I just knew everyone would be super boring and talk about the weather and growing vegetables. I sat on my bed and screwed up my face in concentration. What I needed was an idea; I would stay here until I had come up with a brilliant plan like the kind that detective Sam Silver would think of. Something so clever that it would get me out of going to the farm.

TUESDAY

When I got up the next morning, I still hadn't thought of anything even a tiny bit brilliant, so I decided I'd lock myself in the bathroom.

The thing about our bathroom is that it's downstairs, past the kitchen. Everybody else was upstairs so no one noticed I was in there for a long time. I heard Dad stomping about shouting, 'Where are my socks? Who's had my socks?' Which is a joke because the last thing anyone would want to steal is Dad's cheesy socks. Mum and Simone were having an argument. Mum said, 'Simone, every single item of clothing in your bag is black.'

Simone made this huffy noise and said, 'So?'

And that was the end of the argument.

I started casually whistling, hoping that Mum would hear. She didn't. I tried drumming a solo on the back of the door with a tube of toothpaste and the loo brush. Still nobody came. I ended up singing *The Grand Old Duke of York* using a toilet roll like a megaphone and finally Mum knocked on the door.

'Are you all right, Daniel?'

'No,' I said.

'Are you having trouble trying to do a poo again?'

'No, I am not!'

'Because all that noise sounded like you've got constipation.'

Which is pretty much what Mrs Murphy said when my mum made me audition for the school choir.

'I am not having toilet trouble!'

'Well, if you haven't got a problem, you need to get a move on.'

'No!' I said.

Mum made a noise like a camel snorting.

'What's the matter now?' I heard Dad say.

'Your son is locked in the bathroom.'

Mum always says 'your son' to Dad when she thinks I'm being difficult.

'I'm not coming out,' I said.

'What, ever?' Dad asked.

'Never.'

'You'll miss your birthday. And Christmas. We'd only be able to get you really flat presents that we could post under the door. Like writing paper and a road map. You wouldn't like that, would you?'

I pretended to not be listening.

11

'What will you eat and drink?'

'There's lots of water,' I said. 'And I can eat . . .' I looked around the bathroom. 'There are some mints in the cabinet.'

'I wouldn't eat those if I were you. They've been there since before you were born.'

I rummaged around in between the bottles of shampoo and the tubes of cream.

'There's a packet of pills that look like chocolates.'

'Don't eat them!' Mum squealed. 'You know you mustn't take pills you find.'

'If you eat those, Daniel, you'll be pooping like a carthorse and then you really won't be able to come out of the bathroom.' Dad chuckled like everything was fine. 'Come on, son, out you come. Time we all got in the car.'

I clenched my fists. 'I am not coming out. I am not leaving all my best things behind. I am not missing Josh's party. I am not going to spend a week with a great granny I don't even know. AND I AM NOT GETTING IN THE CAR.'

I ended up in the car.

We'd been driving all morning when I remembered Sam Silver saying that there's always an alternative, and suddenly I thought of an alternative for me.

'Can I come to the wedding instead of going to the farm?' I asked.

'They don't want children there,' Mum said.

'Why not? What's wrong with children?'

'Everything,' Dad said.

'Your cousin Louise doesn't want any interruptions during the service.'

'But I'm not a baby. I'm not going to just start crying.'

'You cried when Dad made you go canoeing,' Simone said.

'That was last year! And canoeing is stupid anyway.'

'You cried when you had that dream about the giant spider,' she went on.

'That was ages ago.'

'You cried when I ate the last of the Chocolate Crispies.'

'That was—'

'This morning! Ha!'

I whacked Simone over the head. She punched me on the shoulder.

'Stop it!' snapped Mum. 'That's exactly the kind of behaviour Louise doesn't want in the church.'

'I know how to behave in a church,' I said.

Simone snorted. 'What about that time we went to the Christmas carol service and we got to the quiet bit where everyone was kneeling down and you farted really loudly.'

'That wasn't my fault! Mum forced me to eat those Brussels sprouts for lunch.'

'Anyway,' Mum interrupted. 'The point is that Louise wants a nice, sophisticated grown-up wedding. I'll bring you back a piece of wedding cake.'

'Couldn't you bring me back a puppy instead?' I asked.

'Not unless they're serving them for pudding,' Dad said.

We stopped at a service station for lunch and then it was

back into the hot, sticky car. Hours later, Mum said, 'We're nearly there now.'

I looked out of the window. All I could see was green. Nothing good is green. Cabbage and slime and bogeys are green. We were right in the middle of a big green nowhere.

We turned off the proper road and went down a bumpy track. We pulled through a metal gate and Mum stopped the car. Behind us was a huge barn-type thing. In front of us was a crumbly old house, beyond that were great big hills. Just hills and trees and fields.

Terrible.

I stumbled out of the car. My left foot had gone to sleep. I looked up at the white house with its thatched roof. There was a creak as the front door swung open.

'Granny!' Mum said, stretching out her arms to a tiny old lady who was making her way towards us, leaning on a stick with a carved top in the shape of a snake. She smacked Mum's arms out of the way.

'Don't call me Granny,' she snapped. 'It makes me sound old.'

Personally, I thought there were plenty of other things making her seem old. Like her white hair, the millions of wrinkles and the fact that she must be about a hundred and three. But Mum just said, 'Oh. What would you like me to call you?'

'Scarlett, you can call me Scarlett.'

Mum stared at her. 'But your name is Ethel.'

'Exactly. Darn good reason for you all to call me Scarlett.' She roared with laughter.

She was crazy. I knew she would be. Perhaps she would be too busy doing mad old lady things to make me go outside with all that mud and the scary, stampy animals. Maybe she wouldn't notice if I stayed in bed all day, reading the single *Silver and Gold* book I'd smuggled in my bag.

'Who are these two donkeys?' Scarlett asked. She pointed at me and Simone.

'They're your great-grandchildren, Daniel and Simone.'

Scarlett sniffed. 'When I decided I'd had enough of travelling the world, I chose this farm because it's so remote, but the relatives keep finding me. I knew I should have bought that hut in the mountains.' She looked at me accusingly. 'Relatives coming out of my ears.'

I looked at her ears. The only things coming out of them were bristly hairs.

Mum put on the face she uses when she's explaining my maths homework. She was trying to be nice, but really she was annoyed with Great Granny. 'I know you like your peace and quiet, but you have remembered, haven't you? You agreed that Daniel and Simone could stay for a week.'

'Oh, yes, yes. They can stay if they must. Plenty of room in the pig pen.'

*

15

It turned out that Great Granny, I mean, Scarlett, was only joking about me and Simone sleeping in the pig pen because after Mum and Dad had scarpered without even apologising for making me miss Josh's party and ruining my chances of beating David Chaplin, Scarlett took me to my real room at the top of the house.

'Your brother has got the room downstairs. You didn't want to share with Simon, did you?'

'No, thank you. I'm sure *Simon*,' I sniggered, 'would prefer his own room.'

I felt a bit better. If mad old Scarlett was going to wind up Simone by calling her Simon maybe this trip wouldn't be a complete waste of time.

We went downstairs and sat at the big wooden table in the kitchen. At least, I nearly sat down, but there was a terrible yowling sound coming from my chair and I don't like to put my bottom on anything that makes a noise.

'It's only the cat, she's having kittens soon and it's making her cross. Children have that effect,' Scarlett said. 'Say hello, Flea-bitten.'

Flea-bitten seemed like an unkind name for a cat until you got a good look at her. Then it seemed like a very suitable name. Flea-bitten and I had a staring contest to see who got the chair. She didn't exactly win; I just decided I'd rather stand up anyway.

Simone stroked Flea-bitten. 'Who looks after all the animals?' she asked Scarlett.

'I have a farmer who runs this place,' Scarlett said. 'And his wife does the cooking, but they've gone to visit their daughter today. She's just had another baby. I don't know why – the last one looked like a potato.' She sighed. 'You'll meet them tomorrow. I mean my farmer and his wife. Not the potato babies.'

I put my head in my hands. The last thing my mum had said to me was that this holiday would be an adventure. I'm not a very adventure-y type of person, but if I was going to have an adventure I'd rather that it was a mystery-solving sort, and what kind of mystery could there possibly be on a stinky farm with a batty old lady and a farmer with potatoey grandchildren?

Scarlett made beetroot sandwiches for her and Simone, but I had cheese instead, and then I was so tired and fed up that I thought I'd go to bed. I'd put one foot on the stairs before I heard Scarlett talking on the telephone in one of the rooms off the hall.

'You'd better make the delivery late on Friday when the nosy parkers are in bed.'

There was a pause while Scarlett listened to the other person. 'Don't worry about that,' Scarlett cackled. 'I'll make sure I finish them off.'

What was she talking about? I could hear the theme tune to *Silver and Gold* in my head. Sam Silver says you learn the most by listening to what people don't want you to hear, and Scarlett was definitely whispering secret plans on the phone.

17

Maybe I'd been wrong to think that all old ladies are boring. This old lady was definitely a little bit mysterious.

I couldn't wait to do some sleuthing.

WEDNESDAY

I woke early and couldn't get back to sleep. I sat up in bed and looked out of the window at the drooping roof of the barn, and wondered about Scarlett. What was that phone call about? Maybe she was the head of a criminal gang. Maybe they used her room as their headquarters and inside she was storing lots of stolen goods like bottles of whiskey and cases of cigars. She would make a good gang leader. She was very bossy. I decided to search the house before anyone else was up.

I tiptoed down the two lots of stairs so I could begin at the bottom of the house. The kitchen was very neat and tidy with a cooker and cupboards and a table with a red and white checked cloth on it; nothing suspicious there. A door off the kitchen led to a utility room with a row of muddy boots by the back door. Propped in one corner was a shovel. I inspected it. It was the sort of thing that would be excellent for whacking someone around the head with. But there were no blood stains on it so I put it back.

The dining room had a huge polished table with twelve chairs around it, and a dresser full of china, but no evidence of criminal activity. The sitting room was crammed with two saggy sofas and three ancient armchairs, all crowded around the fireplace. And above the fireplace hung ... a gun! One of those long pointy ones. I looked closely at it, but I couldn't see any signs of recent use.

The last room on the ground floor was a study. The desk was swamped in official-looking letters. I picked up one that was stamped with the logo of a bank I'd seen adverts for on TV. There were some very large numbers with pound signs in front of them printed on the paper. Was Scarlett super rich? How did an old lady get so much money? She wasn't really a gangster, was she?

Someone was moving about above me. I decided I'd have to leave exploring upstairs till everyone was safely out of the way. Anyway, I needed to use the loo before breakfast.

Simone was standing outside the bathroom wearing black pyjamas and black and green stripy socks.

'What are you doing?' I whispered.

'I'm waiting.'

'Who's in there?' I said, pointing to the bathroom door.

'Must be Scarlett.'

The floorboards squeaked behind me. I turned round and there was Scarlett. She was wearing a red silk dressing gown with a dragon embroidered on it. It was far too long for her.

'What must be Scarlett?' Scarlett asked.

'In the bathroom,' I said.

Scarlett shook her head and turned to Simone. 'Is the little one a bit slow?' she asked.

'Hey!' I said. 'I'm not little!'

Scarlett opened her mouth to carry on, but then I thought of something else.

'Wait a minute, I'm not slow either!'

'Well, you're not quick,' Scarlett said. 'I'm not in the bathroom. *I'm here.*'

'If you're here, who's in the bathroom?' Simone asked.

The bathroom door clicked open and a very large hairy man wrapped in a very small towel came out.

'Morning, all,' he said and walked off down the passage.

'Who was that?' I asked.

'Farmer Gareth,' said Scarlett.

Farmer Gareth and his wife had got back from visiting the potato baby after I'd gone to bed. While I was still gawping after him, Simone nipped into the bathroom. I had to hop up and down the landing because I really needed to go now. When Simone finally came out Scarlett pushed past me.

'I was first!' I said.

'You left the queue,' Scarlett said smugly. 'You didn't even ask me to save your place.'

By this time I had to wrap one leg around the other and twist from side to side to not wet myself. Farmer Gareth came out of one of the bedrooms wearing the biggest pair of dungarees I had ever seen in my life. He looked at me twirling about and said, 'That's a nice dance, lad. You take ballet lessons?'

Before I could tell him that actually I completely refuse to do any kind of dancing and my name wasn't Lad, he had gone downstairs whistling *Jingle Bells* and the bathroom door was finally opening. I got to the loo just in time.

When I was washing my hands, something in the mirror caught my eye.

Hundreds of black somethings all over the bottom of the bath.

Spiders!

I shot out of the room. Simone was carrying a cup of tea up the stairs.

'Simone! Didn't you see in the bath? It's full of spiders!'

'Cool. Let's see.' And she actually put down her cup of tea on a bookshelf and went into the bathroom.

That's how weird my sister is. That's what I have to put up with every day. If I had said, 'Simone, there are snakes in your sock drawer and a lizard is trying on your pants!' She probably still would have come running.

I stood outside the bathroom at a safe distance. Inside, Simone giggled, which was too weird even for my bug-loving sister. I peered round the door.

'Daniel!' She hiccupped with laughter. 'They're not spiders.'

I had a closer look. All the black spikey bits that I had thought were legs turned out to be ... hairs. 'Where did they come from?' I asked.

'I'm guessing Farmer Gareth's back.'

I gave a shudder.

'Don't tell me you're afraid of hairs as well as spiders?'

'I'm not afraid of spiders,' I said. 'I was just a bit surprised to see a whole . . . *herd* of them.'

'You're not afraid of spiders?'

'No.'

'You won't mind that one crawling up your neck then.'

I think it's fair enough that while I was swatting away the made-up spider, I 'accidentally' whacked Simone on the nose.

I was looking forward to breakfast. I knew exactly what Farmer Gareth's wife would be like because there was a farmer's wife in one of my *Silver and Gold* books. I was sure she'd be plump and jolly and a really good cook, the kind that makes cakes and pies. There were bound to be bacon and eggs for breakfast.

Down in the kitchen Simone and Scarlett were already at the table. Farmer Gareth's wife was standing by the cooker. But she wasn't plump, she was short and slim. She smiled at me. 'You must be Daniel. I'm Jill.'

I nodded but didn't manage to smile back. She wasn't at all cosy-looking. And she was wearing a mini dress instead of an apron.

'Just making the breakfast now,' she said.

I looked about for the bacon and eggs, but there weren't any. Instead she spooned out natural yogurt with fruit and muesli.

22

'I don't really like those things,' I said.

'Daniel only eats the same stuff over and over again,' Simone said.

'I just like my favourites,' I explained. 'Don't worry, I brought some with me.' And I ran upstairs to fetch the jar of peanut butter I'd packed in my bag.

Simone and the others ate the yucky muesli while I had toast. I was happy with that; even bacon and eggs can't beat peanut butter on toast.

'What are you going to do today?' Jill asked me.

I shrugged. 'I was supposed to be going to a swimming party tomorrow. Is there a pool around here?'

'No. We've got a pond. You could swim in that.'

I didn't much fancy swimming in a pond. It sounded cold and mucky.

Simone shuddered. She doesn't like doing anything that involves removing her fifty-seven layers of black jumpers.

'You could take a look around the farm,' Jill said, stacking dishes in the sink.

'No, thanks. I think I'll just watch TV,' I said.

'There isn't a TV.'

Simone fell off her chair.

I dropped the milk jug.

'Not to worry,' said Jill. 'There are the animals to feed, the river to see, the woods to explore. And if it rains you've got a barn to make a racket in.'

I looked at Simone.

23

Simone looked at me.

I put my head on the table and moaned, 'What are we going to do all week?'

After I'd got my strength back by having a final piece of toast, I went outside and found Farmer Gareth.

'Have you got a dog?' I asked.

'Yep,' said Farmer Gareth. He whistled. 'Come here, Lollipop!' he called.

Lollipop sounded like a nice friendly dog. Maybe he'd enjoy helping me solve crimes.

Lollipop came around the corner.

'*Ah-rah-rah-rah-rah*!' he barked and snapped his teeth at my thighs.

I took a step backwards. Lollipop took a step forward.

'He's keen on you,' Farmer Gareth said.

I thought the only thing Lollipop seemed keen on was getting a bite of my bottom, but I said, 'Do you think he'd be interested in some detective work?'

'He's already got a job, I'm afraid. How about Blackberry?' He pointed to the pony in the stables. 'She'd make a fine sidekick.'

I shook my head. Who ever heard of a detecting pony?

The sky had clouded over and it was spitting with rain so I decided that now everyone else was busy, I could take a look around the upstairs rooms. Even if I didn't find anything suspicious maybe there was a laptop somewhere.

The only interesting thing in the bathroom was that the medicine cabinet was stuffed with pill bottles. In some of the *Silver and Gold* stories, criminals use pills to drug their victims. Simone's room only had a bed and a wardrobe and a nasty smell of Simone's perfume, and I didn't like to poke about too much in Gareth and Jill's room, but everything seemed ordinary enough.

Scarlett's room was right at the end of the passage. The door was closed. I looked over my shoulder and reached for the door handle ... it was locked! Why would she keep her door locked? Sam Silver says locked doors hide guilty secrets.

'What are you up to?'

I jumped. It was Jill with a feather duster.

'I'm just exploring,' I said.

'Don't go exploring in there. That's Scarlett's room. She doesn't like people touching her things.'

'Doesn't she ever open the door?'

'I reckon she must do to get in and out, mustn't she? But I've never seen inside. Not even to clean. Don't think it's been dusted in there for many a year.'

I trudged back to the sitting room where Simone was making a tower out of playing cards. It was pretty good. She'd leaned pairs of cards together and then cards flat across the top. There were four layers of the tower.

'I didn't know you could do that,' I said.

She raised an eyebrow. 'I'm very talented.' She picked up

25

a roll of sticky tape from the coffee table and bit a piece off, then stuck on another card.

'That's cheating!' I said

'Yep, that's what I'm talented at.' She picked up the whole tower and put it on my head. 'I'm bored,' she said. 'I'm so bored that I'm even talking to you.'

By lunchtime I'd already read half of the only *Silver and Gold* book I had with me. This was what I had been afraid of. None of my favourite books to read, or shows to watch. And no computer to brush up my skills before I had to battle with David Chaplin next week. I couldn't believe my parents had done this to me.

It was mushed up vegetables and something called couscous for lunch. I didn't like the look of it so I had a peanut butter sandwich instead. You can't beat peanut butter. When we'd finished, Scarlett said, 'You can take me for my afternoon walk.' She was looking in my direction. I hoped she was talking to someone behind me, but when I turned around there was only Flea-bitten, and even though Scarlett is tiny I didn't think Flea-bitten could manage giving her a ride.

'Get my chair out,' Scarlett said, and she pointed at the wheelchair under the stairs. Scarlett isn't the sort of person you say no to, so I pulled it out and backed it into the kitchen. I hoped she wasn't going to make me walk a long way. Scarlett picked up her handbag and lowered herself into the wheelchair. I pushed her down the hall and was just about to heave the wheelchair over the front step when she flung her legs out on either side of the door so that I couldn't push any further.

'Stop!' she shrieked.

I thought I must have trapped her finger in the wheel or something. 'What?' I asked. 'What is it?'

'I haven't got my lipstick on!' she said.

I tried to tell her that the sheep weren't going to notice, but she still made me run all the way upstairs to the bathroom. When I handed the lipstick to her, she screwed her lips up to dab on the greasy, orange stuff. Her mouth looked like a cat's bottom with lipstick on it.

'That's better,' she said.

I wasn't sure that it made any difference but I nodded anyway. Scarlett has a way of looking at you that makes your head do whatever she wants it to do.

Once we were outside, Scarlett said I should push her down the lane that leads to the village because it was a smooth surface for the wheels on her chair. When we were halfway down she shouted, 'Stop!' again and made me swing her chair round so that we could look at the view. We could see right across the valley. The cows on the other side of the river were so far away that they looked like toys.

'I could stare at that all day,' Scarlett said. 'Doesn't it make you feel cheerful?'

It was quite nice. Standing at the top looking down on the tiny buildings below us made me feel a bit like a giant.

27

The sun was warm and the breeze was ruffling my hair. 'I'd be happier if I could see a McDonald's,' I said.

'There's more excitement here than you could find in a McDingle's,' she said. 'All sorts happens here. Especially behind closed doors.'

I wondered if she was talking about her own closed bedroom door. 'What sorts of things?' I asked.

'There have been feuds and fights aplenty. And even worse. When I was a girl living in the village there was a shoot-out at this farm. A bank robber had hidden in the barn. There are still bullet holes in the beams.'

My mouth dropped open. 'No way! That's amazing.'

Farmer Gareth came up behind us whistling *Santa Claus is Coming to Town*.

'Come along,' he said to me. 'Flea-bitten's just had her kittens.'

'Now that really is something amazing,' Scarlett said. 'Seeing the start of a life.'

I thought I'd rather see a shoot-out, but since Scarlett said that she wanted to sit a while and smoke her pipe, I decided I might as well go with Farmer Gareth.

I've always thought that cats aren't as good as dogs, but I have to say that Flea-bitten's tiny kittens, all snuggled up in a nest of hay in the barn, were pretty cute. At least they helped pass the time till I could go to bed.

On the way up to my room that night, I tried opening Scarlett's door again, but it was still locked. There was something different though. There was a mark on the door frame. It was a handprint. A red handprint. It couldn't be blood, could it? I remembered Scarlett grinning at the view across the valley. Surely she couldn't be involved in anything nasty? It was about the right size to be Scarlett's handprint and she had looked pretty vicious when Simone tried to take the last piece of apple pie at teatime. I remembered the shovel and the gun; Scarlett certainly had enough weapons if she wanted to hurt someone. She even had pills to drug someone and keep them quiet. But how had it got there? Maybe it was paint. Of course, it must be paint.

One thing was for sure: the farm wasn't nearly as boring as I'd thought it would be.

THURSDAY

As I went downstairs next morning, Jill was cleaning the landing window. I crept up behind her. The handprint on the frame of Scarlett's door was gone. I looked at Jill, who was polishing the window with a rag, then back at the doorframe. It was suspiciously shiny. Did this mean the whole household was in on whatever Scarlett was up to? I needed to watch out for more clues.

After breakfast, (Jill tried to make me try a kiwi fruit, but I reminded her I only like my favourites and had peanut butter on toast again), I walked along the lane. The sun was already beating down and I was glad I'd put on my shorts. I wondered if David Chaplin was busy practising *Vampire Vengeance*.

Behind the hedge, someone was playing a harmonica and when I went round the bend I saw a boy about the same age as me sitting on the fence. I don't normally like meeting new people because sometimes they're not very nice, but as soon as I saw him, thoughts popped up in my head like bubbles. This boy must have a house, and houses have computers. I could use that computer to play *Vampire Vengeance*, which I had smuggled in my bag under my pants. It was a shame that my head was totally full of those thoughts because when I got close to the boy, he said, 'What's your name?'

And I said, 'Computer!'

'Your name's Computer?' He wrinkled his nose. 'Do your parents not like you?'

'No. I mean, yes.' Then I remembered that it was Mum and Dad who had dumped me in this stupid place. 'Actually, it's hard to tell sometimes,' I said. 'Anyway, what's your name?'

'Brandon.'

Which I thought was even worse than Computer.

'You're new,' Brandon said.

'I'm staying at the farm.' I thought this might be a good time to do some of what Sam Silver calls 'sniffing about'. 'Have you ever seen anything suspicious round here?' I asked.

He thought hard. 'I heard your farmer once had a pig that could play Snap.'

'I meant like mysteries, you know, strange goings on.'

He thought again. His cheeks were starting to get quite pink with the effort.

'There was a lad called Alex. He went to our school. Then he left. Then he went to the big school. Then he worked at your farm.'

'That's nice,' I said. He seemed to have forgotten my question.

'It's not nice. Because he disappeared. I haven't seen him for a month.'

'Maybe he's on holiday.'

'Nope. Because his sister was still at our school right up until we finished on Friday. She can wiggle her ears.'

'That's nice.'

'It's not nice. Our teacher says if she keeps making people laugh with her wiggling ears, when they should be doing their sums, she'll be sent out of the room. To the corridor.'

His voice made it sound like a fate worse than death.

'Is it not nice in the corridor?'

'Extremely not nice. You have to look at all the portraits they've done in art. The eyes glare at you.'

I wanted to get back to the mystery, even though it didn't sound like a very good one, so I said, 'Where do you think Alex disappeared to?'

'Dunno, but I'll tell you what, I heard that old lady at your place—'

'Scarlett?'

'She told me her name was Trixibelle! Anyway, I heard her telling Alex that if he didn't stop eating her strawberries she'd lock him up and throw away the key, or else tie him up and use him for target practice when she's doing her knife throwing.' He squinted at me. 'What do you think about that?'

This was more like it! 'That's very interesting. She could have locked him in her room, couldn't she? And kept him there, although, obviously she'd have to feed him. And if she had thrown a knife at him then he might be bleeding and that would explain the blood, but I wonder . . .' I trailed off.

Brandon was staring at me so hard that I was starting to understand how those kids at his school with the art watching them felt. Then he said, 'Do you want to go swimming in the pond with me, Computer?'

Even though I still wasn't sure about swimming in a mucky pond, I wanted to ask Brandon some more questions, so I said, 'All right then.'

The pond was not at all like the pool where Josh was having his party. The pool has a wave machine and a spiral slide. In a couple of hours' time I would have been shooting down that slide if it hadn't been for my parents dragging me here.

There were no slides or waves at the pond and swimming in it was like getting into a bath of ice-cold water full of bugs and little wriggling things. It was muddy, freezing, covered in pondweed and absolutely . . . brilliant.

When you swim in a pool it's all warm and chloriney, but in the pond it was like taking a bath in nature. I didn't think I'd like it, but actually the cold water and all the splashing about made me feel like my skin was buzzing.

I floated on my back and sculled my hands so that I could turn in a circle and look at the bank. Sam Silver says you should always keep an eye on your surroundings.

'I'm going to be a detective,' I said. 'What about you, Brandon? What do you want to be when you grow up?'

'Old enough to buy fireworks,' he said.

'Yeah, but what job will you do?'

Brandon smiled. 'Firework maker.'

That afternoon, Brandon showed me how to make a pea-shooter out of a plant called Cow Parsley. It was growing at the side of the lane; chunky green stalks with tiny, white frothy flowers on top.

'Find a bit with a good thick stem,' he said, pulling up a piece. 'Then chop a length ...' He got out a penknife and started hacking at the Cow Parsley. 'Hollow, see?'

I peered down the stalk. He was right; it was hollow like a straw.

'Then you get your dried pea ...' He took a pale, hard little thing out of his pocket and pushed it into the stem.

'And ...' He lifted the stalk to his lips and blew.

Thfffpt!

The pea shot out the end and hit me on the forehead.

'That's brilliant!' I said. 'Can I make one?'

33

'All right, but remember it's for peas. Don't go thinking it'll work with the rest of your dinner.' He gave me a stern look. 'Mash isn't any good.'

I imagined Brandon filling his pea-shooter with mash and I started to laugh.

'What about custard?' I asked.

'Terribly messy,' he said.

By the time I got back to the farm it was teatime and I was starving.

'What's this?' I asked, eying my plate suspiciously.

'Jambalaya,' Jill said, fixing me with a steely gaze. 'I know you like your favourites,' she said. 'But you'll never find any new favourites if you don't give something different a go once in a while.'

I thought about that. Imagine if there was something that I liked even more than peanut butter that I haven't found yet. I gave the Jambalaya a go. It wasn't as good as peanut butter.

But it wasn't bad.

After tea, Scarlett went upstairs and Farmer Gareth taught me and Simone how to play poker using chocolate buttons to bet with. When I'd managed to win most of Simone's buttons, I made my sleepy way to my room, but I couldn't resist the temptation of stopping and listening at Scarlett's door.

At first it was quiet and I thought she must be asleep. But then there was a low murmuring. It sounded like people were talking. Who could she be talking to? Maybe she *had* got Alex in there. Maybe she kept him tied up and forced him to listen to her rambling stories.

'Yah!' Scarlett shouted from inside the room. I flinched backwards. The next thing Scarlett said was in a low growl, but I was pretty sure I heard, 'I'll have your head off!' Then there were footsteps moving towards the door so I scarpered off up the stairs before Scarlett could come out and find me.

FRIDAY

I didn't sleep well. I couldn't work it out. I'd thought I knew exactly what Scarlett would be like, but she wasn't the doddery, forgetful old lady I'd been expecting. After everything I'd seen and heard, I was starting to think something odd was going on, but that didn't seem right either. By morning, I was desperate to talk to someone about it. If only there was someone older and smarter than me that I could trust.

But there wasn't anyone.

There was only Simone.

I did my best to explain things to her, but by the time I'd finished she was wearing the 'I don't believe you face' that Mrs Murphy uses when I tell her that I'm too ill to do the maths test.

'So you're saying that you think Scarlett has kidnapped a boy and is keeping him in her room?' she asked.

35

'Not exactly. I just … there are some strange things going on.'

Simone looked at me for a long time. 'Sometimes weird stuff happens. Sometimes people are weird. You can't get freaked out just because someone isn't how you expect them to be.'

'I'm just saying it's not normal.'

'When you think about it, no one is normal. No one is exactly like anyone else.'

I puffed out a sigh.

'I tell you what,' Simone said. 'For the next couple of days, we'll both watch Scarlett. If she's up to anything criminal then we can tell Mum and Dad when they get here on Sunday.'

It was probably the most sensible thing I'd ever heard Simone say. It was almost as if she was trying to be a good sister. I nearly spoiled it by pointing out that she'd got breakfast-egg yolk on her chin. But it didn't seem fair when Simone was being … nice. I had to screw up my face to stop a rude comment slipping out and Simone said, 'Why are you grimacing like that? Have you farted? Gross!'

Which meant everything was back to normal and I could call her 'Eggy Face' as much as I wanted to.

Later, I found Brandon by the pond and I remembered what I'd meant to ask him the day before. 'Have you got a computer?' I asked.

'Yep. But I don't get on it much because my mum uses it for her work.'

'Her work?'

'Yeah, she works from home.'

My mouth dropped open. Imagine your mum hogging the computer like that! I decided to give up on *Vampire Vengeance* for a bit. Instead, we spent the rest of the morning fishing. I'd never tried fishing before but Sam Silver says you have to create opportunities to quiz witnesses and I had more questions for Brandon.

'Has Alex turned up?' I asked, after he'd shown me how to cast my line.

'Nope.'

'Do you think Scarlett might have locked him in her room?'

Brandon's eyes bulged. 'She might've. Once she tried to shut me in the barn when I'd only borrowed hardly any apples out of her orchard.'

When I tell Josh my theories about things that might be mysteries, he doesn't pay much attention, but Brandon listened hard to everything I told him about what I'd heard and how I'd tried to investigate. He even suggested that I searched the barn to see if there was anything suspicious in there. We didn't catch any fish, but I decided that fishing wasn't as boring as I always thought it would be.

After Brandon had gone home for lunch, I managed to make friends with Lollipop. Well, not exactly friends, but he stopped chasing me with his tongue hanging out like I was a walking sausage. I was quite surprised when it got to mid-afternoon and I hadn't even been bored.

Simone called me into the sitting room.

'Got anything to report?' she asked.

'I haven't really had much time to watch her. I did see inside the boot of her car.'

'What was in it?'

'Wellies and a violin case.'

Simone chewed her lip. 'I've noticed that she does a lot of digging in the garden, but I've never seen her actually plant anything.'

'Do you think she's burying something?'

Simone didn't get to answer because Scarlett appeared in the doorway and said, 'Daniel, come down to the meadow with me.'

I froze. I wasn't sure about going out on my own with Scarlett again. What if she got ideas about locking me in somewhere?

'Er . . .' I said. 'What about your chair? Will it be all right in the fields? Isn't it a bit bumpy?'

'Don't you worry about me,' she said, beckoning me to follow her.

I gave Simone a last look, hoping for some help, but she said nothing, so I was forced to follow Scarlett outside.

In one of the sheds, she showed me her mobility scooter. Only this one wasn't like those little rickety ones you see old people going to the shops on. This one was big. It had a strong frame and huge ridged wheels.

She was right. There was no need to worry about her. I just hoped that nothing small and fluffy got in her way.

I trotted along through the fields beside Scarlett for about half an hour. I decided that as long as we were out in the open I was probably safe enough. When we got to the meadow she gave me a rug to lay out.

Scarlett unpacked a flask of tea, some beetroot sandwiches and a cherry cake. She broke the cherry cake in half and gave me one of the huge pieces.

'I've already had lunch,' I said.

'It isn't lunch.'

'It's a bit early for tea, isn't it?'

'It isn't tea.'

'What is it then?'

'It's cake, you prune.'

So I ate my cake and drank my tea. Then I leaned back on my elbows and stared into the woods.

'There are some campers in there,' Scarlett said. 'Do you think you would like to spend a week living in the woods?'

She wasn't thinking of making me sleep in the woods, was she?

'I'm not sure about that,' I said.

'Lovely and fresh when you wake up,' she said. 'Nothing like seeing the very beginning of the day.'

Scarlett seemed keen on beginnings.

39

'I don't know if I could manage it,' I said.

'Well, life is all about finding out what you can do. You never regret trying.'

Just when I thought she was going to give me one of those talks that grown-ups love to bore you with, she pointed up at a cloud.

'Doesn't that look like a dragon eating Christmas pudding?'

I looked at the cloud and then at her wrinkly finger. Whether she was a gangster or not, I had to admit that I was having quite a good time with her. In fact, even though I'd always thought that old people were super boring, Scarlett was actually quite fun.

Scarlett pointed to another cloud. 'And that one looks like a baboon sticking his bottom out.'

She was bonkers too, but she was definitely fun.

'Do you want another cup of tea?' Scarlett asked.

I shook my head. I'd already had buckets of tea. I didn't have room for another drop. In fact ... I was starting to feel quite uncomfortable.

'What's the matter?' Scarlett asked. 'You're staring like a cod fish.'

'I need to ...' I could feel my face going red. I lowered my voice. 'I need to go to the toilet.'

'Do you mean you want a wee? Why didn't you say so? If you're going to guzzle tea like that then of course you'll need a wee. I expect you'll be weeing like a fountain.'

I was so hot and embarrassed that I thought I might melt

into a puddle. Uh oh, it wasn't a good idea to think about puddles or I'd be making one.

'Not to worry,' Scarlett went on. 'No problem.'

I thought she was going to offer me a lift back to the farmhouse on her scooter, but instead she said, 'Don't be shy then; there's nature's loveliest lavatory over in the woods.'

I darted off to the woods. I couldn't see a loo anywhere. It didn't seem like the kind of place for a toilet block. Maybe there was a portaloo. Or a cafe with toilets. I squinted through the greenery. Nope. Nothing but trees.

Then I realised. Scarlett meant that I should just *go*, right there. In the middle of the open air!

I knew boys at school who went camping and peed in the woods. Once David Chaplin did it around the back of the bike sheds. But I had never peed anywhere except in a nice clean toilet. What if somebody saw? I was going to have to go somewhere, though, and soon.

I found a few trees packed close together. I turned round in a circle to make sure no one was coming and then ... I did it. It wasn't bad actually. A bit breezy, but fine. Maybe I could spend a week in the woods after all.

We had a Mexican thing called burritos for tea. At least that's what I found out afterwards. When I sat down at the empty table and asked Jill, 'What are we having?' she put a finger on her lips.

'I'm not telling you. And I'm not showing you. First,

you've got to close your eyes and take a mouthful. If you don't like it you can have your peanut butter toast or a beetroot sandwich like Scarlett, but I'm not having you tell me you don't like it before you've tried it.'

I didn't much fancy eating anything I hadn't inspected first, but I was starving and Jill clearly meant business. I closed my eyes.

'Open up.'

I opened up and she popped a forkful of food into my mouth. It was delicious. A soft chewy outside with a tasty meaty inside that was just a little bit spicy.

'That was worth it, wasn't it?' Jill asked.

I nodded.

'Doesn't do anyone any good to go round always assuming anything different'll leave a nasty taste.'

I supposed that was true. I decided to put burritos on my list of new favourites.

SATURDAY

On Saturday afternoon, Scarlett came clattering down the passage into the kitchen, where I was playing cards with Simone, and beckoned me over with her stick. She sniffed me and said, 'You'd better have a bath, ready for the barn dance tonight.'

'A barn dance?'

'Yes, a barn dance,' Scarlett said. 'All the barns in the

village get together and the boy barns ask the girl barns to dance.'

'Oh, Scarlett! We know what a barn dance is,' Simone said.

I nodded my head. Then I shook it. 'Wait a minute, what is a barn dance?' I asked.

'A dance. In a barn,' Simone said.

'Oh. I don't really like dancing. It's not one of my favourite things to do.'

Scarlett sniffed. 'It's not one of mine either, but I put up with it for all the snacks and fizzy pop. And the music and jumping about on hay bales. You could do the same, couldn't you?'

'I suppose.'

So I had a shower and got changed into clean jeans. Scarlett decided to go for something much more fancy, and appeared in a purple shiny ball gown that crackled when she walked.

'You look like a giant Quality Street,' I said.

Scarlett beamed. 'Marvellous. Everybody loves those sweeties, don't they?'

I couldn't argue with that.

The dance was at another farm on the other side of the valley. The barn was decorated with bunting and fairy lights. There was a band at one end and a table full of food and drinks at the other. People were sitting on hay bales at the sides and a man with a microphone was organising a bunch of people in the middle into squares and telling them how to do the dance.

They were all laughing and joking like it was great fun.

I still hadn't decided if I was going to do any dancing. I didn't really know how. When Faye Wright had a disco, me and Josh just jumped up and down to the music. Until Josh jumped on Faye's foot. Then Faye's mum sent him to sit on the stairs and think about what he had done.

I went to the food table, but I wasn't really hungry so I just had a couple of sausage rolls, a scotch egg, three handfuls of crisps, two fairy cakes and a tomato cut into the shape of a flower.

Scarlett's purple dress caught my eye. I watched her reach behind a hay bale and pull out her violin case. Even though I was starting to doubt whether Scarlett really was a secret criminal, for a second I imagined her opening it and pulling out a machine gun, but when she did open it there was only a real violin. Gareth took Scarlett's arm and helped her into a chair next to the band. When they started up the next song Scarlett lifted the violin and played. I was so surprised that a little bit of Scotch egg and several crisps fell out of my mouth. That explained the violin case in the boot of Scarlett's car. She was actually really good. You could hear her bouncy, cheerful notes above the rest of the band.

The dancers were spinning each other round and smiling like anything. Simone was dancing with Brandon's brother even though no one had made them and I noticed that when he swung Simone around he lifted her right off the ground.

'Fancy a go?' Farmer Gareth asked, jerking a thumb at the dancers.

'I don't know anyone to dance with.'

'You know me.'

'I can't dance with you! You're a boy!'

'Two lads can do just as well as a lad and a lassie.'

Farmer Gareth pulled me into the circle and then swung me up into the air.

I'd always thought dancing was boring but this was so fast that I could hardly catch my breath for the whole of the swirling, twirling song.

'Phew!' I puffed when we sat down to drink lemonade with Jill. 'You're really good,' I said to Gareth.

'Aye.' Jill nodded. 'He used to be county champion.'

'Did you win competitions?' I asked.

'He won all the competitions.' Jill looked at Gareth and beamed with pride.

'With you?'

Farmer Gareth shook his head. 'No, she was busy with her own competitions. Jill plays football.'

I stared at Jill. 'Really?'

Jill chuckled. 'Just local league. But I do enjoy it.'

'She's dynamite on the wing, this one,' Farmer Gareth grinned.

'Wow!' I looked at Jill's sparkly frock. 'I can't imagine you running about a muddy pitch,' I said.

'Good job I don't have to live in your imagination then, isn't it?' Jill said.

I had to think about what that meant for a minute. I

45

suppose Jill was saying you should do what you want to do and not what other people think you're capable of.

The barn dance was much more fun than I thought it would be. There was a lot of dancing and eating and singing. A barn is a really good place to make a lot of noise.

When we came back to the farm, everyone was so tired that no one was speaking. It wasn't the kind of not speaking like after Mum and Dad have had a row. But the kind where you don't talk because you don't need to. We were all tired and happy together. Jill squeezed my shoulder. I thought about her football skills and Farmer Gareth's dance competitions.

I wondered what else I didn't know about Jill and Gareth. Or Scarlett. Or even Simone. Maybe in future I should remember that even the most normal-looking person might be a secret dance champion.

I climbed the stairs to bed and pulled the covers around me. Out of the skylight I could see a patch of starry sky.

Maybe there were even secrets about myself that I didn't know yet.

SUNDAY

It was our last day on the farm so I wanted to do all my new favourite things. I played gangsters with Brandon, until we were hot and dusty, and then we swam in the pond. Jill made burritos for lunch, then I went to the meadow with Scarlett, and later I played with the kittens in the barn.

On my way upstairs to pack my bag I heard a sound. I tiptoed down the landing. The door to Scarlett's room was ajar. At last I could take a look inside.

All of my suspicions about Alex and the knife throwing came back to me. Then I remembered Scarlett wearing her sweet-wrapper dress and playing her violin while winking at Farmer Gareth last night. Scarlett was a good person. Sometimes rude and silly, but definitely good. If she wanted to keep her bedroom a secret then I would let her. I turned away.

'Come in,' someone in the room whispered. 'Come here.'

The hairs on the back of my neck stood up. I took a breath and flung the door open.

There in front of me was a white-faced vampire.

I gasped.

But he was only on a huge computer screen.

'*Vampire Vengeance*!' I said.

Someone clapped a hand down on my shoulder.

I jumped.

It was Scarlett. She beamed at me as if everything was fine. I couldn't believe it.

'You've got a computer?' I looked around her room. 'And a TV? And a DVD player?'

Scarlett shrugged.

How could she have kept all this secret? 'You mean old ... meanie. Why didn't you share any of your things? I've been here all week and ... and ...'

'And you've had a marvellous time,' Scarlett said.

I opened my mouth to tell her what a pig she was, but I thought about the cherry cake and the clouds and I closed it again. Then I remembered missing Josh's party and I opened it again, but she did have a point about me having a marvellous time so I shut it again.

'Are you doing your fish impression?' Scarlett asked. 'It's quite good.'

I started laughing. I couldn't help it. 'I haven't watched any TV all week!' I snorted. 'I've been outside! I've been swimming! I played with the animals!' I gasped for breath. 'And all this time, you've had this lot in here!'

Scarlett chuckled and pointed to the computer. 'Fancy a game?'

We played *Vampire Vengeance* for half an hour.

'You're quite good,' I said.

'I'm better than you, shorty.'

'No, you're not. You don't even wait to see if the shadows behind gravestones are vampires or angels. You just bash everything over the head.'

'I like bashing.'

'Scarlett, can I ask you something?'

'Go on.'

'Was there a red handprint outside your door the other day?'

'I didn't expect you to be the housekeeping type. Jill did tell me to watch where I lean when I've been slicing the beetroots.'

48

Her beetroot sandwiches! That explained it.

'What happened to Alex?'

'He's gone to stay with his girlfriend in London.'

'What about that phone call about the delivery?'

I thought Scarlett might tell me off for eavesdropping, but instead she made me come downstairs to the kitchen and opened the door of the utility room. She pulled open the door of the little fridge in there. Inside were two fancy cakes in huge boxes. On top, in swirly writing, one said, 'Goodbye, Daniel' and the other one, 'Goodbye, Simon'.

'Oh,' I said. 'That's nice. That's very nice.'

'What did you think I was talking about taking a delivery of? A machine gun?' Scarlett cackled with laughter. Then she saw my face. 'Gracious me, child! What do you think I am? A gangster?'

I looked at my feet. 'Erm . . . no. Not any more.'

'A gangster!' She said under her breath while shaking her head. 'As if I'd be a gangster!' she helped herself to a cold sausage from the fridge. 'I'm not a gangster,' she said to me gently. She shut the fridge door. 'I'm a diamond thief.'

I knew she was joking, but I was pretty sure if she wanted to be a diamond thief she would be a very good one.

Soon after that my parents arrived and we had a lovely tea with the cakes that Scarlett had bought and all the fancy dishes Jill had made. I tried a bit of every single one.

'We'll be setting off early tomorrow,' Mum said to me after tea. 'Do you want to have one last look around?'

49

We went out together in the dusk and had a walk around the farm. I showed Mum the kittens and the rest of the animals. Then I took her to the spot where you can see right across the valley and pointed out the pond where I went swimming with Brandon.

Mum looked into my face. 'It sounds like you've tried all sorts of new things.'

I remembered what Jill had said. 'You have to try things to find new favourites.'

Mum nodded. 'I thought perhaps you'd like to try something else new.'

'What's that?'

'Well, we really haven't got room for a dog, Daniel, but I thought perhaps, when they're old enough, we might give one of the kittens a home.'

'Brilliant.'

She smiled at me.

I looked around at the moonlit farm. I thought about how I'd got all those silly ideas about there being a mystery to solve, but really the biggest thing that I'd worked out this week was that you can't know exactly what something or someone will be like before you've given them a go. Real life is much more surprising than any detective story. And burritos are even better than peanut butter.

THE UNFORTUNATE CAREER OF SUPER OLD-AGED PENSIONER (AND WONDER GRANNY)!

STEVE COLE

Stanley Sweetman lived at 92 Bongo Street. Really, he should've changed his name to Stanley Rottenhorridman, because he was not very sweet at all. But there was already a *Mrs* Rottenhorridman living at number 73, and Stanley didn't want anyone to think he was married to that old trout.

So, 'Sweetman' he was – by name if not by nature.

Stanley had lived alone his whole life – chiefly because he was revolting. The only things he ate were pickled onions and baked beans. He filled his house with them so he hardly ever had to go out. People always told him he was crazy for only eating pickled onions and baked beans.

'YOU'RE CRAZY, STANLEY SWEETMAN!' they said.

But Stanley didn't care because he was a hundred and five years old. He was doing pretty well on all those beans and onions.

Some people say that the secret of reaching a great age is

clean living. You know the sort of thing – eating healthily, lots of exercise, taking baths and brushing your teeth, going to bed early ...

Stanley disagreed.

Violently.

'WHAT ARE YOU ON ABOUTTTTTTT?' he raged. 'The secret of reaching a great age is DIRTY ROTTEN LIVING!'

Stanley had many ways to prove this. For instance, he only owned one pair of underpants, which he cleaned once a month by dipping them in left-over pickling vinegar. And he had not taken off his socks since 1967.

''COURSE I HAVEN'T!' he shouted. 'If I took my socks off, my feet would get dirty, wouldn't they?'

Stanley never took a bath. Once every six weeks, on a rainy day, he would stand beneath the broken drainpipe outside the sewage works and shower in dirty rainwater.

The miserable old man never cleaned his house either. It was older than he was and three times as rickety.

He had no carpets – the falling-apart floorboards were covered in squashed cardboard.

The crumbling walls were held up with cobwebs.

His windows were so dirty you couldn't tell day from night.

'SO?' Stanley cried. 'Saves on curtains, doesn't it!'

And his saggy bed had no sheets or blankets. He slept in old newspapers.

'I LIKE TO READ IN BED!' Stanley snarled.

Worst of all, the toilet got blocked in 1978 and Stanley had never fixed it. From that day on he did his business in empty bean tins and for toilet paper he used labels torn from pickled onion jars.

'THEN I THROW THE WHOLE LOT IN THE GARDEN!' Stanley explained. 'DON'T WANT GERMS IN THE HOUSE, DO I?'

It was, in short, a despicable place to live. But dirty living wasn't the only reason for Stanley's immensely great age.

Stanley never put the tiniest strain on his body. He never worked, and he never worried. He never did anything very much. All his life, he had taken things slowly.

Very slowly.

Verrrrrrrrrrrrrryyyyyyyyyyyyy slowwwwwwwwwwwwwly.

Even as a child, he'd prided himself on being the ultimate slowcoach. Once, on sports day at school, he ran the three-legged race in six-and-a-half days. It very nearly got in the World Record books for the longest short race ever, but sadly he was disqualified when the boy he was racing with starved to death just before they reached the finish line.

Ever since then, most days, Stanley stuck to the same routine. He got out of bed at ten o'clock (which took him an hour), walked carefully downstairs (which took two hours), ate a tin of cold baked beans (forty-five minutes), had a nap to recover his strength (six hours), ate half a jar of pickled onions (one hour), walked carefully back upstairs (two and a half hours) and finally got back into bed, exhausted, and fell asleep until morning.

But on the warm July day of Stanley's one hundred and sixth birthday, things did not move slowly at all.

In fact, parts of it were moving at one million miles per hour!

Way out in space, a strangely glowing meteor was streaking through the blackness. Where had it come from? No one knew. Space is a very spacious place, after all. But as for where it was going? Well. That question was easy.

The meteor was headed for Earth.

More specifically, it was heading for the particular part of Earth where Stanley Sweetman lay sleeping, tucked up in his vest, pants, socks and an old flat cap, snoring underneath his flimsy newspaper blanket.

As the meteor entered the atmosphere, it began to burn up, as meteors do. It glowed red hot and broke apart into smaller chunks. Some of those smaller chunks made it right the way through the atmosphere to crash into the surface of the Earth as 'meteorites' ...

And one of those meteorites came SMASHING through Stanley's filthy bedroom window!

'Eeeek!' yelped Stanley, shocked awake.

Fortunately, the meteorite missed him by milimetres and hit the damp old mattress. THUD! It sat there, caught by the rusty springs, smoking, bathing Stanley in a ghostly green glow (which was the closest thing to a bath he'd had in about fifty years).

'Phew!' said Stanley, gazing at the eerie emerald light. 'That was a close one.'

No sooner had he said the words than the mattress caught on fire.

'AAAAAAGH!' Stanley moved faster than he had ever moved before. In less than four minutes he had rolled out of bed before the flames could burn him.

Unfortunately – WUNCH! – Stanley fell right through the mouldy cardboard-covered floorboards.

'OOOOGH!' Stanley gasped, waving his arms and legs.

Fortunately, he landed on the sofa in his living room.

'EEEEEEEE!' he said happily. 'A soft landing!'

Unfortunately, the burning bed crashed after him. It landed on one end of the sofa and tipped it up like a seesaw. Stanley was sent flying into the air. He crunched his head on the ceiling, and then fell back down to the floor – right on top of the glowing meteorite!

His bottom burned and stung. A fierce fizzing fuzzed through his furred-up veins. His ancient pants smoked and sizzled, and the flat cap spun about his head.

'Nggggggggggggggggggggggggg!' he cried. Not the spiciest pickled onion nor the mouldiest bean had ever left Stanley in such a tremendous tizz.

WHOOSH! Stanley bounced off the meteorite, faster than he had ever moved before, and smashed through the old front door. In a daze, he staggered out into the street in his vest, pants and flat cap. 'Help!' Stanley yelled. 'Fire! Fire!'

Fortunately, a fire engine was passing and quickly stopped.

Unfortunately – CRUNCH! – it ran over Stanley first.

'ARRRGH!' Stanley groaned.

Fortunately, an ambulance was close behind.

Unfortunately – WHAM! – the ambulance ran Stanley over too.

'URRPH!' he moaned.

Fortunately, a second ambulance was travelling close behind the first ambulance.

Unfortunately – SQUISH! – the second ambulance parked on top of Stanley.

'THAT DOES IT!' Stanley shouted from under the tyres. Without thinking, he flexed his wrinkly muscles ...

And suddenly—

incredibly, impossibly—

Stanley found he was tossing the ENTIRE AMBULANCE aside like a toy! It flew across the road, skidded onto the pavement and crashed into a wall.

'HOO HOO!' Stanley chortled. 'Take that, young'uns!'

'Whoa,' said the ambulance driver, as he climbed out through the window. 'What happened?'

Stanley stared down at himself in wonder. He had big muscly arms like a bodybuilder. Beneath his vest, his chest was broad and firm. And, poking out from his pants, his legs bulged in an extremely athletic fashion. 'I'll tell you what happened, sonny!' Stanley breathed. 'I reckon ... that ... I happened!'

'Yeah, sure you did, you old nutter,' said the driver of the first ambulance. 'Must've been a freak tornado ...'

'A FREAK TORNADO?' Stanley frowned. By now, the fire in his house had grown as hot and fierce as an ogre's indigestion. Orange flames danced flickering can-cans at the windows, but Stanley found he was unafraid. He suddenly felt as if he could do anything.

'I'll show you a freak tornado!' Stanley took a deep, wheezy old breath ... then blew it out again as hard as he could.

WHOOOOOOOOOOOOOOOOSH! That mega-blow was like a hurricane, scattering firefighters and extinguishing the flames as easily as a child might blow out birthday candles. Stanley's whopping, wheezing breath almost knocked over his whole house, and filled the whole street with the pong of pickled onions.

'Ha!' Stanley cried. 'I knew I could do it!'

'Wow!' A little girl came running up to Stanley. 'You're like ... a superhero!'

'You're right, pipsqueak! Somehow I have acquired incredible powers.' Stanley stared at his smoking house, took off his cap, thought hard and scratched his stubbly head. He had never felt so strong and powerful. Through a broken window he saw the meteorite still glowing inside.

'There's only one possibility,' he muttered. 'MY **DIET!** All these years of BAKED BEANS and PICKLED

ONIONS have turned me into … SUPER OLD-AGED PENSIONER!'

Stanley jumped into the air, and took flight with all the power of a keen (if slightly doddery old) pigeon. 'I must get MORE of my fave foods!' he declared, 'so that I become even stronger!' He flew so fast that his ancient pants-elastic very nearly snapped, leaving his undies to flap about his ankles while the rest of him traumatised the town. But, with heroic sticking-power, Stanley's pants stayed up and his socks clung onto his feet – even as he accidentally flew into a washing line full of clothes drying in the summer breeze.

'Oooh!' said Stanley, pulling a pink fluffy dressing gown from his face. 'This will make a fine superhero cape!' He tied the arms around his neck and zoomed onwards.

'Look out, world!' Stanley boomed as he landed in the street outside the supermarket and stood with his hands on his hips. 'Super Old-Aged Pensioner is here!'

No one in the street took a whole lot of notice. They thought Stanley was just a nutty old man.

'Eee, I'll show them,' Stanley muttered. He noticed a grey-haired woman standing by the side of the road, watching the traffic go past. 'Bah! No one ever takes any notice of old folk. Especially ugly old boots like this one.' He hovered above the road, pulled off his flat cap and hurled it at an approaching truck. THWOOM! The truck crumpled up like the inside of an accordion and stopped dead. Cars crunched into the back of it and horns began to blare. A big motorbike was coming the other way. 'Horrible noisy thing!' Stanley uprooted a set of traffic lights from the pavement and swung them like a bat. SMUNCH! The motorbike was sent crashing into a bus stop and its driver landed in a litter bin. Passers-by screamed and ran for cover, and more cars honked their horns.

'Ta-daaaa!' Ignoring the commotion, Stanley pointed at the grey-haired woman. 'You can cross, now, ugly-face! SUPER OLD-AGED PENSIONER generously permits it!' He scowled. 'Say thank you, then.'

The old lady looked baffled. 'But . . . I don't want to cross the road. I'm waiting for my son to collect me.'

'What?' Stanley's scowl grew deeper. 'You mean, I demonstrated my powers and super-strength for nothing?'

'Er, yes.' The lady smiled proudly. 'My son's a scientist working for a secret organisation, you know. He's ever so clever. His special subject is meteorites. Especially the extra-dangerous glowing green ones.'

'That sounds boring!' Stanley retorted. 'Whoever cares about extra-dangerous glowing green meteorites? Anyone sensible in the world knows that the only things that matter are pickled onions and baked beans! Your son should study them instead – the idiot!'

Just then a policeman ran up, alerted by the chaos. He saw shocked drivers and startled pedestrians pointing at

Stanley, and frowned. 'Excuse me, sir. Are you responsible for attacking this traffic?'

'Traffic!' Stanley cried. 'Eee, there's too much traffic on the road today. In my day it was all horse-and-carts. The milkman rode a donkey and stuff.'

The policeman cleared his throat. 'Be that as it may, sir, perhaps you'd like to accompany me to the station—'

'Accompany you?' Stanley frowned. 'Ahhh. You want to be my partner, eh? Well, sorry, copper – SUPER OLD-AGED PENSIONER works alone! Especially when there are baked beans and pickled onions to buy. Now, look over there!' Stanley pointed past the policeman. As the policeman turned to look, Stanley took off into the air with a power-packed *PARP!* and streaked into the supermarket in a wrinkly blur.

Ha! he thought. That showed the uniformed young'un!

After a lifetime of moving slowly, Stanley found the sudden speed felt incredible! Recklessly he turned a loop the loop over Tesco – but it made his stomach feel funny and he landed by the supermarket's sliding doors with a vinegary burp.

'Ugh,' he muttered. 'Tasted better first time around.' He scratched his bum, which still stung from when he'd fallen on the meteorite. 'Funny, I never normally get indigestion . . .'

As Stanley walked inside the supermarket and picked up a basket, he found there were young people with trolleys blocking the way.

'I'm not having this,' he cried. 'PENSIONER POWER!' With that, he leaped over their heads in a single bandy-legged bound into the middle of the baked-bean aisle.

Normally Stanley chose the El Cheapo Economy brand. But today, hoping to boost his superpowers further, he swept twenty tins of the finest branded beans into his basket.

''Ere!' came a squawk from behind him. 'Wait a minute!'

Stanley turned to find a hunched, pink-haired old lady with a tartan shopping trolley standing in the aisle. She peered at him through thick glasses.

'Eeeeeeeeeeee! Stanley!' she said. 'Is that you, pet?'

Stanley groaned. Of all the people to run into! It was his neighbour, Mrs Rottenhorridman, from number 73! Like him, she really didn't live up to her surname: Mrs Rottenhorridman was actually a very sweet old lady, and Stanley didn't like that at all.

'Er, Stanley? Who's he? I don't know what you're on about,' he said. 'I'm Super Old-Aged Pensioner.'

'Oooooh, yes,' said Mrs R. 'I've always thought you were a *super-duper* old-aged pensioner, Stanley. But why aren't you wearing that dressing gown properly? You'll catch your death of cold in just your vest and pants.'

'Stop your moaning, Mrs R! After years of munching beans and pickles, I've got superpowers, haven't I?' Flexing his muscles, he pushed apart the shelves of the aisle and strode through it to the pickled-onions section. With a swipe of his hand he pushed ten jars into his overfilled basket. 'There! You see?'

'Oooooh, yes, very super, Stanley.' Mrs R smiled. 'But, er, how are you going to pay for them, you daftie? I bet you've come out without your pennies, haven't you?'

Stanley cursed. It was true! He'd forgotten about payment. 'Well . . . I'm SUPER OLD-AGED PENSIONER, aren't I? I'll just take them!'

'You can't do that, Stan! We can't have a supervillain living on Bongo Street! It'll lower the tone of the whole area.'

Stanley thought hard. He'd already tricked a policeman, knocked over some firefighters and brained an ambulance driver. All three emergency services must be cross with him. 'I suppose I'd best not make things worse,' he told himself. 'I don't want the army coming after me – they'll be disturbing my nap time!' Grumpily he began putting back the things in his basket.

'Oh, no, no, no, dear,' said Mrs R, 'don't you worry. I'll buy your groceries for you.'

'You?' Stanley frowned. 'Why would you do that?'

'Not many men can pull off the "pink dressing gown around the neck" look.' She fluttered her lashes behind her thick glasses. 'Perhaps you'll invite me to share some of your beans, eh? And nibble your pickles?' She snapped her gums together. 'Of course, I'll have to put me false teeth in first . . .'

Disgusting! thought Stanley. But he just mumbled and

grumbled and shoved the basket in Mrs R's direction. Let the old boot buy his shopping if she wanted – but she wasn't getting a single bite!

It took a long time for Mrs R to finish paying for Stanley's groceries. She'd brought along her jar full of pennies, and had to count out £22.67 in 1ps. The people queuing behind her got impatient and started to complain, which made her lose her count around the fifteen-pound mark so she had to start again.

Stanley complained loudest of all and said some very rude things, but luckily by then Mrs R had turned down her hearing aid so she couldn't hear him. At last the haul of baked beans and pickled onions were paid for, and Mrs R stuffed them in her tartan bag-on-wheels.

'Right! I'll have that,' Stanley informed her, the moment they stepped outside. 'Thanks, I'm off now. Bye!' He grabbed the tartan bag handle and leaped into the air . . .

But Mrs R didn't let go. She came shooting through the skies with him!

'EEEEEEEEEEEEE!' she cried, clutching onto the strap with one bony hand while the other tried to keep her hat on her head. 'Heavens! I'm glad I wore my thermals today!'

Stanley turned another loop the loop to try and shake her loose, but Mrs R was clinging on tighter than a sloth with bionic claws, and his aerobatics only gave him more indigestion. This time the gas escaped from the other end.

'Manners!' Mrs R called to him. 'I do like the wind in my hair, but not quite like that!'

Cursing her stubbornness, Stanley landed outside his house, and Mrs R fell tumbling into a box hedge. 'Eeeee!' she said, shaking tiny leaves from her hat. 'Thanks for the lift! Much quicker than the bus.'

'And much more expensive too,' said Stanley. 'In fact, I'm charging you £22.77. So that's paid for all my shopping, *and* you owe me 10p.'

She looked up at him. 'Really?'

'Of course, really. Pay up!'

'A once in a lifetime experience like that for only £22.77!' Mrs R beamed and threw a handful of pennies in the air. 'You lovely, generous man! You really are a super old-aged pensioner!'

'Ugh!' Stanley groaned, picked up her bag, and stomped off into his house through the broken front door.

Two things struck him as he came inside.

The first thing that struck him was that the meteorite was still glowing green in his living room.

The second thing that struck him was a giant robotic fist. It knocked him over onto his front. Then cold fingers closed on his bottom, grabbed hold – and hurled him outside.

'OOOF!' cried Stanley, as he landed in the garden.

'EEEEEK!' cried Mrs R, who was still crawling out of the bush. 'What happened, Stanley? Are you all right?'

''Course I am, you old halibut!' Stanley jumped back up.

He wasn't sure what was going on, but he wasn't going to take it lying down – not now he had special powers! 'It'll take more than a big metal man hiding in my house to get the better of SUPER OLD-AGED PENSIONER.'

'A metal man?' Mrs R frowned. 'What does he want, d'you think?'

'I don't know, but he's going to get a thumping!' said Stanley, marching back inside. 'Oi! You! Come out and face me!'

The enormous robot DID come out and face him. Although it didn't actually have a face: just a blank, gleaming oval of steel crowned with little lights blinking red and gold. Its body was an upturned triangle, bobbing about on three metal tentacles for legs, while its two chunky arms stuck out from either side, each ending in a whopping iron claw.

One of those claws had closed about the glowing green meteorite. The robot was dropping it into a kind of metal box bolted onto its back.

A box that was glowing brightly with MORE meteorites . . .

'Hey, it's carrying a load of those stupid green rocks,' Stanley realised.

'Oooh!' Mrs R had crept up behind him. 'The meteor must've broken up in the atmosphere and fallen all around – and this fine metal chap is picking up all the pieces.'

'I'll bet I know what it's REALLY after,' Stanley grumbled. 'My beans and pickled onions!'

Just then, the robot turned to go out of the back door. One

of its spidery metal legs caught on the tartan bag's handle and dragged it along.

'SEE? TOLD YOU!' spluttered Stanley. 'Give me back my shopping, you walking scrap-heap!' He hurled his flat cap at the robot. KROOOM! The robot was knocked forward and crashed through the kitchen wall. Stanley lunged for the tartan shopping bag but the robot was already on its feet again. WHAM! It sent Stanley flying through the kitchen window.

'THAT DOES IT!' In a cloud of bean-gas Stanley jumped out and hammered his fist down on the robot's head, knocking it into the ground. The green rocks in the box on its back were jolted loose and fell all around the garden. Stanley picked them up and started throwing them at the robot. 'Urp! BLUG!' His stomach made the most extraordinary noises as he went on chucking the glowing stones. He was starting to feel quite peculiar. 'Here!' He tossed a couple of meteorites to Mrs R. 'Make yourself useful, woman! It's your stupid shopping bag it's got, after all!'

'Oooooh!' said Mrs R as she caught them neatly. 'Aren't these pretty stones . . .'

The robot stalked towards her, clearly wanting the rocks back. Stanley kicked out his leg at super speed and his sock – one of the very socks he hadn't taken off since 1967 – flew off and hit the robot right in the face. FWAP! The shocking stink was enough to swamp even the robot's mechanical senses. It jerked about in a mad metal ballet, the tartan bag still hooked about one metal claw-like foot.

'Stop it!' Stanley shouted, grabbing for the bag, a split-second late each time. 'You'll dent me tins! You'll crack me jars!' He looked back at Mrs R. 'How about a little help, you old haddock?'

But Mrs R couldn't hear him. The rocks were bathing her in their eerie green light. She'd had a herbal bath just that morning, but this was even better. She could feel her skinny arms bulking up, and her legs growing muscles. Her thermal vest glowed with uncanny energy . . .

'Oooh, Stanley! Look!' Mrs R could feel her spine growing straighter and her pink hair growing curlier. The shining rocks slipped from her grip. 'I'm changing,' she cried. 'Faster than before! Stronger! Better at knitting!' She threw back her head and punched the air. 'Where once stood Enid Rottenhorridman, now stands . . . WONDER GRANNY!'

'For flipping heck's sake!' Stanley groaned. 'Just stop showing off and help me stop this grocery-snaffling robot— ARGHHHH!'

The metal man socked Stanley into a tree and grabbed the green meteorites from Mrs R's feet. Mrs R hardly noticed. She had started knitting a scarf at incredible speed, her hands a blur as the needles click-clacked together. Soon it was as long as a cowboy's lasso and she roped it about the robot's tentacle legs. FWOMP – BOING! It tried to move away but its legs tangled and it fell crashing to the ground once more.

'Take that, you big bully!' cried Mrs R, 'with the compliments of WONDER GRANNY!'

'Stop showing off,' moaned Stanley. 'Look! The thing is trying to hop away!'

It was true. BOING! BOING!

FROOOOSH!

On its third bounce, with all the meteorites regathered – jets leaped from its shiny steel base and pushed it up into the air like a robot rocket.

And STILL the tartan shopping bag held on.

'It'll burn up!' cried Mrs R. 'Eeeeeeee, I've only had it a couple of years. There's loads of wear left in it.'

'There's loads of lovely grub left in it!' Stanley staggered to his feet, hiccupped and ran after the bag. 'Come on!'

'Wait!' came a voice from the front of the house. 'Stop! Stay where you are!'

It must be that copper, thought Stanley. But there's no time to get a ticking off from the police. I need to keep my strength up with tinned and jarred delights! He ran across the garden. 'Up, up and . . . up a bit more!' Seconds from the garden fence, he took off into flight.

'Wonder Granny TO THE RESCUUUUUUUE!' Mrs R hopped heroically after him into the air – and quickly overtook him!

''Ere!' Stanley shouted after her. 'How are you doing that?

YOU'VE not been eating baked beans and pickled onions!'

'It's them rocks that have given us powers, you daftie!' Mrs R called back to him. 'Ooooh, look at that man down there in your back garden, waving at us and jumping up and down. He seems like a nice boy. And who's that with him?'

Stanley looked down. He recognised the woman he'd tried to help across the road outside the supermarket. The one who was waiting for her son, the scientist.

The man with her wasn't the policeman. It was a man in a white lab coat.

'So her son DID collect her,' Stanley muttered. 'But why did he take her to MY house . . .?'

He decided to worry about that later. There was a tartan shopping bag to rescue!

The robot put on a burst of speed.

'You can't get away from us!' Mrs R threw off her hat and flew even faster. She grabbed hold of one of the robot's tentacle legs. It began to kick and jiggle, trying to throw her clear. ''Ere! Super Old-Aged Pensioner, give us a hand!'

'Coming!' *PARRRP*! The extra gas propelled Stanley just that little bit faster, and he managed to grab hold of the tartan shopping bag. But it was still tangled in the robot's claw-like foot, and he was sent spinning in a spiral as he fought to hold on. 'Urgh!' he groaned. 'I don't feel well.'

'I've got an idea!' Mrs R bellowed. 'If it keeps flying in this direction it'll reach the beach. If we can only force it down into the sea, perhaps it'll blow a fuse!'

'Hmm. That's quite a good plan.' Stanley grimaced at her. 'In fact, I thought of it first! You copied me!'

'If you say so, dear!' Mrs R was too busy holding onto the steel coils of the robot's leg to argue. Below her, she saw the beach come into view, a lovely long slice of golden yellow beside the deep blue sea. She noticed a Jeep driving along the seafront. It was the nice lad in the white coat and the old lady again. And they were still waving!

Maybe they're superhero fans? thought Mrs R. Well, we can't have them disappointed, can we?

She pulled back her fist and smashed it into the robot's side. CLANG! A dent appeared in its triangular body, and the lights on its head flashed red. KA-KLANG! Another wondrous old-woman punch and one of the robot's legs fell off!

'I'm not letting you have all the fun!' Stanley declared. He clung onto the robot's arms, shinned up its trunk and with a bellowed roar of 'PENSIONER POWER!' he nutted the robot right in its solid steel face.

PRANGGGG! The crown of lights around the robot's head blew a fuse, while its rocket jets sparked and went PHUT! and went out.

'Going DOWWWWWWWWWWWN!' shrieked Mrs R. 'Come on, pet – let's leave it to make a splash and get back to shore.'

'Not without my shopping!' Stanley shouted. He went on tugging at the tangled handles of the shopping bag, pulling and yanking and straining as the robot spiralled down towards the choppy ocean ... drawing closer ... closer ... CLOSER ...

With a last desperate heave, Stanley pulled off the robot's foot and freed the tartan bag. 'Got it!' he shouted in triumph. 'PENSIONER POWERRRRRR—!'

Then the robot, the shopping bag and Super Old-Aged Pensioner all hit the water with a climactically catastrophic KER-SPLAAASHHHHHHHHHH!

'Eeee, the great daftie!' sighed Mrs R. 'He'll be wet through! He'll catch a chill, him in his vest and pants and flat cap and only one sock, eeeeeeee!' She dived down like a big wrinkled heron and grabbed Stanley from out of the ocean by his fingers.

'There we are, then,' she cooed. 'Eee, Stanley, you're holding my hand, you romantic old devil!'

'I've lost me beans!' he sobbed. 'And me pickled onions broke open in the water. They're ruined!'

'Oh, give over,' said Mrs R. 'We beat a deadly robot that was nicking green rocks. We're heroes! We'll be given medals and prizes and certificates and money-off vouchers and a LIFETIME'S SUPPLY of your favourite groceries, more than likely ...'

'You think?' Stanley grinned as they neared the shore. 'Oh, look, it's that daft old woman and her scientist son again. They saw the robot at my house, they must've come to congratulate us!'

Mrs R landed on the beach with Stanley and laid him down on the sand, shivering and hiccuping and clutching his tum. The man in the white coat came rushing up.

'Hello, pet!' Mrs R beamed. 'Have you come to thank us – Wonder Granny and Super Old-Aged Pensioner?'

'*Thank* you?' The young man looked appalled. 'I'm furious with you. My name is Doctor Pota, from the IOWSFSWSP.'

Mrs R frowned. 'Pardon, dear?'

'That's the Institute Of Weird Stuff From Space With Special Powers.'

'Oh,' she said. 'Er, doesn't it take as long to say the initials as it does to say the whole thing?'

'Yes,' Dr Pota agreed. 'That's just one example of the weird stuff we deal with. ANOTHER example is bits of weird space meteorite with special powers . . .' He sighed. 'I suppose it's a good thing they're all lying out of reach in the ocean, now. But I'm quite upset that you've destroyed my highly expensive, super-complicated PLASMA-bot!'

'Eeeeeeee! PLASMA-bot?' She frowned. 'Whatever are you on about, love?'

'PLASMA-bot – short for Prioritise, Locate And Secure Meteorites ASAP-bot.'

'ASAP?'

'As Soon As Possible.' Dr Pota nodded seriously. 'We shorten that bit because PLASMASAP-bot doesn't sound as cool.'

'Mmmmm,' said Mrs R sympathetically. 'Well, the silly

thing took Mr Sweetman's shopping, love. We had to destroy it, didn't we?'

'And now my beans and pickles are lost at sea!' Stanley groaned. 'I should sue you and your rotten robot!'

'I fear you do not understand.' Dr Pota looked down at Stanley. 'I sent out the PLASMA-bot to locate and secure all the lumps of meteorite that landed around these parts.'

'They landed around MY parts,' said Stanley indignantly. 'I sat on one, and then your daft "bot" clobbered me ON the bot!'

'My PLASMA-bot is programmed for self-defence,' said Dr Pota. 'But I imagine there must have been a speck of space rock stuck in your bottom.' He nodded even more seriously. 'Even the tiniest fragment can cause terrible problems. That's why I sent the PLASMA-bot to tidy them all away.'

Mrs R tutted. 'What sort of problems do you mean, love?'

'These meteorites glow with special space radiation that has the power to transform old people into superheroes,' Dr Pota explained. 'But the effects are not always stable.'

'URRRP!' Stanley belched loudly. 'What are you on about?'

'Well, so long as you eat a balanced diet, exercise, wash regularly and stay cheerful and kind into your old age, you're probably fine,' said Dr Pota.

'Eeeee!' Mrs R smiled and clasped her hands together. 'That's nice!'

'But if you've spent your life being miserable, eating nothing but pickled onions and baked beans, never washing and barely moving on a day-to-day basis ... I'm afraid the outlook is not so rosy.'

'Eh?' Stanley got up unsteadily and belched again. 'But ... I do all them things, and look at me. Just look at me!'

'Er, yes.' Mr Pota *did* look at him. And the sight did not seem to make him happy. 'The outlook is even LESS rosy if the decades of dirt holding you together are suddenly washed away by a sudden splashdown in the sea ...'

'Oh,' said Stanley.

'Eeee, whatever will become of him?' wailed Mrs R.

'I'm afraid it's very serious,' said Dr Pota. 'Mr Sweetman, judging by your gas issues ... I'm afraid you may be about to EXPOLDE.'

'Eh?' Stanley blinked and burped. 'Eeee. For a moment there, I was worried. I thought you said "explode".'

'Oh, no, no,' Dr Pota assured him. 'I said, E-X-P-O-L-D-E, *expolde*. It's a special medical term we doctors of weird stuff use. You see, when someone becomes too old and rotten to blow up in the *normal* way, they EXPOLDE instead.'

'Ridiculous!' cried Stanley. 'Preposterous! Flapdoodle!'

BOOOOOOM!

He 'expolded'.

'Ooo, 'eck,' said Mrs R, as bits of Stanley slopped down like sticky rain into a nearby rockpool. 'Have you got a bucket, so I can take him home?'

'Sweet, man!' said Dr Pota's mum. 'He's gone from Super Old-Aged Pensioner . . . to SOUP of Old-Aged Pensioner!'

Dr Pota nodded. 'And you know, there's a moral to this story . . .'

But no one ever heard it, because a moment later, another enormous meteorite whizzed out of the sky and struck the beach, squashing them all flat.

'SUPER METEORITE IS HERE!' boomed the living space rock, looking all around. 'Uhhh . . . Where'd everybody go?'

CRUEL

JONATHAN MERES

I say it before we even reach the end of the street. And the street where we live isn't a particularly long street, either. But I say it anyway. Those five little words that I always say at the beginning of every single journey. Well, not *every* single journey. But definitely at the beginning of every *long* journey. And definitely at the beginning of every holiday. Which this is. And anyway they've been expecting me to say it since the moment I shut the car door and fastened my seat belt – when I say *they*, I mean my parents and my charismatic brother, Isaac – but it's almost become like a tradition or something. *They* know I'm going to say it. *I* know I'm going to say it. So I say it. It was only ever a matter of time.

'Are we there yet, Dad?'

'Very funny, Bonny,' says my dad. Without laughing. And, as far as I can see, without smiling either. It's kind of hard to tell, what with me sitting in the back and only being able to see a bit of his face reflected in the rear-view mirror. But it's enough to notice that he's somehow managing not to split his sides.

'What kept you?' says my mum. And I can see that she definitely *is* smiling because I'm sitting on the opposite side of the car to her and I can see her whole face. Well, not her *whole* face, obviously. But one side of it, anyway. And that side is definitely smiling. And I'd imagine the other side is too. Be a bit weird if it wasn't. Anyway I don't reply. Because there's no need to reply. Even though it was a question. It wasn't a *proper* question. My mum's being sarcastic.

Isaac doesn't say anything, either. Which could be because he can't actually hear anything. Or it could be just down to the fact that Mum once told him if he hadn't got anything nice to say then he shouldn't say anything at all. I reckon Isaac must have taken it a bit too literally because he hasn't said anything since. Or hardly anything, anyway. And practically nothing that I've been able to understand. It's ridiculous. Just because he's a teenager doesn't mean he has to suddenly start mumbling like a caveman.

Actually, I take that back. Compared to Isaac, most cavemen were like Winston Churchill. And if you don't know who Winston Churchill was, he was this guy from the olden days who used to do these really amazing speeches about fighting on beaches and never surrendering and stuff. At least I think that was him. The point I'm trying to make is that Isaac doesn't say very much. That's all you need to know. Dad says it's got something to do with his hormones. Isaac's hormones. Not my dad's. I don't think my dad's even got any hormones. I think they run out when you're, like, forty or something. But I'd prefer not to think about that.

Oh, and if you haven't already realised, I was being ironic when I described my big brother as 'charismatic'. Because if you're charismatic that means you've got this kind of magnetic personality. And Isaac has no personality whatsoever. Let alone a magnetic one.

'Why do you always ask your father, by the way?' says Mum.

'What do you mean?' I say.

'Why do you never say, "Are we there yet, *Mum*?"'

I think for a moment. I wasn't even aware that I *didn't* ever ask Mum. But now she comes to mention it, I don't.

'Because I'm the driver?' says my dad.

'So?' laughs my mum.

My dad doesn't reply. Either because he genuinely can't *think* of anything to say, but more likely because by now he's too busy concentrating on joining the main road and merging into the traffic. Which, in fairness, is pretty horrendous. Proper bumper to bumper. As if the whole world has suddenly decided to go on holiday today and not just us. Which is pretty annoying. Actually it's *really* annoying, as we've got a ferry to catch. And I doubt very much it's going to wait for us. I doubt ferries ever wait for anyone. Even pop stars. Although why you'd want to catch a ferry in the first place if you're a pop star, I don't know. They probably have their own ferries. One of the perks of the job, I'd imagine.

Everything goes very quiet for a bit. So quiet that I can hear whatever rubbish music Isaac is listening to on his headphones. Which as far as I can make out seems to mainly consist of drums and a sort of tinny hissing sound and someone screaming as if they're giving birth. Enough for me to be quite glad I can't hear it any louder. And how Isaac ever got headphones to actually fit his stupid-shaped head in the first place is a complete mystery to me. But that's another story. Apart from that, though, everything is very quiet and I wonder if everyone's thinking the same thing as me. What if it's like this the whole way? The traffic, I mean. What if it's going to be bumper to bumper between here and the ferry? Because if it is, we're stuffed, basically. We'll never make it. And then what? We wait for the next ferry? Or we simply turn around and drive back home again?

Which wouldn't be the end of the world, by the way. If we drove straight back home again. Because I didn't particularly want to go to France in the first place. I still don't. Not that I've got anything against France. I'd like to make that crystal clear. I have nothing whatsoever against France. Quite the opposite. Or, as they say in France, *au contraire*. I really like France. It's just that, well, a) I've been there about a thousand times already and b) everyone else is going to Florida. Well, everyone else I *know*, anyway. Actually they're not, thinking about it. Only Amy C and Amy D are going to Florida. But no one else is going to France. Just us. Same as usual.

Of course I did actually *try* and suggest we went somewhere a bit different this year. Fat lot of good that did. If you're still actually allowed to say 'fat' lot? And you're probably not. You're probably supposed to say calorifically-challenged lot of good, or something equally stupid. Anyway, it made no difference. Mum and Dad looked at me as if I'd just told them they weren't my real parents and that I'd adopted them when I was a baby.

Mum said, 'But we're going to a different *campsite*.'

'Exactly!' said my dad. 'What more do you want, Bonny?'

What more do I want? Well, some place with actual walls and a ceiling would be nice for a start. Ditto a bed and maybe a TV. Also it would be quite good to be able to pee in the middle of the night without stumbling about with a torch and tripping over tents in search of a communal toilet block. Not that you ever actually *need* a torch, of course, because you can smell the toilet block a mile off, or however many kilometres that is. But maybe I'm being unreasonable and just a bit *too* demanding?

Honestly, though. A different campsite? Great! Thanks, Mum. Cheers, Dad! I mean don't get me wrong. They *are* usually really nice campsites that we go to. I was exaggerating a bit there for comedy purposes. The toilets don't generally smell *that* bad. But I mean, come on. Give me a break. How about we go to a hotel with its own private beach instead? Or our very own fancy-schmancy villa with a private pool? But I suspect my parents have no intention of ever giving me a break. At least not until we've been to every single campsite in France anyway. And there are still plenty to go yet.

I look out of the window. Is it me or is the traffic not quite so bad all of a sudden? Maybe I've just been a bit distracted thinking about ferries and campsites and minging toilets. But it's definitely got better since I last looked. Or since I was last *aware* of looking anyway. Because instead of being all bumper to bumper like they were, the cars are much more spread out. Which is good. Obviously. Because now we're moving nice and smoothly and not stopping and starting all the time. Which means that it looks a lot more likely that we'll make the ferry. It also means that the mood in the car has noticeably changed again. All of a sudden it feels like we're actually going on holiday, as opposed to going to a funeral. Which is what it's felt like for the last few minutes, if I'm totally honest. OK, so I'm exaggerating again for comedy purposes. Not that there's anything funny about funerals, of course. But you get my drift. Things have been a bit tense for a while. And now? Not quite so tense. In fact, not nearly so tense. It's almost as if a great big weight has been lifted from our shoulders. Which I know is just an expression. But that's actually what it feels like. To me it does, anyway. I've no idea what it feels like to my mum and dad. I couldn't care less what it feels like to Isaac.

'Music, guys?' says my dad, pressing a knob on the dashboard before anyone even has a chance to answer. Yeah. As if we actually have a choice in the matter. He was always going to put music on at some point. It was just a question of when.

'Prefab Sprout,' says my mum, as Paddy MacAloon starts warbling away about what happens when love breaks down. 'That makes a change.'

It doesn't, by the way. Make a change, I mean. Mum's being sarcastic again. Dad's always playing Prefab Sprout. Which is the only reason I know the singer's called Paddy MacAloon, by the way, in case you were wondering. I'm not some kind of expert on 80s musical trivia. Anyway, they were Dad's favourite band 'back in the day', as they say. And because they were *Dad's* favourite band when he and Mum first met at university, they soon became my *mum's* favourite band too. Resistance was futile! Although unlike my dad, Mum's musical tastes actually continued to evolve. She likes all kinds of stuff these days. I even caught her dancing around to Taylor Swift the other day. It was hilarious.

That's why Isaac's called Isaac, by the way. And why I'm called Bonny. Because they're both Prefab Sprout song titles. I perhaps should have said. Or maybe not. I mean it's not that interesting really. Oh, and I'm twelve, in case you're wondering? Isaac's just turned fifteen. I perhaps should have mentioned that too. That's slightly more interesting, I suppose. And now I come to mention it, the song that

Isaac's named after is actually called Green Isaac. But they couldn't very well call him that. Unfortunately. Anyway, blah blah blah.

'Got any other CDs with you, Dad?' I say, knowing it's highly unlikely that he has.

'Nothing wrong with a bit of Prefab Sprout, Bonny,' says my dad, without answering the question. 'They were a proper band, they were. Not like some of the rubbish you get these days.'

I can't help smiling. The way Dad goes on sometimes, you'd think he was a *hundred* and fifty, not fifty. But he's right. There *is* nothing wrong with a bit of Prefab Sprout. It's just that ... well, other bands and types of music are available. And, anyway, I only said it to get a reaction. And I got one. Bingo.

My phone pings. I've got a text. It's from my brother.

Seriously. I'm not even joking. I wish I was. A text? From my brother? The one sitting next to me in the back of the car right now? Well, obviously the one sitting next to me right now. I've only got one brother. Thank goodness. But, I mean, honestly. I've always known he was weird. But this? This is weird on toast.

He nudges me in the ribs with his stupid pointy elbow and nods at my phone. You know, as if to say, *'Look, I've just sent you a text'*. Yeah, thanks, Isaac. Because I'd never have known otherwise, would I? Idiot.

I open it.

Did you check on Graham?

Just five little words again. But, unlike the previous five little words – the ones I said right at the beginning of the journey – these are totally unexpected. They hit me quite literally like a bolt from the blue. Well, not *literally* like a bolt from the blue. That would be quite painful. But they come as a surprise. And not a very welcome surprise, either.

I look at Isaac. He looks at me. And just for a couple of nanoseconds I think I can detect the very faintest glimmer of a smile on his stupid lips. Because he knows perfectly well what he's doing. Or rather, he knows perfectly well what he's just done. And he's done it on purpose. And he knows that I know that he's done it on purpose. And I know that he knows that I know that he's done it on purpose. And I also know that he knows the precise effect it will have on me. Has *already* had on me. That was the whole point of him doing it. To make me worry. Because my brother is essentially evil. I can read him like a book. Yeah. A really *stupid* book.

You're probably wondering who Graham is, right? Well, I'll tell you. He's my hamster. And he's *not* named after a Prefab Sprout song! He's named after the breakfast cereal. Golden Grahams? And he's a kind of golden colour. Simple. Also, Graham is just a funny name. Well, for a hamster it is. No offence to anyone called Graham. Anyway, he's called Graham and he's my hamster. At least we *think* he's a he.

But let's not go there right now, eh? Because right now I'm thinking, *did* I check? That he's got enough food and water? That he's got plenty of nice fresh hay to curl up and fall asleep in? That the little wire door flap thing in his cage is securely fastened? Because there *was* that one time when I didn't close it properly and he got out and we didn't find him again for two whole days and . . .

NOOOOOOOOOOOOOOOOOOOOOOOOOO!!!!!!!!!!!!!!! !!!!!!

I mean, I *did* check. I *know* I did. But why did Isaac have to say that? Or text it, anyway. Did *he* leave Graham's cage open? On purpose? No, surely not. He's evil, but he's not *that* evil. But it's too late. A teensy-weensy seed of doubt has already been planted in my mind. Which I know I'm just not going to be able to shake off. And which, if I'm not too careful, will quickly germinate and become a seedling of doubt, then a tree of doubt and then a whacking great big forest of doubt. Because what if I didn't check? Even though I know I did. But just what *if* I didn't? What would happen then? Or what *could* happen? Because that's the way my mind works. A niggling little worry can quickly escalate into something I can't stop thinking about. And Isaac knows that only too well. Which is precisely why he texted me. And which just goes to prove he's not quite so stupid as he looks. Mind you, he couldn't possibly be as stupid as he looks.

I take a moment to try and assess the situation as calmly

as possible. We've given a spare set of keys to Chloe so that she can pop round and feed Graham every couple of days, because she only lives round the corner. She can feed him and make sure he's got plenty of water. And clean him out at the end of the first week. But what if she doesn't? Or can't for some reason? What if she's lost the keys or something? Or what if she just forgets? Which she won't, of course. I know she won't because Chloe's my best friend and she loves Graham almost as much as I do. She really wants a hamster of her own but her mum won't let her because she's allergic. Or hamster-intolerant or something. Her mum, I mean. Not Chloe. Anyway there's no way she's going to forget to go round. But what if she does? Graham could die. And I mean *literally* die. Or escape. Or escape and *then* literally die. And it would all be my fault and I'd never forgive myself and I'd feel guilty and have recurring nightmares and be in therapy for the rest of my life.

So much for assessing the situation as calmly as possible.

'WE NEED TO STOP!' I suddenly blurt. I can hear my own voice. I sound ever so slightly mad.

'What?' says my dad. 'What do you mean, "we need to stop"?'

'Why do we?' says my mum, turning around and eyeballing me in the eyeballs. 'What's happened, Bonny?'

'Nothing.'

'What do you mean, nothing?'

'Nothing yet,' I say. 'But it might.'

91

By now we're on the motorway. I see a sign whizz past. Or, strictly speaking, we whizz past a sign. A sign that says, 'SERVICES 2 MILES.'

At 60 miles per hour that means I've got two minutes to say something. I glance at the thingy-ometer. The speedometer. We're going 70 miles per hour. I quickly calculate that means I've got . . . even less time than that.

'I need the toilet.'

'Pardon?' says my mum.

'I need the toilet.'

'Why didn't you go before we left?' my dad says.

'I did.'

'What?'

'I did go,' I say.

'When?'

'Just before we left. But I need to go again.'

'Can't you wait?'

'No.'

'Stop at these services, Jeff,' says my mum.

'But . . .' begins Dad.

'Stop at these services!' says my mum again, only much more insistently. 'The next ones aren't for another thirty miles.'

My dad doesn't say anything. And the bit of his face that I can actually see in the rear-view mirror looks anything but happy. By now we can see the slip road ahead approaching fast. Or rather, we're approaching the slip road. And we're approaching it fast.

Dad huffs and puffs like he's blowing out a thousand candles, then indicates. We leave the motorway and slow down before parking. Well, I mean, obviously we slow down before parking. That goes without saying, but I thought I'd say it anyway. I'm just trying to paint a picture. You know? Ramp up the tension a bit, rather than just describing what happens next? Not that I actually know what happens next, because it hasn't happened yet. It's fair to say, though, that there's something of an atmosphere in the car again. Well, there's always an atmosphere. On Earth there is, anyway. What I mean is that there's a *bad* atmosphere. And if it wasn't for Paddy McAloon singing something about hot dogs and jumping frogs (no, really), it would be a darn sight worse.

'Come on then,' Dad says, opening his door.

'Where are you going?' my mum asks.

'Toilet.'

'But I thought . . .'

'Yeah, I know,' says Dad getting out of the car. 'But I might as well go now we're here. Better safe than sorry and all that.'

'What about you, Isaac?' says Mum. 'Do *you* need to go?'

Isaac shrugs and grunts at the same time. Which for him is quite a feat. Doing two things at once? Who said guys can't multitask? I have no idea what the grunt actually means, by the way. I don't speak Caveman. But whatever it means, Isaac gets out of the car and follows Dad into the services. I'm pretty sure it's all part of his cunning plan.

93

'Well?' Mum says, after a few moments of me showing no signs of going anywhere. 'You'd better hurry up. They'll be back in a minute. You don't want to keep your dad waiting.'

Mum's right. I don't want to keep my dad waiting. But there's something I have to say. And I'd better hurry up and say it.

'I don't need the toilet, Mum.'

Mum swivels round and eyeballs me in the eyeballs again. 'Pardon?'

'I don't actually *need* the toilet.'

'But—'

'I was scared.'

'Scared?'

'In case Dad went ballistic.'

Mum frowns until her eyebrows almost meet in the middle. 'Why would Dad go ballistic?'

'If he knew the real reason I wanted to stop.'

'Which is?' asks Mum, starting to sounding just a little bit stressy and cheesed off. 'Come on, Bonny. Spit it out!'

So it all suddenly comes pouring out. About how Isaac texted me – yes, actually *texted* me and about how that then immediately made me panic, even though deep down I knew that I was completely overreacting and that I had absolutely nothing to actually panic *about*, because Chloe could always go round and check Graham and make sure he was OK.

Mum suddenly stops being stressy and actually starts

being surprisingly sympathetic. I don't why I say *surprisingly*, by the way. After all, she's my mum. It shouldn't exactly come as a major surprise that she's being sympathetic. But somehow it still does. She says something about completely understanding where I'm coming from and how *she* takes longer and longer to leave the house because she has to check that the front door's locked about three hundred times first. She smiles. I think she might be exaggerating just a little bit.

So now Mum knows. Knows why we needed to stop. Because I needed to check. And because the longer it went on and the further away from home we were, the more anxious I was going to get. If we were going to have to turn back, turn back now and not later. Mum also knows that I didn't want Dad to know the real reason, because I didn't want things to get even stressier than they were already. And trust me, they *would* have done. Which is why I *pretended* I needed the toilet. What can I say? I panicked. I had to think quickly. It was the best I could come up with!

Anyway, Mum says I'd better hurry up and check with Chloe, to put my mind at rest once and for all. Or at least try and put my mind at rest once and for all. Not only that but Mum says that she and I should follow Dad and Isaac. Not *all* the way obviously. I still remember accidentally walking into the boys' toilets at school once and it's not an experience I'd like to go through again any time soon. Or ever. Talk about gross. It was like something out of a horror movie. But

Mum's right. We should definitely follow Dad and Isaac into the services. That way it will look like I've been too, if we happen to bump into each other.

So that's what happens. Mum and I head into the services and as we do, I'm texting Chloe and asking her to nip round and check on Graham. She texts back about ten seconds later and says, 'Yeah, no probs, Bon'. Which is what she calls me. Obviously. Immediately that makes me feel a bit better. Actually it makes me feel *much* better. Not a hundred per cent better. More like ninety-five. But that'll just have to do, I suppose. Better than nothing.

Inside the services it's properly mobbed. Absolutely heaving. Mainly with gangs of marauding French school kids, by the looks of things. I presume they're French, anyway. And they're not exactly *marauding*. More like mooching about and being all moody. Marauding makes them sound like they're pirates or something. Although actually one does look a bit like a pirate, come to think of it. He's got long black wavy hair and a dangly earring. He's even wearing a blue-and-white stripy t-shirt. You know. The sort that *all* French people are supposed to wear, but actually only your dad wears? I half-expect him to be nibbling on a baguette. But he's not. He's eating a burger. He turns round and sees me staring. I can instantly feel myself turning bright red like someone's just flicked a switch. Which is dead annoying for a start. Because I definitely don't fancy him. And I'm definitely not in the least bit bothered if he happens to be on the same ferry as us. Why on earth would I be? It's not as if we could ever be boyfriend and girlfriend or anything. That would be ridiculous!

I look round to say something to Mum. There's just one teensy problem. Mum's not there any more. Well, I mean obviously she's there *somewhere*. She's not just vanished or been abducted by aliens or anything. At least I hope she hasn't been. What I mean is that Mum's not right next to me like she was a moment ago. Before I got distracted by Captain Hook.

I try and think. Well, I don't try and think. I do think. Where would I go if I was Mum? The shop, that's where. And why would I go to the shop? To stock up on puzzle magazines. Obviously. Because there's only one thing better than sitting in a tent in the pouring rain in a field in the middle of France, and that's sitting in a tent in the pouring rain in a field in the middle of France, doing a crossword. Well, if I'm my mum there is, anyway. Which I'm not, thank goodness. Because life's too short to do crosswords. No offence to anyone who likes doing crosswords, by the way.

Anyway, I go to the shop. And guess what? Mum's not there. Or at least if she is, she's not in the bit that sells magazines. So now my mind *really* goes into overdrive and I start imagining all kinds of crazy scenarios. So crazy that I'm not even going to say what they are. And the weird thing is, I *know* they're crazy even as I'm imagining them. But try telling my mind that!

'There you are!' shouts my dad from the entrance to the shop. 'We've been looking everywhere for you!'

'Everywhere?' I say, wondering why he couldn't have just come over and said that without raising his voice so that everyone within a half-mile radius could hear him.

'Don't get smart with me, Bonny! You know perfectly well what I mean.'

Dad's right. I do know what he means. Rather than stand here and argue about it though, I decide it's probably best to say nothing. And anyway Dad's already gone.

By the time I get back to the car Dad's started the engine and is reversing out of the parking space. I think he's making a point. He stops just long enough for me to open the door and get in. Which is nice of him, I suppose.

Mum turns around and looks at me as Dad accelerates just a little too sharply and we head back onto the motorway. She doesn't say anything. Just raises her eyebrows. I have no idea what that's supposed to mean. Maybe it doesn't mean anything. Maybe she just felt like raising her eyebrows. I can't help noticing something in her lap.

'Is that a new puzzle magazine, Mum?'

'Yes, why?' says Mum.

I shrug. 'Nothing. Just wondered.'

From the corner of my eye I can see Isaac's shoulders going up and down ever so slightly. Like he's doing his best not to burst out laughing. I'm not going to say anything, though. Or do anything. Not now, anyway. I refuse to give him the satisfaction. Because I know that he's loving this. I also know that he's going to pay for it too. I'm not sure how. Or when. But he'll definitely pay for it at some point. Nothing's ever been more certain.

'OH, FOR GOODNESS' SAKE!' yells my dad.

'What is it?' says my mum.

'What do you mean, what is it?' says my dad, staring straight ahead through the windscreen. 'LOOK!'

My mum looks. And so do I. It's not a pretty sight. Stationary traffic as far as the eye can see. Which isn't very far, on account of all the stationary traffic. It's like a solid wall. Well, a solid snake, anyway. And now we're stuck in it too.

'Something must have happened up ahead,' my dad says.

'Mmmm,' says Mum.

'Probably an accident.'

'Mmmm,' says Mum again.

'While we were in the services.'

I glance up and catch sight of Dad's eyes in the rear-view mirror. He's looking right back at me.

'If we hadn't stopped we'd have missed it.'

Right. I see. So it's all my fault. And now if we don't make the ferry in time I'm literally never going to hear the end of it.

'She needed the *toilet*, Jeff!' says Mum. 'We *had* to stop!'

Good old Mum, I think to myself. Still sticking up for me even though she now knows that wasn't the real reason we had to stop. Though if I'm honest I'm not that crazy about having my lavatorial habits being discussed as if I'm not here. And actually, thinking about it, if we hadn't stopped when we did, then maybe we'd have been involved in the accident ourselves. Maybe by stopping when we did, we actually *avoided* an accident. So, actually, you're welcome, Dad. Don't mention it. No really. It was nothing.

I look out of the window on my side and see nothing but bus. It's completely obliterated everything else that was there before. Almost like there's been an eclipse or something. But there hasn't. It's just a bus. And right there, staring directly down at me, is the piratey French guy. He smiles and straightaway I can feel myself going bright red again. Oh my goodness. Please don't let him be on the same ferry as us.

My phone pings. It's a text. Not from my stupid brother. From Chloe. The good news is she's already popped round to our house. And Graham's absolutely fine. He hasn't escaped. And he's got plenty of food and water and lots of nice clean hay. Phew! Chloe's even done a little hamster emoji and a smiley face because she knows that'll make me happy. And it does.

The bad news is that I now need the toilet. I mean genuinely need the toilet. And apologies if that's too much information. But I really do. I should have gone while I had the chance, I suppose. But I wasn't thinking straight. I got distracted.

There's no way I'm going to say anything, though. How can I? Dad would go completely bonkers. I'm just going to have to sit and suffer in silence. Fingers crossed we get going soon. Legs crossed too. Ha!

I look out of my side of the car again. The bus isn't there any more. Either *it's* moved or *we* have. Either way, *something's* moved. And now I see. Yes, the traffic's definitely started to flow.

My dad visibly relaxes. Well, the bit of him that I can actually see does, anyway.

'Music, guys?' he says, reaching forward and pressing the knob on the dashboard before anyone has a chance to object. Not that anyone was ever going to object. I certainly wasn't. I honestly don't mind a bit of music. Even Prefab Sprout! Anything to keep my mind off, shall we say, more *pressing* matters?

Ah yes, I recognise this song. I've got no idea what it's about. All I know is that it's called Cruel. Which under the circumstances seems quite appropriate.

THE WOFF

JEREMY STRONG

I – AN UNEXPECTED VISITOR

If ever you ask someone to describe a creature from Outer Space, they are likely to give you a wicked grin. They will tell you in a chilling whisper that space creatures are green, hairy and enormous. They have six legs, covered with poisonous, rustling hairs; twelve bulging eyes that never sleep and a mouth like a car crusher. You will be told that these monsters eat human beings for breakfast, lunch and tea, not to mention a late afternoon snack. They also adore milkshakes – made from whole cows, shaken, but not stirred.

Do not believe such tales. Just think about it a moment. Think how many creatures of different sizes and shapes there are on our small Earth. We have everything from animals so small you cannot even see them, right up to the Blue Whale. This is so large that you need forty tape measures just to calculate its waist-size. Remember that out of all these thousands of animals only a few are actually a nuisance: lions, snakes, sharks, brothers and sisters ...

It is the same in Outer Space, except that they do not have lions and sharks and so forth, but many different creatures. Possibly, out there, deep in space, there may be some six legged, green ghoulies as big as Mount Everest. But there must also be many thousands of smaller creatures which are bound to be harmless ... like the Woff.

A Woff is pretty small. Its head is little larger than a marble, and the body only slightly bigger than that. It has four short arms, but no legs at all, not even titchy ones that would require a magnifying glass to find them. Instead, the Woff manages to move around by breathing.

On top of its head is a tiny hole, which is really a sort of nose. It breathes in through this, but it can't breathe out through it. This makes the Woff rather like a back-to-front whale. A Woff blows the air out at the bottom of its body, as a hovercraft does. It can move around very happily on a cushion of air, though being a bit lazy, it prefers to stay in the little egg-capsule and motor around instead.

The head is rather strange. The Woff always wears a helmet with a special hole through the top so it can carry on breathing. On each side of the helmet are two large round blobs, like swollen earphones. These are ears but they are capable of translating different languages into the Woff's own speech. Between the ear-pods and on the front of the head are two perfectly round eyes, shielded by a wide visor.

Perhaps the oddest thing of all is the mouth. It is only there when the Woff needs it. As it begins to speak, the mouth appears on the face. As soon as the Woff stops speaking it disappears without a trace. It even vanishes between words.

The Woffs are great space travellers. They live millions of light years away, on the planet Meron. Unfortunately this planet is totally flat, smooth and one shade of violet. It has no rivers or seas and the weather is always the same, day in, day out. Consequently, the Woffs get a bit bored with life on their planet. They have developed a superb means of travelling through space. All they do is *think* themselves to where they wish to go.

This may sound easy, but try it yourself. The Woffs have spent many years perfecting this method of space travel. Using it they can cross vast differences with no trouble at all.

Unfortunately the particular little Woff that I am talking about had rather lost concentration. He had been trying to finish a crossword puzzle at the same time as piloting his ship. Now the egg craft was completely out of control. It hurtled towards Earth, spinning crazily. At the last moment the Woff pilot pulled the machine out of its death-dive. It skidded across a school playground and hurtled through a classroom window, shattering it into seven thousand and

sixty-three pieces. It hit the wall at the far end, slid down to the floor, tilted to one side and stopped. And that is where the story begins.

For several hours the battered space craft lay silent and still upon the classroom floor. It was only as evening came and long shadows stretched themselves lazily that there was some movement.

A hatch on the roof of the craft slid stubbornly back. It stuck several times as if the crash landing had rather spoilt its operation. A head lifted slowly from the egg-hull.

The Woff's eyes were screwed up tight. He gingerly felt all around his head with four hands. Then the eyes opened wide and blinked, just once. Without turning his head, the Woff glanced from side to side and then looked down at the control panel. Perhaps because there was no visible mouth, the face showed neither pain, nor worry.

The Woff began to press a sequence of buttons. A row of tiny lights flickered and a quiet hum drifted from the machine. It began to turn slowly on the spot and then, rather jerkily, it lifted into the air. The Woff kept the little craft hovering while he checked over the controls. He eased his hands over the levers and the craft pulled forwards.

Carefully, the pilot manoeuvred his space ship in and out of the table legs and chairs, gradually increasing his speed as he tested the craft's performance. When at last he was satisfied, the Woff began to cruise over the desk tops, peering intently at this strange new world that he has entered so suddenly.

The growing darkness did not seem to bother him. Even though the machine had no searchlights of any kind, the Woff was able to see. He hovered for several minutes in front of displays of work. He tried to read what the children had written about 'Foxes' and 'What I did in the Holidays'. He even turned his space craft upside down but it still made no sense to him at all.

Eventually the Woff came to the teacher's desk. That looked quite interesting. There were piles of books on it and all sorts of smaller things like broken necklaces and rubbers and half-chewed pencils.

He also found a small hyacinth in a flowerpot, sitting shyly on a shelf. The Woff wondered if that would bounce too. He prodded the pot until it overbalanced and fell on the floor. The plastic tub broke and dark, crumbly earth dotted the floor. The little hyacinth lay on its side in the middle.

The Woff was very pleased and there were twelve more flowerpots, which the children had planted during the winter. The Woff went to each pot in turn and nudged it to the edge until it toppled over. Then he burbled with pleasure while the pot plunged to the floor and shattered.

After the spectacular muddy display made by the last pot the Woff quickly got bored. Scissors and staplers did not seem to do anything. And then he found the old bird's nest. It had once been the home of an elderly blackbird but had

109

been deserted. One of the girls had brought it in only the previous week.

The Woff stared at it for ages. Of all the things he had seen, the old nest was by far the most interesting. He cruised round it slowly several times and at last came to a halt right above it. Then very slowly he began to descend, until his purring craft was lying snugly in the smooth-sided nest. The purr died away. The little marble head retreated into the egg-hull. The hatch squeaked, jerked and then closed. The space-egg went to sleep.

2 – THE WOFF WAKES UP

The day after the Woff's arrival was a Monday and it was a school day. Soon after half past eight children and teachers began to arrive. Mr Pringle drove into the car park and stopped. He closed his eyes and began to yawn. His mouth opened wider and wider and wider. Then wearily he gathered up his bag and walked to his classroom.

The first things that Mr Pringle saw in his classroom were twelve little hyacinths lying in twelve large and muddy messes. The second thing he noticed was that one window was missing. Instead of filling the window frame it was lying in little pieces all over his floor. Mr Pringle's eyebrows slid slowly up his forehead.

'Thieves!' he muttered, and went straight off to find the headmaster.

In the meantime three children appeared outside the broken window. They stared at it excitedly. Nine-year-old Evie turned to the other girls.

'Who did that?' she asked. 'Somebody must have broken in.'

'I don't see why anybody should want to break into a school,' said Tamako. 'I'd want to break out!'

Asmita peered into the classroom. 'It's ever so messy in there,' she whispered. 'It looks as if there's been a fight.'

'Can you see a body?' demanded Evie.

Asmita shook her head. 'No, but they wouldn't leave the body behind, would they?'

'Of course not,' said Tamako. 'They'd burn it in the school incinerator.'

Asmita gave a shudder. 'Urrgh,' she said. 'Who'd be murdered in our classroom, anyway?'

Tamako clapped her hands together and grinned. 'Mr Pringle, of course!'

At this point several more children arrived and asked what was going on. Evie began to fill in the details, talking at breakneck speed.

'Mr Pringle's been murdered by a gang of parents and there are pools of blood all over the floor and half the desks are smashed and the body is smouldering in the incinerator . . .'

So it went on. Within five minutes the whole school had heard that poor Mr Pringle had been stabbed, shot,

111

strangled, drowned and poisoned. A crowd of thirty children gathered outside the scene of the crime.

Even as they watched, Mr Pringle and the headmaster walked into the classroom. Tamako gave a groan and so did a lot of the other children. They wandered off to play football, now that they had been cheated out of a dead body.

The police arrived a few minutes later, having been called by the headmaster. They could not work out what had happened and were quite baffled by the affair. The beak-nosed sergeant suggested that it was the work of hooligans, but he did not sound too sure. When they left, Mr Pringle got a broom and swept the floor. He stuck a large sheet of card over the smashed window and finally let the children into the classroom. Evie hurried over to her teacher.

'Has there been a robbery, Mr Pringle?'

'No, Evie.'

'Are there any dead bodies?' She gave a little giggle and Mr Pringle sighed.

'No, Evie. There are no dead bodies ... yet.' After that Mr Pringle had to spend twenty minutes answering all the questions about the window and the floor. All this time, the Woff was sleeping peacefully in the old blackbird's nest on the nature display table.

It was nearly playtime before anybody happened to glance at the nature corner. Evie walked past and looked idly at the nest. She suddenly realised that something was different about it. She peered more closely and then picked up the egg. It was cold and hard and heavy. Evie ran her fingertips over the smooth surface. She was about to tell Mr Pringle about the strange object when something stopped her. She glanced quickly round the classroom to make sure that nobody was watching and then carried the Woff back to her desk and put it inside.

'Is something the matter, Evie?' asked Mr Pringle suspiciously. 'You look as if you've just laid an egg.'

Evie turned bright red and shook her head vigorously. She heard one of the boys make faint clucking noises but Mr Pringle glared at the boy so hard it soon stopped.

When playtime came, Evie grabbed the precious egg and went out to her friends. 'Look at this!' she whispered excitedly. 'I found it in the nest on the nature table.'

'What is it?' asked Tamako, turning it over in Evie's hands.

'An egg, of course. But it's very heavy.'

'Perhaps it's a dinosaur's egg?' suggested Asmita.

At that moment the egg cracked. The tiny hatch slid back and the little round head of the Woff appeared. The only trouble was that he came out sideways because Tamako had just turned the egg over. The Woff blinked and stared up at the girls.

Evie almost dropped the thing, she was so startled. There was a hollow 'clunk' as all three girls leant forward to see more clearly and banged their heads together. Asmita jumped back and waved her hands wildly.

113

'It's a man!' she cried.

'Don't be silly, it's too small,' snapped Evie.

'Well, it looks like a man,' insisted Asmita.

'I'd like to see a man with a hole in his head like this!' Evie pointed out.

Tamako giggled.

'Ollie Parker says that Mr Pringle has got a hole in his head.'

'That's probably why Ollie Parker keeps on having to do extra work. Look, it's come out further. It's got ear-muffs on and it's staring at us. Here, you hold it. It's a bit scary.' Evie held out the Woff to Tamako and Asmita, but neither of them would even touch it now.

Just then a small, wriggly mouth appeared on the Woff's face, and he spoke. 'Izzawompatrubbadubbapoolyglompervowvowvow?' he demanded excitedly. The mouth disappeared and he looked up at the girls expectantly.

'Did he say something?' asked Asmita. 'Or was that a sneeze?'

'He spoke,' said Evie. 'But what did he say?'

'Something about a rubber bow-wow, I think?' murmured Tamako.

'I know that!' Evie cried. 'You try talking to it.'

'Izzawompatrubbadubbapoolyglompervowvowvow!' repeated the Woff, even more loudly. For a creature so small his voice was surprisingly deep and musical. Asmita began to jump up and down.

'I think it's French,' she said excitedly. 'You went to France last year, Tamako!'

'I know, but I can't remember much and I don't think it sounded like that either.'

'Oh go on, try!' said Evie.

Tamako stared up at the passing clouds for a few moments, thinking hard. Then she turned to the Woff.

'Bonjoy, Mooswer. Havay voo ur glassay por sank euros?'

'Wow! Was that French?'

Tamako blushed and nodded.

'What did you say to him?' asked Asmita.

'I said "Hello, man," – well, something like that anyway. "Hello, man, have you any ice-creams for five euros."'

Evie's mouth opened and shut and opened again. 'You asked him for an ice-cream?'

Tamako nodded.

'What on earth did you do that for?'

'It's the only French I remember.'

'Izzawompatrubbadubbapoolyglompervowvowvow!!' boomed the Woff, even more loudly. Then suddenly he took off from Evie's hand and zoomed up to the level of her face. He stared at her for a second and then did the same to Asmita and Tamako. Finally he hovered politely, midway between all three. A short series of musical chimes broke from the Woff as he pressed several buttons.

'Wow!' squeaked Evie. 'He's got four arms!'

115

'Wore,' said the Woff, slowly, as if he were practising. 'Wore, woe, wee ... where ... where am I?'

Tamako grinned at Evie and Asmita. 'He speaks English!'

'Where am I?' repeated the Woff patiently.

'Er, um, bonjy monsewer. Oh, bother, I mean, hello and welcome to Worsley Junior School.'

'Where am I?' repeated the Woff calmly.

Tamako turned to Asmita and began to whisper angrily.

'I've just told him where he is. What's the matter with him?'

Evie nudged her friend. 'I think I know what he means.' She turned to the little creature from Outer Space. 'This is Worsley Junior School, Downsview Road, Manchester, England, Great Britain, Europe, the Earth, the Milky Way, the Universe. Is that what you wanted to know?'

A series of tiny lights flashed up on the Woff's control panel.

'That is quite sufficient, thank you,' he sang. 'What are you?'

'What are we?' repeated Asmita, looking at the other two. '"What are we?" We're girls. Isn't that obvious?'

'Don't be silly,' said Evie. 'He may come from another planet. How should he know?'

Evie addressed the Woff once more. 'We are people,' she explained hopefully. 'We're children. I'm Evie and that's Tamako and the tall one who talks too much is Asmita.'

'Ah,' sighed the Woff. 'Human beings. That explains

a lot.' The Woff told them briefly how his people think themselves from one place to another. 'I was on my way to visit my granny on one of the seventeen moons of Meron. Unfortunately I tried to do a crossword puzzle at the same time and the extra thinking made my craft go out of control and I crash-landed in your school. Let me introduce myself. I am Azmantha Perrix Scobbalob.'

'Azzmanwhat?' asked Evie immediately.

'Azmantha Perrix Scobbalob.'

'Hmm,' murmured Evie warily. 'That's rather a lot to remember.'

'Then just call me Woff,' suggested the Woff, giving them a happy smile.

3 – THE WOFF TYPES A LETTER

'Where are you going to put the Woff?' asked Asmita, as the children came off the playground and drifted back into Mr Pringle's classroom.

'On my desk, I suppose,' Evie replied.

'I shall be quite all right,' chimed the Woff. 'There's no need to worry about me.' The Woff tried to make his vanishing mouth stay on his face long enough to smile, but because he was only used to making noises he gave a growly leer instead.

Tamako jumped back. 'What's that supposed to be?' she asked anxiously.

117

'I was trying to copy your smile,' the Woff explained.

'*My* smile! I don't smile like that. That's what crocodiles do.'

The Woff buzzed busily up and down between the girls.

'What's a crocodile?' he sang.

'It's a long green monster with an enormous mouth full of sharp teeth,' said Asmita.

'Oh, you mean a Thropp,' the Woff murmured.

'No I don't,' said Asmita. 'I mean a crocodile.'

'Thropps are long green monsters with sharp teeth,' the Woff said. 'But they're not called crocodiles. They're called Thropps.'

'So you keep saying,' interrupted Evie. 'Watch it, here comes Mr Pringle.'

There was a sudden hush in the class as Mr Pringle walked to his desk and sat down.

'Why is everybody so quiet?' sang the Woff cheerfully.

Mr Pringle jerked up and glared round the class.

'Mathew! Stand up! Why did you say that and why are you talking like a robot?' Poor Mathew seemed to be in a state of severe shock, as if he had just been arrested for murder. He stared wide-eyed at his teacher.

'It wasn't me, Mr Pringle, honest!' he protested.

Evie urgently bent over her desk and whispered to the Woff, who was sitting on the top and humming brightly to himself as he watched Mr Pringle.

'Just keep quiet!' hissed Evie.

'Why?' chimed the Woff.

'Who said that?' Mr Pringle stared angrily at Evie. 'What are you doing, Evie?' Are you licking your desk? Didn't you have any breakfast this morning?'

Evie straightened up and turned bright red all over. Before she could think of a reply the Woff demanded, 'Why do you let that giant over there speak to you like that, Evie?'

Mr Pringle leapt from his chair with such ferociousness that his seat spun backwards and hit the wall. 'What is going on!' he spluttered. 'Who is it that keeps interrupting?'

The Woff was about to say more and he had started to take off from Evie's desk. She hastily clamped one hand over him.

Mr Pringle's eyes narrowed.

'Now what are you doing, Evie?' What have you got there?'

Evie's mind was blank. She couldn't think what to say. She could hardly tell Mr Pringle that she had her hand over a Woff called Azmantha Perrix Scobbalob who'd just crash-landed in the classroom. Evie slowly shrugged her shoulders. She could feel everybody's eyes upon her, especially Tamako's and Asmita's.

Mr Pringle folded his arms.

'It's a ball!' he cried. 'I can see it's a ball. Is it yours?'

Evie gave a silent sigh of relief. 'No, Mr Pringle,' she said.

'Then take it to the Lost Property Box in the secretary's office. At once.'

119

'Yes, Mr Pringle.' Evie was stunned. This was almost worse than Mr Pringle discovering what the ball really was.

'And Luca, you go with her and make sure she does as she's told.'

Luca got up slowly from his seat and the two of them left the classroom. 'Now perhaps we can have a bit of peace,' pleaded Mr Pringle. He seemed to have forgotten all about the strange voice.

As they walked across to the secretary's office, Evie tried to explain to Luca about the Woff. He just laughed at everything she said. That was the trouble with Luca. He liked being difficult. He chuckled and said, 'If that thing is a space monster, then my name's King Kong.'

'It is,' insisted Evie. 'And it can talk too.' She turned to the Woff.

'Go on, tell Luca about Meron and your granny and everything.' But the Woff had retreated into his space craft to sulk and would not even poke his head out.

'See, told you!' said Luca, as they reached the office. 'Go on, hand it in.'

He watched while Evie anxiously placed the Woff on top of the pile of Lost Property. 'Goodbye,' she whispered. Luca stuffed his hands in his pockets and rolled his eyes.

'You're daft,' he muttered.

Evie went back to the classroom sadly, wondering if she would have a chance to rescue the Woff later. Mrs Raja, the secretary, had not even noticed the children come in. She had her back turned to the door as she was busily typing out a letter for the headmaster.

The Woff hovered silently behind Mrs Raja's head. The hatch slid silently back and he came slowly out of his craft, with just the top of his head poking over the edge, so that he could see what was going on.

Then he came out a little further, his eyes fixed upon the computer screen. It was tremendously interesting.

Now the Woff watched intently as row after row of strange little black marks appeared on the screen, while Mrs Raja's slim fingers danced over the buttons of her keyboard, The Woff thought it was one of the most extraordinary things in the Universe – but what was it?

He leaned out of his craft and gently prodded Mrs Raja in the ear.

'What are you doing?' sang the Woff politely.

Mrs Raja jumped several feet from her chair, turning in mid-air as she did so. She came down with an awful whump on the keyboard and leapt into the air again with a startled scream clutching her bottom.

'What are you doing?' repeated the Woff, wondering if the secretary was perhaps performing a special dance to celebrate his arrival. Mrs Raja clapped both hands over her face and screamed. It wasn't a very loud scream because her face was covered. 'What are you doing?' asked the Woff for a third time, trying hard to understand this extraordinary human behaviour.

Mrs Raja lowered her hands and stared at the Woff. Her

mouth fell open like a dropped bucket and her eyes rolled upwards and almost disappeared. Then she slid slowly down the edge of the desk and folded into a heap on the floor. She had quite fainted away. The Woff buzzed around the motionless body for half a minute or so.

'Hello? Why are you lying on the floor?' he asked, several times. Since he wasn't too sure where Mrs Raja's ears were, he asked her feet first, then her knees, then her elbows and nose. Finally he gave up and went to the computer.

The Woff began to examine the machine from all angles. He gingerly extended one arm and pressed down. Unfortunately he had his back to the screen and couldn't see anything happening. He tried another key and another. Soon he was pressing every key he could find. He punched them harder and harder, trying to make something happen, and getting crosser and crosser.

At that moment Evie came hurrying into the office. She had managed to get out of class by pretending that she needed to go to the toilet. Evie stood horrified at the doorway. There was Mrs Raja lying on the floor while the Woff was pounding furiously up and down on her keyboard.

At first Evie thought the Woff must have killed the secretary but then Mrs Raja groaned and began to wake up.

'Woff!' cried Evie. 'Come on, quick! We must get away and hide!'

'Why won't this silly thing work?' demanded the Woff angrily.

'Come on! We must go!'

'Oh, all right, if I must.' He gave a last bounce on the 'h' and 'j' keys and then flew towards Evie. As he reached the office door he spun round and let off a short laser blast at the computer that left the machine a melting wreck of hot metal, fizzing and sparking noisily.

'Woff!' squeaked Evie frantically. 'Why did you have to do that?'

'It was boring and wouldn't play,' the Woff grumbled.

'I think you'd better get into my bag when we get back to the classroom,' suggested Evie. 'And for goodness' sake don't come out or say *anything* until I say you can.'

'Why not?' asked the Woff sensibly. 'Is it because of those giant things?'

'What giant things?'

'That thing you call "Ringo" or something.'

'Pringle, Mr Pringle! Don't let him hear you calling him names like that!'

'Why?' asked the Woff. 'Is he dangerous?'

'Yes,' snapped Evie, hurrying back across the hall.

'I could blast him with my stun-gun,' offered the Woff.

Evie began to giggle.

'What are you doing now?'

'I'm giggling. It means that I think you're funny.

'I don't think I'm funny,' sulked the Woff. 'Hee hee hee hee,' he droned. 'There I can giggle too.'

123

'Sssh!' Evie hissed. 'We're back at the classroom. Now remember, into my bag and stay there, quietly.'

'Oh, all right,' said the Woff. 'I'll remember.'

But he didn't.

4 – THE CASE OF THE DISAPPEARING PENCILS

Inside the secretary's office, Mrs Raja gradually recovered and managed to stagger to her feet. For several seconds she gawped at the smoking remains of her computer and almost fainted again. She clutched at the table and made a sort of 'ooooooooh' noise as if she were about to be ill, then she rushed into the headmaster's room and burst into a frenzied babble.

' . . . and this flying egg thing was right behind me all the time, and it poked me in the ear and it was vile, ooh, it was horrible, and its eyes glowed and it kept saying, "What are you doing? What are you doing?" – just like that, it did – and when I woke up there was the computer – exploded!'

The headmaster smiled calmly and drummed his fingertips together. 'Sit down, Mrs Raja, you look dreadful. Now what is all this about exploding computers and eggs? Have you been asleep?'

'I fainted, and I'm not surprised neither. You should have seen it. Oh! It was gruesome!' Mrs Raja leant forward and her eyes bulged. 'It leered at me!' she added.

The headmaster raised his eyebrows. 'Leered at you?'

Mrs Raja nodded her vigorously and gave a shudder at the same time.

'It's wrecked my computer,' she went on, and suddenly burst into tears. It was the shock.

'I think we'd better take a look.'

The head went into the secretary's office. Wisps of blue smoke hung over the mangled machine and a smell of hot metal filled the air. The head stumbled to Mrs Raja's desk and rescued the letter she had sent to the smouldering printer. The letter was charred round the edges. He read it.

Dear Parent,
  Soon it will be time for our Summer Concert and we would like to qwertyuiop = *) (MBV + ¼ "BKJHfdscvbUYTmliyew. ½ 2/3 = 1/4 *) (1876mnBVCC"

And there the letter came to a jumbled stop. Silently the headmaster took the letter back to his room and showed it to Mrs Raja. She promptly burst into tears once more.

'It wasn't me, I don't type like that! It must have been that egg!'

Mrs Raja was in such a state that the headmaster had to get out his secret bottle of brandy and give her a drop. The secretary gulped, coughed, almost choked and rapidly turned purple.

The headmaster anxiously slapped her on the back.

'Is that better? Now, there must be a simple explanation

for all this, Mrs Raja. Why on earth should your computer go up in smoke like that? Did you spill your tea on it?'

The secretary winced and wrung her hands. 'I keep telling you, it was that little round thing. It was foul – it had a face like a squashed snail.' It was a good thing that the Woff could not hear this remark, otherwise Mrs Raja would have gone up in smoke too. The head drummed his fingers on the desk.

'I really don't think it could be anything like that, Mrs Raja. We must be reasonable. It can't possibly be a flying egg.' He reached for the telephone. 'I'd better order another computer. I think you ought to go home, Mrs Raja. You've been overworking.'

The secretary nodded and twisted her fingers together. She glanced at the bottle of brandy and coughed. 'Do you think . . .?' she began. Without saying a word the headmaster poured out another tumblerful of brandy, and Mrs Raja sipped it gratefully.

Meanwhile, in Mr Pringle's classroom there was peace and quiet. The children were listening to their teacher talking about prehistoric monsters. Evie was paying her usual attention, staring out of the window and watching a tractor mowing the school field. The Woff stayed still and quiet for a little while. He had closed his hatch for a doze.

After half an hour he woke up with a strange feeling. At first he wondered what it was, and then he realised that he had not eaten since leaving Meron. He was starving hungry. Back on his home planet, the Woff was used to having regular, large meals. But things were different on Earth. The Woff wondered if he would find anything to eat at all. He hunted around at the bottom of Evie's bag. Suddenly he gave a delighted sniff and pounced on the stub of a pencil. It was ideal and he cheerfully chewed up the whole lot.

That was enough to whet his appetite. He definitely wanted more. There was nothing left to eat in Evie's bag, so the Woff tried to get out. Evie had made sure it was well zipped up. The Woff silently went to work with his laser and cut a Woff-sized hole in the side of the bag. He purred out and hovered amongst the chair legs.

Within one minute the Woff found three pencils lying on the floor, so he quietly ate those, leaving a trail of sawdust behind. Then he began to peer over the table-tops in the hope of finding some more lunch.

Mr Pringle was showing the class some pictures of dinosaurs on a large poster. For some while nobody saw the Woff working his way from desk to desk, eating all the pencils. Sanjeev was the first to realise. The Woff had just settled on his desk and was about to consume Sanjeev's pencil. With a startled yelp Sanjeev slapped his hand down on the desk and the Woff zoomed off in alarm.

Unfortunately, Sanjeev's hand caught the end of his pencil where it poked out over the edge of the desk, and he catapulted the missile right across the room so that it speared Mr Pringle's picture of a Stegosaurus munching a prehistoric carrot.

'Who did that?' roared Mr Pringle.

Sanjeev slowly raised his hand. 'It was an accident, Mr Pringle. I'm very sorry.'

'Look at my poster, it's ruined!' Mr Pringle plucked the pencil from the Stegosaurus' eye and put it on his desk. 'Make sure there are no more accidents like that,' he warned.

Behind him, the Woff silently ate up Sanjeev's pencil.

By this time nearly all the children had noticed the Woff at his lunch, eating his way steadily through the class supply of pencils. They were delighted. They began to whisper to one another and point at the wandering space-egg. At last Mr Pringle put down his poster in despair.

'Why are you all so fidgety all of a sudden?' he enquired.

'It's that egg!' blurted Kieron, pointing wildly.

'What egg?' Mr Pringle turned to look. But the Woff had just disappeared beneath the desk and made his way back to Evie's bag, with a very full stomach.

Gemma glimpsed it and scrambled onto her chair with a shrill squeak, gathering her skirt round her knees.

'There's a flying mouse in the classroom,' she shrieked. 'I saw it!'

'It was an egg,' argued some of the others.

'It was a mouse!' repeated Gemma.

Mr Pringle thumped his desk with both fists. 'That's

enough!' he bellowed. 'Eggs don't fly, and neither do mice. Stop being silly, Gemma, and get down from there.'

'But . . .'

'But nothing!' Mr Pringle said sternly. 'Get out your writing books and write down what we have been talking about this afternoon.'

The class sighed and opened their desks to get their books. Sanjeev put up his hand, then Kieron, then Evie, then Luca and so on, until nearly everybody had their hand up.

'Now what is it?' cried Mr Pringle. 'Gemma, what is it?'

'I haven't got a pencil,' she said lamely.

'Luca?'

'Neither have I.'

The rest of the class began to mumble the same thing. Nobody had a pencil. Mr Pringle clutched his forehead.

'I don't believe it! What have you done with thirty-two pencils? Eaten them?'

'No,' said Kieron. He grinned. 'The egg ate them.'

'What egg?'

'The flying egg!' chorused the whole class.

'Oh no, not that again!' Mr Pringle started forwards and stared incredulously at the floor. 'Why is there sawdust everywhere?' he demanded. Kieron put his hand up. 'No, no! Oh no!' said Mr Pringle. 'Kieron, I don't want to hear any more about flying egg-mice, thank you. Next thing, you'll be telling me the Martians have landed. Just sit still, all of you, while I fetch some new pencils from the stock cupboard.'

As soon as Mr Pringle left the classroom there was uproar. Everybody was asking the same question. 'Did you see it? It was a flying egg, wasn't it?'

Evie fished around in her bag and proudly brought the Woff out. In an instant she was surrounded by fascinated friends. They had to stand on chairs and tables to see over each other's shoulders.

The Woff was asked so many questions that he had to explain everything from the beginning.

'How long are you going to stay?' asked Kieron.

'Are you on holiday?' said Wiktoria. 'When are you going back?'

'I can't get back,' the Woff sang in an unhappy drone. 'I don't suppose I shall ever see Meron, or my granny, again.'

'Why ever not? What's the matter?' asked Evie anxiously. But before the Woff could answer there was a warning shout from behind.

'Look out, Mr Pringle's coming.'

There was a rush for chairs and Evie thrust the Woff back into her bag. 'Be good!' she hissed at him.

'Hee hee hee hee,' was all the reply she got. Then everybody had to get on with their work, while Mr Pringle began to wonder what was wrong with his class this particular morning.

5 – WOFFS CANNOT SWIM

Azmantha Perrix Scobbalob managed to keep out of further trouble until lunch-time. Mr Pringle even began to think that things were getting back to normal. There was not a murmur from his class as they wrote with their new pencils. Twelve o'clock came and Mr Pringle invited them to stop working.

With sighs of relief, Evie and her friends handed in their work and got themselves ready for lunch. Mr Pringle went off to the staffroom for a well-earned rest. As soon as he had gone Evie opened her bag. 'Come on, Woff, are you asleep?' she called.

There was a mumbling hum from the depths of the bag and then the Woff poked his head over the top and peered at the faces all around him.

'I was asleep,' he droned. 'But I'm not asleep now,' he complained. 'I don't think all those pencils agreed with my stomach, you know. We have much better food on Meron.'

Evie clasped a hand over her mouth as she recalled what the Woff had said earlier that morning. 'Are you sure you can't get back to Meron?' she asked. The Woff came out of her bag and flew up to her shoulder. He perched there, wobbling slightly.

'My craft has been damaged. When I crashed through the window and hit the wall I was travelling rather too fast. The bang broke part of my motor. It isn't actually a motor, but it

131

would be too difficult to describe it to you any other way. It's a small part of the motor, but it's very important and I don't suppose I shall be able to fix it on Earth.'

Some of the children looked at each other, then Luca said, 'Why not?'

'It needs a diamond,' the Woff sang gloomily.

'But there are plenty of diamonds on Earth!' exclaimed Luca.

Tamako groaned. 'Oh yes,' she said. 'Millions. The ground is absolutely covered with diamonds!'

The Woff looked carefully at the ground. 'I'm sorry,' he began slowly. 'I can see only sawdust.'

'Take no notice of her,' said Luca. 'What I meant was that we do have diamonds on Earth, so it shouldn't be too difficult to find you one.'

Asmita and Tamako shook their heads slowly.

'Diamonds are expensive,' murmured Asmita.

'My mum's got one!' Evie cried. The Woff bounced eagerly up and down.

'Do you think she'd let me use it?' he asked hopefully.

Evie collapsed back into her seat. 'I don't suppose so. It's in her wedding ring you see, and she's rather fond of it.'

There was a depressing silence for a while, which was only broken when they were called for lunch.

'Are you coming?' Evie asked the Woff.

'Oh, yes. I should like to see what human beings eat.'

At the lunch table the Woff sat quietly on Evie's lap.

Occasionally he hovered and watched forkfuls of food pass from plate to mouth and disappear. He stopped to watch Evie sprinkle salt on her chips.

'What is that white powder?' he asked.

'Salt. It makes the food taste nicer. Do you want to try some?' Asmita poured a tiny heap of salt on the side of her plate and the Woff dipped his craft and ate some.

An instant later his head vanished and his hatch snapped shut. The space craft sat on the table, still and silent. Evie became anxious.

'Woff? Woff? Are you all right?' She tapped on the egg-craft with her knife, but there was no reply. Evie shrugged her shoulders. 'I hope he's not poisoned,' she said seriously.

Just then the Woff's hatch slowly grated back and his tiny head began to rise cautiously into view.

'Oh, Woff!' cried Evie. 'Are you all right?' His eyes were screwed up tight. He opened one and gave Evie a severe scowl.

'No,' he grunted. Then he added huskily, 'I don't like salt.'

'I should think you need a drink,' suggested Tamako. The Woff eyed the big, glass water-jug suspiciously.

'What's in it?' he demanded.

'Water. There's nothing wrong with water. It's tasteless.'

'Why do you drink it then?'

Tamako frowned. 'I don't really know. We just do.' She took a sip from her beaker to show how harmless it was.

The Woff drifted to the top of the water-jug and cast a

glance over the lip. He had never seen water before and didn't know what it looked like at all. So far as he could tell, the jug was empty.

'There's nothing in there,' he sang, and before anybody could stop him, he had dived into the jug. There was a loud 'plop!' and a spray of water pattered onto the table. Evie leaned over and peered in. The Woff was lying on the bottom and staring back at Evie with a look of startled bewilderment. There was a muffled explosion and a great, gurgling gloop of bubbles burst upon the surface.

'I don't think Woffs can swim,' cried Evie with dismay and hurriedly rolled up her sleeve. She plunged her arm into the water-jug.

'Phew!' sighed Evie. 'That was close!' She brought out the Woff. There was a film of water beneath his visor and his eyes were tight shut. Evie shook him hard. The Woff gave a tremendous sneeze and in one go got rid of all the water he had accidentally sucked in by blowing it out. He soaked the whole of Evie's front.

'Urr!' she squealed. 'I'm wet through. Oh Woff, did you have to do that?'

'I'm sorry,' he said. 'I don't like water. It's cold, and wet.'

Evie plucked at her sopping blouse. 'I know,' she said.

6 – WOFF AND CHIPS

After lunch, Evie and her friends went out to play and the Woff decided to explore. The school kitchen was a fascinating place. There were enormous ovens and stoves with fat gas rings. There was a giant potato-chipping machine and a mixing bowl with whisks as big as footballs. Huge saucepans boiled and steamed, vats of hot fat sizzled and the five cooks busied themselves with cutting and cleaning, chopping and washing up.

The Woff had never seen anything on Meron so complicated as this kitchen. Soon he was idly wandering round and coughing every time he flew through a cloud of steam.

All at once he stopped dead and began to tremble with excitement. There, just below him, sitting in some kind of special space-transporter, were three Woffs! Azmantha Perrix Scobbalob was overwhelmed. His planet must have traced him and sent a rescue party all the way to Earth!

Eagerly, the Woff descended. A delighted hum broke from his craft as he settled himself next to the egg-box. He began to talk excitedly in his own language, bleeping and buzzing like a faulty radio. The three eggs did not say a word. They did not even move.

The Woff was upset and he looked sharply at the eggs. Fancy coming all the way from Meron and then not bothering to speak to him. Perhaps they were asleep? He spoke sternly to the egg nearest to him and then gave it an angry prod. The egg fell out of the box, wobbled to the edge of the table, flew gracefully towards the floor and broke.

The wet splat was followed by a moment of horrified silence as the Woff stared at the runny mess of white and yellow oozing slowly across the kitchen floor. He dived down upon the smashed egg, babbling away in his own language.

'I'm sorry, I didn't mean it! Speak to me, please speak to me!' The egg spread further still, while the frantic Woff sped backwards and forwards, bleeping miserably to himself. He didn't know what to do.

The Woff went back to the table and tried to explain everything to the remaining Woffs.

'It wasn't my fault. Why won't you talk to me? I only touched him to see if he was awake or not. Why won't you speak to me? Have you brought the diamond I need?'

There was still no sound or movement from the two eggs and the Woff was working himself into a fine state. He was convinced that the eggs had come to rescue him, yet they would not even speak. Perhaps they too had suffered some awful accident when they reached Earth?

The Woff was struck by an idea. He knew how to repair his own little machine so he could easily check out the new arrivals'. He parked his craft next to the eggs and hovered out, carrying his tool-kit with him. The Woff fetched his laser-driver and began to remove what he thought was the engine panel from the side of a Woff-craft.

The laser-driver burned a large hole in the side of the egg and the rather runny, half-scrambled contents dribbled out onto the table. Quite certain now that he had murdered two of his fellow beings, the Woff dashed back madly to his craft, slammed the hatch and switched himself off. He wanted nothing more to do with that dreadful craft. The shock would give him nightmares for a week.

The head cook returned from preparing a bucketful of chips and began mixing up the ingredients for her pudding. It was a minute or two before she turned to the egg-box. Her hand hovered over it for a second and then she frowned. She looked about her. There was a smashed egg on the floor. That was odd. What was even more strange was the half-scrambled egg in the box.

The head cook carefully lowered her large wooden spoon and stood, hands on hips, trying to work the problem out. One of the other cooks walked past and glanced at her.

'Something the matter, Mavis?'

'Yurss,' said the head cook slowly. 'Look at them eggs.'

'You've dropped one. That's not like you. You're so careful, so you keep telling us.'

'Yurss, I am, and it's not like me, and it isn't me, Sophie. I didn't drop that egg. Did you?'

Sophie shook her head.

Mavis bellowed across the steaming kitchen. 'Who dropped one of my eggs?'

There was a loud chorus of, 'Wasn't me!'

'And it weren't me, neither,' muttered Mavis staunchly. 'And look at this,' she said to Sophie, pointing at the half-scrambled egg. 'What do you make of that, then?'

Sophie bent forward and stared at the neat hole. She bent closer and sniffed it. She cocked one ear and listened to the shell. Then she gave it a little tap.

The head cook humphed impatiently.

'I didn't ask you to give it a medical examination, Sophie. How do you explain that half-scrambled egg?'

'I don't know, Mavis. It's a mystery.'

'Yurss,' drawled the head cook. 'I had three eggs and now there are four. Perhaps you've got an answer for that, too?'

Sophie gave up. She didn't know how to answer any of the cook's awkward questions.

'I'd better get on with the washing up,' she murmured and hurried off to the sinks.

Mavis eyed the eggs in the box suspiciously and then decided she'd better get on or second sitting lunch would be late. She picked up the first egg, broke the shell on the side of the mixing bowl and added it to everything else. Then she picked up the Woff and tapped him smartly on the edge.

He wouldn't break. Mavis tapped the egg harder, and then once more.

'This is a bloomin' tough shell!' she complained. She held the Woff more firmly and brought him down with a sharp crack against the bowl.

Suddenly the hatch sprang back and a furious Woff

appeared. He skidded out of the head cook's grasp and buzzed angrily around her head. He was still extremely touchy about the eggs, not to mention being kicked around the playground.

'Eeek!!' squawked Mavis. 'It's a giant bee!' She hastily ducked behind the table as the Woff swooped out of a cloud of steam. 'Here, you can't do that!' she cried, plucking up courage. She seized her wooden spoon and hurled it after the disappearing Woff. It was wildly off target, and clunked one of the other cooks on the back of the head.

'Who did that?' cried the astonished cook, just as the Woff whizzed past her nose. By this time all five cooks had realised that something unusual was sharing their kitchen with them. Panic broke out.

Every time the Woff was sighted, the cooks hurled a pan or a potato or a bag of sugar at it – whatever came to hand. They were poor shots and the Woff easily dodged the missiles. Azmantha Perrix Scobbalob was beginning to enjoy this little game. The tables and the floor were gradually disappearing beneath a muddled mess of food, cutlery and crockery. The cooks began to slip and slide. They were hitting each other more often that not.

'I'll get you!' bellowed Mavis, plunging after Azmantha through a sea of currants and wooden spoons. 'No little insect can get the better of me!'

The Woff turned and came diving back at the head cook. She, in turn, seized the bucket of prepared chips and flung it at him. All at once Azmantha Perrix Scobbalob saw three hundred and sixty-five uncooked chips hurtling towards him. With lightning reactions he frazzled the whole lot with a long burst from his laser gun. The chips fell to the floor, perfectly cooked.

While Mavis stared dumbfounded at the pile of steaming chips, the Woff sped out of the kitchen, determined to find Evie's bag and a bit of peace. Silence slowly settled over the battlefield. Two of the cooks had fainted. One had been knocked unconscious by a flying saucepan. Mavis and Sophie stood next to each other, breathing heavily. Sophie cleared her throat.

'I think the second sitting will be a bit late, Mavis.'

'Yurss,' said the head cook dreamily. 'I don't believe it, Sophie. It's not true. Tell me I've been asleep.'

'Oh no, you never sleep on the job, Mavis. So you keep telling us.'

Mavis examined one of the chips. She gave a start. 'Right! Come on! Action stations! Let's get this mess cleared up, there's a lunch to be cooked and as soon as it's done I'm going to see the headmaster about this.' Mavis bustled about the kitchen. 'Throw a bucket of cold water on those three, Sophie. I'll not have them sleeping on the job!'

Under the iron rule of the head cook, order quickly returned to the kitchen and the second sitting was only twenty minutes late. As soon as lunch was finished, Mavis marched off to the headmaster's room. She knocked sturdily on his door and went straight in.

'Cook! What can I do for you?' he asked in surprise, hurriedly shutting the confiscated comic he had been reading.

'I've got a complaint.'

'Oh dear. Nothing serious, I hope?' The headmaster smiled at Mavis but when he saw her grim expression he quickly tried to look sympathetic.

'Very serious, headmaster. We've had a nuisance in our kitchen today. It's a wonder the children got a second lunch. My cooks had to work like beavers,' she added proudly.

'I'm sure you managed admirably. Now what was this nuisance? Not one of the children, I hope?'

'No. It was a flying egg.'

The headmaster blinked, trying to remember where he had previously heard about such a thing.

'A flying egg?' he repeated.

'Yurss. It scrambled half my proper eggs for me and then it fried up all the chips. A whole bucketful ... just like that – *ZZZZZZZZ*!!' The headmaster leaped back several feet.

'Goodness! Are you sure, Cook? I mean, eggs don't usually fly, do they?'

Mavis folded her brawny arms and fixed the headmaster with a glare of steel. 'No, they don't, and that's how I know this was one. I don't know where it came from and I don't know where it's gone, but it had better not come back to my kitchen!'

141

'No, of course not.' The headmaster frowned as he recalled Mrs Raja and the exploding computer. 'I'll get this business sorted out at once. Thank you for telling me, Cook.'

Mavis gave a curt nod and returned to her kitchen.

The headmaster walked thoughtfully down to the staffroom, wondering what he could possibly say to his staff about the menace of the flying egg. He winced. They would think him quite mad.

As for Azmantha Perrix Scobbalob, he was sitting quietly at the bottom of Evie's bag, enjoying the peace. Earth seemed a rather noisy, hectic place and he was getting a bit tired of the constant hustle and bustle. Meron might be flat and boring but it was far more suitable for Woffs than Earth. At least he didn't keep falling into water-jugs or getting kicked sky-high. Besides, his granny would be getting worried by now, wondering what had happened to him.

The Woff was homesick.

7 – THE PAINTING ON THE FLOOR

When the headmaster walked into the staffroom he found Mr Pringle staring thoughtfully out of the window as he sipped at a mug of tea.

'What's so interesting out there, Mr Pringle?'

Evie's teacher grunted. 'If only I knew headmaster, if only I knew.' Mr Pringle thought about telling the headmaster about the peculiar events in his classroom but decided against it. The headmaster would probably think him mad.

The headmaster cleared his throat.

'Mr Pringle, I expect I sound a bit silly, but have you by any chance seen ... um ... well ...' He coughed. Words failed him. Then he blurted, 'Have you by any chance seen a flying egg?'

There was a clatter and a crash as Mr Pringle dropped his empty tea mug on the floor and both men gave frightened jumps. Mr Pringle hastily began to pick up the bits and pieces.

'I'm terribly sorry. You gave me a bit of a shock,' Mr Pringle explained with great embarrassment.

The headmaster got down on his knees and began to pick up pieces too, taking the opportunity to whisper fiercely to Mr Pringle beneath the staffroom table.

'So, you *do* know something!' hissed the headmaster in an urgent voice.

'Quickly now, have you seen this flying egg, or are Mrs Raja and the cook mad?'

Mr Pringle gave a start. 'Mrs Raja? The cook? What do they know?'

The headmaster briefly told of the exploding computer and the battle in the kitchen.

Mr Pringle added his own information, which wasn't much, but the headmaster seemed interested. They got into a deep discussion, quite forgetting that they were still beneath the table. Other members of staff came into the room and cast queer glances at the couple whispering on the floor, but Mr Pringle and the headmaster were too concerned to notice.

When Mr Pringle reached his classroom he felt too nervous to teach anything. He decided that the children had better do some artwork. They could paint some pictures of prehistoric animals to go with this morning's writing. The class thought this was a marvellous idea.

Tables were moved together to make large painting surfaces and the children fetched the paints and brushes and water-jars.

Their noise disturbed the sleeping Woff and he soon ventured out of Evie's bag, so that he could see what was going on. It was fascinating to see the bright coloured marks appear on the paper, as if by magic. It was even better than the computer and Azmantha dearly wanted to have a go himself. He carefully avoided Mr Pringle and hovered down to Evie. She was busily painting a large Triceratops.

'What are you doing, Evie?' he sang brightly.

'Oh, hello, Woff. I wondered what had happened to you. I'm painting.'

'I would like to paint.'

Evie shook her head and smiled.

'I don't think Mr Pringle would like that. Anyway, look what happened at lunchtime, when you fell in the water-jug. I think you're safer just watching.'

The Woff went off and tried to persuade other children to let him borrow their paintbrushes, but they were all too busy on their own pictures. He grew crosser and crosser. Everything was going wrong. His motor had been broken. He'd had pots and pans hurled at him and he was stranded for ever on this strange planet Earth because he needed a diamond which he didn't have. Now he wanted to paint.

He wanted to paint a stirring picture of a Thropp, and nobody would let him. They were the creatures that Tamako thought were crocodiles. Azmantha decided that if nobody would give him a paintbrush, he would have to get one for himself.

He tilted his craft and went into a low dive, swooping down over the art-table. Just as he passed over the water pot he reached out and grabbed a brush, holding onto it with grim determination as he sped upwards once again. Unfortunately, as the Woff plucked the brush from the pot, he also managed to knock it over. Murky water began to trickle everywhere.

'Oh no!' Sanjeev shouted in despair, as a brown stain spread across his toothy Tyrannosaurus-rex.

'Look what you've done!' yelled Evie, trying to stop the flood seeping over her Triceratops.

Mr Pringle hurried over.

'Get some paper quickly and mop it up,' he commanded. 'Don't stand there gawping while all the animals drown!'

The Woff had disappeared, of course. He was hiding beneath the art-tables, watching curiously as water dribbled over the edge and pattered onto the ground. He flew slowly over the spreading pool, making swirling patterns with his stolen brush. It wasn't a very good picture – not nearly lively enough. He needed a bit of colour, especially if he was going to paint a Thropp.

Silently he poked his tiny head over the table-top. Everybody seemed busy, cleaning the water off their paintings. With great care, the Woff began to pull the paint tray towards the edge of the table. It overbalanced and clattered to the floor, upside down. Azmantha darted under the table once more.

'Who did that?' cried Mr Pringle, his nerves thoroughly on edge. 'Was that you, Kieron?'

'No, Mr Pringle.'

'Honestly, you children are so clumsy. Pots of water, paint trays! Look at that mess down there. You had better get that cleared up sharpish.'

Kieron went to get the mop. Meanwhile the Woff was tearing around at breakneck speed, dipping his brush in the paint, scooping it up and completing his magnificent Thropp portrait beneath the shelter of the art-table. He put the finishing touches to it. Azmantha Perrix Scobbalob thought it was quite brilliant and he sprayed it thoroughly with a clear, hard varnish. Then he went off to hunt for diamonds in the bookcase.

Kieron returned and mopped up the spilt paint without noticing the Thropp. It was not until the art lesson was over that anybody saw it. When the children moved the tables back to their normal positions the picture was revealed. There was a tremendous, terrifying, purple, green and spotty, seven-legged, seven-horned, two-headed Thropp, galloping across Mr Pringle's floor. It was really quite a superb painting.

For a moment nobody could do anything. They gathered round and stared at the wonderful picture. Mr Pringle gulped and looked from face to face.

'Whose is that?' he said at last, speaking in an unnaturally hoarse voice. He had a dreadful feeling in his stomach that the flying egg had been at work once more. 'Who painted that picture on the floor?'

Nobody answered, and in his heart of hearts, Mr Pringle knew that not even he could have painted a picture as good as that.

At that moment the headmaster wandered into the classroom to check that everything was all right. He peered over Mr Pringle's shoulder at the picture on the floor. His eyebrows shot up.

'Mr Pringle? Do you normally let your children paint on the floor?'

Mr Pringle gave a startled jump. 'Um, no, of course not. I don't know how it happened. It appeared as if by magic. Wash it off at once, Evie.' Mr Pringle turned away to speak with the headmaster.

Evie touched his elbow, looking worried.

147

'It won't come off, Mr Pringle,' she said.

The headmaster interrupted.

'Don't be silly, Evie. It's washable paint. Of course it will come off.'

'It won't,' Evie insisted. 'I've tried.'

'Your mop must be dry,' cried the headmaster. 'Here, give it to me.' He snatched the mop from Evie so that a spray of mucky water flicked across Mr Pringle's clean shirt.

The head went red.

'Oh! Sorry, Mr Pringle. Really, Evie, fancy making a mop as wet as that!'

Evie looked at her friends and rolled her eyes. The headmaster pushed the mop furiously backwards and forwards, but the Thropp galloped on. He got out a little penknife and, on bended knees, scraped at the painting. That had no effect either.

The headmaster got slowly to his feet. 'Right!' he snapped. 'Which one of you did this?' He glared at the children. 'Come on, who did it?'

Evie knew. Kieron knew. Tamako and Sanjeev and Gemma knew. Everybody in the class knew, except Mr Pringle and the headmaster. Nobody was going to tell them. There was a cold silence until Mr Pringle gave a little cough.

'I don't think it can possibly be the children's work, headmaster. It's too good. Besides, it's not any dinosaur that I know of.'

The two men looked at each other, both thinking the

same thing. They went into one corner of the classroom and had a rapid consultation.

'If it's the flying egg,' the headmaster hissed. 'It means that the little beggar is still in here!'

Mr Pringle nodded and glanced around anxiously. 'What shall we do?' he asked.

'We can't leave the children in class with a dangerous egg. We shall have to evacuate them. You take them into the hall, Mr Pringle. Tell them a story or play them a record to keep them quiet. I shall start a search.'

The headmaster drew himself up to his full height and gritted his teeth. 'By hook or by crook I'll catch this thing, if it's the last thing I do!'

8 – GOODBYE!

'Why are we going into the hall, Mr Pringle?' Evie asked, stopping in the doorway so that nobody else could get through.

'We're going to listen to a story, now go on in.'

'Why can't we listen in the classroom?' she asked.

'Because I'm going to play a record as well. Now go in, please.'

Evie still didn't move. 'Why can't we listen to the record in the classroom?'

Mr Pringle rolled his eyes as he pushed Evie through the doorway. 'Because, Evie, we don't have an old-fashioned record player in the classroom. You won't be listening to a CD or an mp3. The headmaster wants to play an old-fashioned vinyl record, called an LP, to everyone.'

'Is that because the headmaster is old-fashioned?' asked Sanjeev.

'No, it isn't and don't be so cheeky,' snapped Mr Pringle. 'This is a famous old recording of some extraordinary music. If you must know, the head wants us out of the classroom so that he can look for something he's lost.'

'Oh.' Evie went into the hall, wondering what the headmaster would want to look for in her class. Her stomach turned right over and almost fell to her feet. The Woff! Was he searching for the Woff? Evie turned and stared back at her classroom. She could just see the shape of the headmaster moving behind the closed door. The Woff was in there, trapped, and there was nothing she could do.

Evie whispered urgently to Tamako and Asmita as they sat down. The three girls could not take their eyes off the door.

'If I could have your attention, girls ...' Mr Pringle said stonily, 'I shall play you a wonderful old piece of music that sounds like prehistoric monsters stamping around and roaring. It was written by a man called Stravinsky. He was Russian and lived in France.'

Sanjeev shot his hand up.

'Yes, Sanjeev?'

'How could he be Russian if he lived in France, Mr Pringle? He must have been French.'

150

'No,' said Asmita. 'He must have lived in Russia if he was Russian so he couldn't have been French.'

'He would have been if he had lived there,' insisted Sanjeev.

'Where?' Luca demanded.

'In France.'

'Not if he was Russian,' said Luca.

'Maybe he was French and lived in Russia?' Asmita murmured.

'For goodness sake!' Mr Pringle shouted. 'Stop talking gibberish. Stravinsky was French and he lived in Ru ... oh! Now you've got me at it. Never mind where he came from. Just listen to the music, all of you.'

Inside Mr Pringle's classroom the headmaster could hear the heavy throb of the music. So could the Woff. He listened for a few seconds and decided that some strange creature was talking a most odd language. Then he went back to his search for a diamond.

So there it was. The headmaster searched at one end of the classroom for the Woff, and Azmantha searched the other end of a diamond. Having rifled through all the cupboards, the headmaster began crawling beneath all the tables, peering into corners and looking in the children's bags to see if the Woff had slipped into one to hide.

'Urrgh,' the headmaster grumbled. 'The things they leave in their bags.' He paused to unstick his fingers from a half-chewed toffee, then he looked in Evie's bag.

The Woff flew up quietly and watched for a second. 'That's Evie's bag,' he sang. 'What are you doing?'

'Aaagh!' cried the headmaster, trying to jump to his feet. His head smashed against the table-top and he even managed to stand right up, with the table clinging to his back for a moment, like a tortoise shell, before it toppled backwards, upside down. The headmaster clapped one hand over his injured head and tried to ward off the Woff with the other.

'What are you doing?' repeated the Woff, eyeing the headmaster earnestly. He came a little closer and the headmaster immediately took a step back and tripped over Evie's table. He sat down on an upturned leg and leapt into the air once more.

'Ge . . . ge . . . get away from me, you monster!' the head cried, still clutching the rapidly growing bump on his head. 'You'd better be careful! Don't come any nearer, I'm armed!' So saying, the head seized the nearest weapon, which happened to be Mr Pringle's empty coffee mug.

The Woff suddenly noticed a sparkle on the headmaster's hand. His eyes fixed on the little object wonderingly. Yes, it was! The head had a diamond on his wedding ring! Azmantha surged forward excitedly.

'Excuse me,' he began, but the headmaster took another step back and hurled the coffee mug at him. It was a bad throw and the Woff watched the mug whizz past harmlessly.

He turned back to the headmaster, who was now retreating clumsily towards the classroom door.

'Excuse me, but isn't that a ... oh, bother the man. He's gone.' The head had whirled through the door and slammed it shut behind him. The bang was heard even over the throbbing din of the music.

The class swung round to see what was going on.

Mr Pringle gave the headmaster a questioning glance.

'It's in there!' he croaked, leaning against the door to hold it shut. 'It tried to get me!'

'Can't hear you,' shouted Mr Pringle over Stravinsky's stamping drums and buzzing violins. 'What did you say?'

The headmaster wiped the sweat from his forehead. 'It's in there!' he bellowed, and Evie's heart sank. The Woff was trapped.

At this point a small round hole appeared in the door, just above the headmaster's left ear, and the Woff came sailing through gaily.

'No, it isn't!' Mr Pringle gurgled. 'It's just escaped! Oh, it's horrible, all slimy and green, with hundreds of bulging eyes ...'

Evie leapt to her feet. Their Woff, slimy and green? He wasn't like that at all. He was round and sweet.

'He isn't slimy,' she cried, with tears in her eyes. 'He's lovely and all he wants is to go home to his granny on Meron.'

The rest of the class were on their feet now, jumping

153

up and down and shouting about how wonderful the Woff was, but their cries were drowned as the music went pounding on.

Mr Pringle shouted at the children and covered his eyes, the headmaster still clutched the smoking door and the Woff calmly hovered in front of him, wondering what all the noise and fuss was about. He eyed the glittering diamond with longing.

'Is that a diamond?' he began once more. 'Because, you see, I was doing this crossword puzzle on my way to my granny's, and she'll be ...'

The headmaster gave a strangled yell and broke away from the door. He started to run up the hall, with the Woff flying quickly after.

'I only wanted a brief word,' he chimed. 'She's expecting me for tea, and if I could just find a diamond to repair my motor ...'

'Help!' cried the headmaster, leaping over the astonished children. He darted into the kitchen, closely followed by the Woff. A second later they both came dashing out, with a fusillade of pots and pans raining down on them. Mavis and the other four cooks came charging out of the kitchen.

'I said I'll not have that flying egg in my kitchen again!' cried Mavis, brandishing a rolling pin like King Arthur's best sword.

The music from the record player got louder and faster,

filling the air with its pounding beat. Round the hall went the headmaster and the Woff. Round the hall went Mavis and the four cooks after them.

'Stop him!' panted the headmaster, his face purple from all the running.

But Mr Pringle still had his eyes covered, so convinced was he that the Woff was some terrible, ugly monster.

'Oh, bother all this,' droned the Woff to himself. 'All I want is that silly person's diamond.'

Out of the corner of his eye he spotted the record going round and round and he identified it as the strange creature that was making all the noise. He broke off in mid-flight and swooped down to the record player.

'Is there something the matter with you?' asked the Woff kindly. 'Are you ill?' The music blared on and the record went round and round. 'I feel seasick,' he thought, as he lost balance and tumbled into the machine.

There was a loud bang and two clicks as Mr Pringle triumphantly slammed down the lid and flicked over the catches.

'I've got him! I've got the flying egg!'

The headmaster was too puffed to say anything.

The head cook grunted with satisfaction. 'You make sure you keep him there,' she warned, and marched back to the kitchen with her staff.

There was an ear-splitting yowl from the record player and the music suddenly ceased. In the tense silence that followed, everybody looked at each other and then turned to stare at the record player.

Mr Pringle smiled and began to relax. 'I've caught it,' he repeated softly.

Evie, Tamako, Luca, Asmita, Kieron, Sanjeev and Gemma all stood up. 'Please let him out,' they pleaded. 'He's not dangerous at all.'

'I know he wrecked the computer,' said Evie. 'But he didn't mean to. It was an accident'.

'He only wants a diamond,' said Luca. 'Then he can go home.'

Mr Pringle and the headmaster only shook their heads. 'No,' panted the headmaster. 'That thing is a danger to the whole world. We must ...' The words died in his throat as the record player began to tremble violently. It jumped and banged upon the table.

Mr Pringle tried to hold it down with both arms. All at once the lid blew off, sending Mr Pringle reeling backwards. Blue-grey smoke curled upwards from the wrecked turntable, and from the haze of smoke the Woff appeared. The children cheered and then gasped.

There was something magically different about the Woff. It was difficult to say what. Afterwards, some said he was larger; others said he was a different colour or shape. But they all agreed that somehow he looked far, far grander and most splendid.

'Hello, Evie,' the Woff sang. 'I'm glad you're here.

I've come to say goodbye. I've found a diamond.' He bleeped cheerfully.

'Oh, Woff,' Evie sighed. 'I am glad! Where was it?'

The Woff pointed at the smashed record player. 'It was in there. That's a peculiar machine. I don't know why it wanted a diamond because it can't fly, I checked. It had a diamond in its arm, so I took that. I don't think it liked me very much, because it gave a squeaky roar and then stopped talking altogether. I did ask nicely, so you can't blame me. Anyway, I didn't like what it was saying.'

'Are you going right now?' asked Evie sadly.

'Yes. My granny will be worried. I might come back one day, but I must be going now. It's a long way to Meron.'

'Don't do any crossword puzzles this time!' warned Tamako.

'Hee hee hee hee hee,' the Woff giggled. 'Goodbye!'

Azmantha Perrix Scobbalob turned towards the huge glass window at the end of the hall. Lights began to radiate from his egg-hull. A steady, throbbing hum filled the air. He seemed to glow for a moment and then ... gone!

There was nothing left, just the endless crashing tinkle of breaking glass where he had whizzed through the hall window. Mr Pringle sat down heavily.

'I think you'd better ask Cook for some cold water,' he said to Luca. 'The headmaster seems to have fainted.' He looked searchingly at Evie.

'Now, Evie, would you tell me about this, this wasp?'

'Not a wasp!' laughed Evie. 'A Woff. He was a Woff.

Azmantha Perrix Scobbalob,' she added proudly. She stared dreamily out at the sky and sighed. 'I do hope he comes back,' she murmured. 'He was fun.'

Mr Pringle gave a deep groan. 'Time to go home,' he said thankfully. 'I hope I never see a day like today, not ever, ever!'

ORLANDO'S DOOM

JOANNA NADIN

FRIDAY 14TH AUGUST

My birthday

10AM

Presents asked for:

- A new phone, i.e. one that was actually made this century and doesn't look like it's a toddler's toy.
- A schoolbag that isn't a hand-me-down and therefore doesn't have 'I heart Human Rights' in purple gel pen on the front.
- A new name. You can change it by deed poll for only fifteen pounds. Obama Googled it for me. Obama is seven and named after America's first black President. I suggested Obama might want

161

to change her name too, given that she's neither black nor a man, but she says she's proud to be different. I, on the other hand, am really not proud to be Orlando, which sounds like a cat or a Shakespearian person who cries a lot. Plus it can also be a girl's name, which is confusing for some people, and amusing for others, e.g. Denny Potts who likes to point this out a lot.

Presents received:
- A signed photo of Leeds United junior coach Cyril Partridge (from Obama). Obama is obsessed with Leeds United because of Dad. Also with real-life murders and exotic cats. The signature is fake. It's done in red Sharpie and the 'i' has a heart instead of a dot.
- A ten-pound note and a DVD of *Sherlock* (from Dad). The DVD is already used, and also pirated, so not only does it have a spaghetti hoop stain on the cover, but it's blurry and has Hungarian subtitles across half the screen. Dad sent it from the oil-rig where he works. When I was little I used to think he was in prison, but Mam says you can't get put away for swapping your car for a toaster down the Nag's Head, more's the pity. She said that bit, not me.
- A bottle of beer (from Nan and Jeremy). Jeremy is

Nan's dog, named after her favourite TV presenter,
even though she is a girl. I also bet the original
Jeremy was not incontinent with farting issues.
Nan says she won the beer down the bingo, but
Mam reckons she nicked it off her fancy man
Bernie who is partial to brown ale, and fish-paste
sandwiches. He also has farting issues. The beer
has been confiscated.

- A bar of vegan chocolate (from Lady, my big sister).
  Lady's full name is Lady Diana, after Prince
  Charles's first wife who died in a car crash. Mam
  says Lady Di was the 'people's princess' i.e. 'one of
  us' only Obama Googled her and it turns out she
  was the daughter of an Earl and I don't know many
  of those on the Bethlehem Estate. Lady made us
  drop the Di bit after that. She's okay with 'Lady'
  though as she says it's pro-feminist and also sounds
  a bit Tolkien. She is big on Tolkien. Also animal
  rights, women's rights and human rights. The
  chocolate tastes of slightly mushroomy cardboard.
  I've given it to Obama.

Mam is giving me her present later, because the details are
being 'finalised'. Am hoping it's the phone, but I doubt it.
Sometimes I think my family is deliberately torturing me
by refusing to be normal. I Facetimed Dad and he says this
is what happens when you have so many women under one

roof, they all go doolally because of the 'oestrogen' – that's why he's happy on the oil-rigs, which is mostly swearing and talking about football. Obama Googled oestrogen. She says it's a female hormone that can cause mood swings and sensitivity, which explains a lot. She also said it can cause breast growth in boys so I'm a bit worried now I might catch some and have vowed to stay as far away from most of them as possible in case I end up like Manjit Hargreaves who has bigger ones than Lacey Prendergast.

6PM

Mam has revealed her surprise present. It's not a phone or a new bag or even a change of name.

It's a week in a caravan in Wales.

She was just waiting on the keys from Julie Gilhoolie who does nails down at Curl Up and Dye where she works, and who owns the van with her boyfriend Monkey (actual name). We're going tomorrow morning. I begged to stay behind with Nan, but Mam says Nan's coming too and so is Jeremy and besides she's not leaving me home alone, not since Shaniqua from four doors down went to Blackpool for the night and her twins Liam and Noel flooded the bathroom and microwaved a wellington boot. She also said the Carmarthen Clamshell Caravan Park is the 'jewel of West Wales' so I had better blooming like it. Obama Googled it. It has a 'tropical' swimming pool, a 'New-York style burger joint', a 'thrilling' adventure park and 'a prestigious ballroom with all the glamour of a nightly disco'. Mam went mad with excitement at that and has packed her dancing shoes and a dress that barely covers her bottom. She has no dignity.

It's totally unfair. Robbie Knox is going to Benidorm, Manjit's going to see his cousins in Canada, and Britney Briggs has got a fortnight at Disneyworld. Disneyworld! Whereas I'm about to spend seven days in Wales trapped in a metal box with a bunch of weirdos, absorbing hormones like mad.

This is the worst birthday present ever.

SATURDAY 15TH AUGUST

10PM

The Carmarthen Clamshell Caravan Park is not the jewel of anything. The 'tropical' swimming pool is just a normal outdoor pool with three plastic palm trees round the edge, two of which have broken branches, and the other one has a Sharpie drawing of a monkey having a wee on it; the 'New York-style burger joint' is a hut called Daffyd's Buns; the 'thrilling' adventure park is some swings and a seesaw that flings you off one end if you're not careful; and the ballroom is a square of lino at the edge of the canteen with some flashing lights rigged up and Daffyd (of bun fame) with a CD player.

But that's not the worst bit. The worst bit is the caravan itself. For a start the inside looks like a unicorn threw up on it, what with all the pink and glitter. Even the toilet has a fluffy cover on it, which is pointless, because who sits on the lid of the toilet? Lady says it is the epitome of the pathetic feminine masquerade and typical of Julie Gilhoolie, who wears a Wonderbra, which is also the epitome of the pathetic feminine masquerade. Obama started to Google all that but we gave up after epitome, which means 'perfect example'. The only thing it is a perfect example of is doom. There is probably oestrogen soaked into every surface. I stand no chance. Plus, I can't even escape when I go to bed because it turns out the caravan is only four-berth.

Mam said, 'Lady and Obama can bunk up and I'll have the squidgy bench in the dining area.'

'What about me?' I asked.

'You're in with Nan and Jezza,' she said.

'No way. She snores, and Jeremy . . . has no bladder control.'

'So wear ear plugs and take the top bunk. She can't climb up there.'

'Nan?'

'No, Jezza. Now stop mithering. It can't be worse than the car.'

Which at the time I thought was true, because I spent most of that in Nan's armpit with Jeremy on my lap and what definitely felt like a dribble of wee seeping through my jeans. Plus the CD player has Fifty Favourite Nursery Tunes stuck in it so we had to listen to *Row, Row, Row Your Boat* and *The Grand Old Duke of York* for two hundred miles. Only now I'm in a room the size of a normal toilet (as opposed to the caravan toilet, which is the size of a small cupboard) that is shaking with the sound of Nan's snoring and is now about ninety per cent dog fart.

I wish I was on the rigs with Dad. Or that I could just disappear. That would be my superpower if I had one – invisibility. Robbie Knox reckons he'd have flame-throwing fingers, but what's the point of just being able to burn things? You could use matches for that. If I was invisible I could watch films for free or steal anything I wanted. Plus no one would be able to see me and notice how mad my family is. Though I suppose at least no one knows me at the Carmarthen Clamshell, which is almost like being invisible when you think about it. So all I have to do is get through the next six days without drawing any attention to myself, growing boobs, or dying of dog fart inhalation.

Which I'm pretty sure is not your average holiday.

SUNDAY 16TH AUGUST

4PM

Okay, so I'm not dead from the dog farts, and my chest is still normal (I measured it with a piece of string and am going to check on a daily basis), but something weird has happened. Weirder than usual I mean.

I had vowed to stay inside, on the grounds of not drawing attention to myself, and also avoiding falling into the tropical pool (which is mainly being used for target practice for toddlers with peanut missiles, because it's too cold to swim), only Mam and Nan were having a row over Nan's moustache. Mam, who is in charge of tanning and waxing at the salon, says it's a ten-second job and Nan'll be smooth as a baby's bum before she knows it. But Nan says since when have babies had wrinkled backsides and she's keeping it because she's seventy-six and Bernie doesn't mind a bit of tickle so why should she? And on top of that Obama was reciting the 1974 Leeds cup-winning season scores, and Lady was playing guitar, or the one chord she knows on guitar, and singing about the patriarchy i.e. how evil men are. So obviously I had to go out.

I decided I would walk to the shop and maybe buy some fruit with the ten pounds birthday money Dad sent because Mam has mainly brought fish fingers and Alphabites, and I am in danger of getting scurvy, rickets and several other medieval diseases according to Obama, who Googled 'vitamin deficiency' for me. And I was just coming out of the shop (with a Picnic bar, which has raisins in it, which is the closest to fruit Daffyd could come up with) which is when the weird thing happened i.e. I saw Britney Briggs from school sitting by the pool flicking through her phone, wearing a winter coat and a face like a thunderstorm.

I mean, there were other people sitting around on their phones as well, because the only people who aren't are ones like Obama, who's not allowed one yet, ones like me who refuse to be seen in public with a ten-year-old orange Nokia, or ones like Lady who says all iDevices are the epitome of something or other. And the coat wasn't out of the ordinary either because, even though it's August, no one seems to have told the Welsh weather that. But the weird thing is that this was Britney Briggs.

For a start she's supposed to be hanging out with Mickey Mouse and her dad the TV producer and his new girlfriend who's a swimwear model (which I only know because Manjit got it off Robbie who got it off Britney's friend Lacey Prendergast), but instead she's stuck in the Carmarthen Clamshell under a plastic palm tree and a picture of a monkey having a wee.

Secondly she's madly rich and popular. She has new Nikes every term, the latest iPhone, and 511 followers on Instagram, including Luke Bruce who is fifteen and who once had a try-out for Stoke City youth team. She's also the second toughest girl in our year (officially) after Melanie Hills who once ate a worm. Even Robbie Knox is frightened of her. But the point is, why is she here?

I was asking myself these questions as I sat down on the bench and woke Mam up, who it turns out was having a power nap on it.

'Christ on a bike, Orlando,' she said. 'Will you just be loud and proud and announce your flaming presence instead of sneaking around like a flaming Ninja.'

She is obsessed with us standing out and 'letting our freak flags fly', which is code for 'be a weirdo and who cares what anyone thinks'. Only I do care. And that's when I had my idea: that I could be a detective. Because all they do is disappear into the background, which I love doing. And when I make my millions as a Private Investigator, Mam'll realise she's wrong about all the standing out stuff. Maybe she'll even let me change my name. You can't be a PI with a name like Orlando, after all. You need to be Tom or Harry or something normal. Anyway, the point is, my first case is 'Why is Britney Briggs at The Carmarthen Clamshell?' I aim to solve it by teatime without Britney or Mam even noticing I'm doing it.

IOPM

So it turns out that sneaking up on someone from behind only works if they're not taking a selfie at the same time and see you lurking over their shoulder from behind a plastic palm looking suspicious.

'OMG. Orlando Butterworth? Are you, like, stalking me?'

'N–No . . .' I managed to stammer.

But when I looked at her again she seemed more embarrassed than me because her face, which is normally all smooth and kind of like a peach, was bright red and creased and her eyes looked a bit wet, like they might actually cry.

'Are you okay?'

'Why wouldn't I be?' she snapped.

'Er, no reason. I thought you were supposed to be in Florida.'

'I . . . I'm going there next week. This is like an extra thing. Dad . . . Dad's undercover. Testing out the facilities, innit.'

'For what?'

'TV show,' she said quickly. 'There was a report of cockroaches in the changing rooms.'

'Oh right.' I mean, it sounded believable. And also kind of cool. Which is when I had my second brilliant detective-based idea. 'Maybe I could help?' I said.

'Help what?'

'Investigate? You know, look around stuff for your dad.' It could be like work experience, I figured. Plus it had to be better than hanging around our van with oestrogen seeping into my pores, dog fart up my nose and idiocy in my ears.

'Oh, right. Yeah . . . maybe. Listen, I've got to go.'

'So, shall I see you tomorrow?'

She shrugged. 'Whatever.'

And then, even weirder, as she walked off, one of the little kids who'd been chucking peanuts into the swimming pool grabbed her hand and went off with her too.

The plot thickens.

171

MONDAY 17TH AUGUST

The little kid is Britney's half-brother Jackson. So he must
be half-swimwear model too. Though he doesn't look much
like it as he is quite wide and shows no interest in actually
swimming. We ended up spending the morning watching
Jackson and Obama playing in the ball pit. Or rather, Obama
was reading *Oliver Twist* while Jackson threw plastic balls at
her head. I hadn't seen any sign of cockroaches, or Britney's
dad, when she said, 'Orlando's a weird name.'

'You're telling me.'

'Though I s'pose it could be worse. Like Chicago.'

I smiled. 'Or Detroit.'

'Or . . . Truth or Consequences. You know there's actually
a place called that in America. I'm moving to America as
soon as I'm allowed.'

'To Truth or Consequences?'

'No, duh. To LA.'

'Oh,' I said. Then I told her something I'd not told anyone
else before. Which is weird in itself, except it didn't feel it at
the time. 'Only I'm not named after the place,' I said. 'I'm
named after the nightclub on the ring road. So I suppose I'm
lucky I'm not "Speedy Brakes" or "Discount Plumbing".'

Britney laughed. 'Or "Totally Trousers Warehouse".'

I laughed then too. Loud and a bit mad, so it took me a
while to notice she'd stopped. But when I looked up I saw
why: there was her dad, who I'd seen once at school, with

a woman who definitely hadn't modelled anything unless it was hammers and work boots.

'Who's this, then,' he said, nodding at me.

'Orlando,' she mumbled. 'He's from school.'

'Orlando? Like in Florida?'

'Yeah,' I lied. Then I remembered I needed to get him on side for a job doing detective stuff on telly. 'Bet you're looking forward to that, though.'

'To what, son?'

Britney jabbed her elbow into my ribs but I didn't know why so I just carried on gabbling. 'To Florida. Next week. You know, Disneyworld?' He looked at Britney then. 'Florida, eh? Fat chance of that on my pay, kid. There's no cash in my line.'

'In telly?'

'Telly? I drive a TV licence van, son. Jesus, Britney. What've you said now?'

Britney went red but said nothing.

'Oh, it wasn't her,' I said quickly. 'I … I just thought I recognised you. You look like someone off the box.'

'Right.' He nodded his head then but I don't know if he believed me. 'Well, we've gotta be off now. Daffyd's opened the hut up and I'm gagging for a quarter-pounder. Two for one. Can't go wrong.'

Britney stood up to go. 'I'm not hungry,' she said. 'She can have mine.' She nodded at her stepmum, who looked like she'd eat four for two if she could.

'Bye then, Orlando, is it?' her dad said.

I nodded. 'Bye. See you, Britney.'

But Britney didn't say a thing. Just pulled her hood up and trudged behind them towards Daffyd's hut so I trudged back to our van thinking things couldn't possibly get any worse.

But being the Butterworth family, of course they could. Because I got back to find that Nan had somehow dyed her face dark orange.

'What happened?' I asked.

'What? The Nangerine?' asked Mam. 'She couldn't read the St Tropez bottle. Got my fake tan mixed up with her sun cream.'

'It's not even sunny out,' I said.

'You can't be too careful,' Nan said. 'Look at Carol Lovejoy. She's had five moles removed and all 'cause she liked a bit of sun on her face.'

'You can be too careful,' Mam said. 'Because now you look like you've painted yourself with woodstain.'

'Dark Chestnut,' said Obama, who had Googled it.

'Tanning is the epitome of pathetic feminine masquerade,' said Lady.

At that point I went to bed with Jeremy. Who may pee herself and fart every five minutes, but is at least mostly silent. On the plus side, I guess both Britney and me have got stuff we're embarrassed about. And if I was Robbie or Manjit I'd be all over it blabbing and laughing. Only I know what it feels like to be embarrassed by your family. And it's good to know I'm not alone.

TUESDAY 18TH AUGUST

I don't normally go around chasing after girls, especially not on a wet Tuesday round a field full of caravans, but at ten o'clock this morning, that's exactly what I was doing. I figured (using my detective skills) that:

a. Britney's got a kid brother so she'd be up early.
b. She won't want to be hanging round her dad anyway after yesterday so, even if she is mardy with me for finding out about the Florida lie, I might be a better bet.
c. If I leave it too late she might come looking for me and then I'd have to explain Nan's tangerine face, Mam's hot pants, Obama's 'I LOVE LEEDS' t-shirt and Lady's everything. Plus Jeremy had eaten a packet of frozen fishfingers (including cardboard) and everyone was awaiting some kind of bottom-area explosion, Mam with a J-cloth and Obama with a camera.

It took me less than five minutes to track her down. That's the advantage of The Carmarthen Clamshell being small and also entirely run by Daffyd. I went to the shop, bought

175

another Picnic bar and also a packet of beetroot crisps (vegetable intake) and asked if he'd seen Britney. He said she was in the ballroom for the under-fives disco with a packet of Nik Naks and a right cob on.

Daffyd was right.

'Morning,' I said.

She looked up at me from the plastic chair and then looked back down at her phone. 'Brilliant. What do *you* want?'

At this point, most normal boys would walk off, but this is the one time living in a house swirling with oestrogen helps. Because what might sound to the amateur like 'go away' clearly means 'please talk to me and ask me what's wrong'.

'What's wrong?'

'You know what's wrong.'

So I said it. All of it, just like that. I said: 'That you're not actually going to Florida at all. And that your dad doesn't work in telly. And that most of the stuff you've been telling people is a pack of lies.'

'OMG. No need to spell it out. Ugh.' Although the 'ugh' was to something on her phone, which she then clicked off so she could hard-stare me. 'What's it to you, anyway?'

'Nothing. I . . . why'd you do it?'

She shrugged then. 'Why not? For a bit of fun. For kicks.'

'Really?'

'Really,' she snapped. But then she slumped down in her chair, and spoke softer. 'Or maybe because my life is so . . . pants. It's all nappies and "Britney, get this, Britney, do that" and my dad's never even there and when he is he's mostly mardy.'

'But . . . what about your new trainers and stuff.'

'Knock-off,' she said. 'Dad gets them down the Nag's Head.'

I nodded at that, 'cause I knew what went on there. Dad once came home with a talking doll for Obama but when she switched it on it only spoke Korean. Dad joked it was probably swearing like a trooper and Mam said more likely telling us how to lay a patio, and Lady said maybe it was declaring why all dolls are patriarchal and the epitome of something or other. But Obama didn't see the funny side. Just like Britney doesn't now.

'But you'll leave one day, right?'

'Too right. Soon as. I'm going to be a vlogger.'

'What's a vlogger?'

She looked at me like I was mental then. 'Duh, a video-blogger. They make videos and put them on YouTube and make millions of pounds.'

'Videos of what?'

'Their lives? That's the thing. You have to have an excellent life to be a vlogger. Like live in a flash house in somewhere like Brighton with a boyfriend who looks like he's in a band.

'That rules me out.'

'Oh, ha ha. It rules me out and all. Have you looked around the Bethlehem Estate?'

I shrugged. 'Mam says I should be proud of where I come from.'

Britney gave me that look again. 'Vinny Davies has had half a car in his front garden for a year, and there's a dead pigeon outside the betting shop that's been there for a month.'

I nodded. She had a point.

'No way am I proud of that. I'm going to move to America and marry a footballer probably. Or be a world famous singer and live in a penthouse near Buckingham Palace.'

'*Can* you sing?' I asked.

And then she did something incredible. Right there, in the middle of the under-fives disco (which was actually more raucous then the grown-up ones because two boys were fighting over a packet of Wotsits and a girl with glasses was doing a wee on the carpet), she sang. Like proper singing – the kind you hear on the radio. Then she stuck a Nik Nak in her mouth and snapped it shut.

'Wow.'

She shrugged. 'Only I've got to get spotted, haven't I?' she said, still chewing. 'Like on *Show Us Your Talents* or something.'

Her phone pinged then and she looked at it and made a yelping noise.

'What?'

'Lacey Prendergast's only posted a selfie of her drinking a mocktail in Malaga.' She held out the phone so I could see.

It did look kind of excellent. 'Cow,' she continued. 'She's got a private pool and she's dead tanned and all. No hope of that here.'

I looked out at the drizzle. Again, she had a point.

'If I was in Florida I could post stuff like this. But ...' She gave up on that sentence, which was probably for the best, because we both knew there was no chance. Unless ...

'I've got an idea,' I said.

'What sort of idea?'

'The kind that needs you to leave Jackson here for a bit. Can you do that?'

'Like, duh. His mum's there,' she said and nodded at one of the disco helpers. 'How do you think we afforded this even? Donna's working here for the summer, innit. So we get a free van.'

'So you're here all summer.'

'Worse luck.'

'Even more reason to do this then. Come on.'

'What *are* we doing?' Britney asked when we arrived at our van.

I smiled. 'Faking it.'

'Faking what?'

'Well, Florida photos. You know, so you can post them on Instawotsit and pretend like you're having the time of your life. But first we've got to make it look like you've actually been there.'

'And how do I do that, genius?'

179

And this is when I knew I must like her a lot. Because I opened the door and said, 'Ta-dah!'

Britney's eyes bulged like hardboiled eggs. Because there on the bench was Mam, with her make-up kit out, turning Obama into a murder victim with some fake scars and a lot of ketchup.

'Hello, Orlando,' said Obama. 'I've been stabbed five times in the neck and had an eyeball gouged out. Good, isn't it?'

Okay, it wasn't exactly the scenario I'd hoped for, but once I'd explained Mam didn't just do horror make-up but was a fully qualified tanning technician and also three times winner of the West Midlands Highest Hair Challenge, Britney was totally up for it, and so was Mam.

'Okay, kid,' she said. 'How brown are we talking exactly?'

'What do you mean?'

'I mean, two days in Spain or a fortnight in the Seychelles?'

'Oh.' Britney frowned. 'Can you do five days in Disneyworld?'

'Paris or Florida.'

'Paris is Disney*land*,' said Obama.

'Florida it is.' Mam nodded in appreciation. 'Precision. I like that. And a challenge.'

'Just don't make her look like Nan,' I said.

We all looked at Nan then, who was watching *Deal or No Deal* on the portable telly with Jeremy. Jeremy is in love with the presenter. We think it's the beard. Obama said Nan should try to grow one to match the moustache. She'd Googled it and reckoned some testosterone, which is the male hormone, would do it, but Mam told her to keep that one to herself in case Nan got any mad ideas. Mam's still recovering from the time Nan watched a programme on Have-a-Go Heroes and tried to arrest Dane Riley, who is in Year 11, for exposing his bottom in public (his trousers are madly low).

'No chance,' said Mam. 'No one else could look like that if they tried. She's like a flaming Oompa-Loompa.'

Mam did the tan in my and Nan's room. Afterwards I went in to check on Britney but she said Mam told her it won't be ready until tomorrow so we'd have to wait until then to do the pictures.

Then she did something massive. 'What's this?' she asked, and held out a notebook. THIS notebook.

I felt my stomach flip like it does when you go over a bridge too fast, and I snatched it back off her. 'How did you get that?'

'All right, keep your hair on. Your mam made me face the bed to do my back. I just saw it poking out from under the pillow. I didn't read it or nothing. Is it work?'

'No it's . . .' Then I decided I might as well tell her. She'd seen Nan, so she knew I wasn't normal. 'It's a diary.'

She looked puzzled. 'Like a blog you mean?'

'Yeah, only written down. And private.'

She looked even more puzzled then. 'What's the point in that?'

I could feel my face getting hot. 'We don't all want to be looked at,' I mumbled.

'Why not? I'd look at you.'

My stomach flipped again then. But not in a bad way. 'Are ... are you saying I'm worth looking at?'

'No! I ... I'm just saying you're not, like, a freak show or anything.'

'Right. Thanks. I think.'

And even though she'd taken it back, I still felt warm inside. Like when you eat Ready Brek and get that glow going on.

'Yeah, whatever. I'd better go. Dad'll be going ballistic.'

'He'll go even more ballistic when he sees your tan show up, won't he?'

Britney shrugged. 'Doubt he'll even notice. See you.'

The glow went a bit then, and I felt bad for her. 'See you,' I said back.

But now that I'm lying in bed, I can feel it again. That sticky warmth like syrup on porridge. And it's not just hot air from the bunk below either.

It's because of Britney.

11PM

She had so better not read that bit. THIS is why diaries should be private.

WEDNESDAY 19TH AUGUST

Britney showed up at eleven this morning looking totally mint. She had a crop top on and short shorts and her skin was a good brown, not even vaguely woodstained. 'You look ... brilliant,' I said.

'Thanks.' She grinned. 'And it's stopped raining and all.'

I looked up and it was like one of those moments in films which you think are totally made up but aren't, because right then the sun came out from behind the cloud and shone down on Daffyd's burger hut so the picture of the hot dog glinted madly and actually looked edible for the first time. Though it still wasn't warm enough to stop Britney shivering.

'Shall we get going then?' she said, her skinny arms wrapped round her.

'Yeah,' I said vaguely, still mellow in the sunlight. 'Yeah, okay.'

We took five good photos. It wasn't as easy as I thought, not getting anything Welsh in the picture. It didn't help that Daffyd has painted dragons on everything, and also that he kept wandering into shot to see if we wanted a '99, because he said might switch the whippy ice-cream machine on if it was going to stay like this for a few hours. But in the end we got two shots of Britney with sunglasses on dead close-up; one of her drinking a mocktail, which is actually some juice from a tin of strawberries and it's out of a candleholder thing, but it looks dead real; one of her lounging by the pool, and we used a filter so you can't tell she's got goosebumps, and blurring round the edges to hide the cracks in the concrete and the monkey doing a wee. We even got one of her hugging Minnie Mouse. Okay, so Minnie is actually me wearing some plastic ears and a mask we borrowed off one of Jackson's menacing friends, but it kind of works.

She got thirty-three likes in less than a minute, including Luke Bruce. I felt a bit funny at that. Because what if he only 'liked' it because he thought she was rich and in Florida. 'I "like" it too,' I said quickly, handing her back the phone. 'In real life, I mean. In Wales.'

She pulled a face. 'You're weird,' she said. 'But also kind of cool. Thanks for that.'

'Whatever,' I said. Like it was nothing. But it wasn't, and she knew it and all.

'So, see you tomorrow then?' she said.

'Yeah. Maybe we could go scuba diving.'

'Or jet skiing?'

'Or swimming with dolphins.'

'Or . . .' Only she'd run out of made-up things by then.

'Or there's skittles in the ballroom,' I said quickly. 'The prize is a big bottle of Tango and a tin of Celebrations.

'Split it?'

'Done.'

*

184

I was still all glowing when I got back to the van. It didn't last long though. When I walked in the door it was like I'd accidentally wandered into a really bad circus. Mam was trying to juggle three cans of mandarin segments, Obama was reciting Leeds United line-ups, whilst standing on one leg, and Nan was doing something disturbing with Jeremy, which involved holding her front paws and swaying to a One Direction song.

'Er, what's going on?' I asked Lady, who for once seemed to be the only sane member of the family.

'This,' she snapped and held out a piece of paper.

I took it. *Miss Carmarthen Clamshell*, it said. *Pit your lovely lady talents against Wales's finest and take home the golden crown, and also free burgers for the rest of your stay from Daffyd's hut (maximum one a day, fries, sauce and drinks not included).*

'It's outrageous,' said Lady. 'It's—'

'—The epitome of pathetic something?' I asked.

Lady stared at me. 'Exactly.' And she stormed off to her bunk bed to play her one chord on the guitar.

'Good job she's not entering,' said Mam, who immediately lost concentration and flung a tin of mandarins too hard so that it ricocheted off the fridge, bounced on the toilet, and rolled along the floor right to my feet, where I picked it up.

'You'd win if you could pull that off on Friday night.'

'Maybe I will,' Mam said, taking the tin back. 'Us Butterworths have got to let our freak flags fly, after all.'

At which point Jeremy let out a massive fart.

'I swear that dog could chuff the National Anthem if she tried,' Mam sighed.

Now that really would win, I thought.

THURSDAY 20TH AUGUST

Mam waxed Nan's moustache off in the night. I got woken up by a scream and Mam's triumphant face looming over the bunk bed as she held the hairy strip aloft like it was a trophy. I don't know what she's so triumphant about. Now Nan's got a massive white stripe in her sultana face, which is weirder than the hair. Plus she's threatened to wax Mam's whole head. Mam's a bit nervous now because she probably would and all. The reason Nan lives with us is because she got thrown out of Grey Gardens Care Home for 'excessive misdemeanours' including smuggling non-residents into her room (i.e. Bernie), attacking the warden Miss Peason with a KitKat, and being drunk in charge of a mobility scooter (she drove it into Dorothy Perkins and sang *Oh When The Saints* in the knicker section). Plus Jeremy kept weeing on the communal sofa.

Everyone else is in a bad mood as well. It's all over the Miss Clamshell contest.

'Lady says it's totally sexy,' explained Obama.

'Sex*ist*,' said Lady. 'Which it is.'

'I don't see how,' said Mam. 'It's feminist. It's about "lady talents", not "lady looks". You could sing your protest song about bees or whatever it is. I'll do your hair for you if you like.'

'You just said it wasn't about *looks*,' snapped Lady.

'It's not. But no point looking like a homeless person when you've got my makeover talent on tap.'

At which point Lady stormed back to her bunk bed.

'It's sort of sexist,' said Obama. 'Because Orlando can't enter.'

'I don't want to enter,' I pointed out.

'But if you did, you couldn't,' said Obama. 'That's called hypothetical. I Googled it.'

'Hypothetically, I don't care,' I said.

'You should,' said Mam. 'Hywel Hughes is judging it.'

'Who's Hywel Hughes?' I asked.

'Bloke off the telly. Nan's third favourite celebrity after Jeremy and the fat chef,' said Mam.

'Off *The Yes Factor* or whatever it is.'

'*Show Us Your Talents*,' snapped Nan. 'Daffyd's cousin Nesta once did his feet for him. Lovely, she said they were. Not a bunion in sight.'

Normally I would have gagged at that. But I wasn't thinking about bunions. I was thinking about something else entirely.

'Got to go,' I said.

'Where to?' asked Mam.

'To see your *girl*friend?' asked Obama.

'No,' I said, feeling my face get hot again. 'I'm ... playing skittles. And she's not my girlfriend.'

187

'Is too.'

'Oh, what*ever*.'

'Oestrogen,' sighed Obama, as I yanked the door open. 'It happens to all of us.'

'Hywel Hughes?' asked Britney for the second time. 'Here?'

I nodded, for the second time.

'But how?'

'Something to do with someone called Nesta and her feet I think. But what does it matter how? He's here. This is your chance to get spotted.'

Britney's face lit up. Then lit down again, if that's a thing. 'But . . . I can't. I'm not supposed to be here.'

'So enter under a different name.' All the undercover detective stuff was going to my head.

'I . . .' For a minute I thought she was going to say yes. But then her face fell again and she shook her head. 'I need a backing singer.'

'Use a tape.'

'NO!' she snapped. Then she goes softer, like she's scared or something. 'I . . . can't do it on my own, all right.'

'But if you're a vlodger—'

'Vlogger.'

'Right, vlogger, then don't they do it on their own.'

'No. Yes. Sometimes. But sometimes with their best friend or boyfriend. Those are the ones I like. Anyway, I'm not doing it. End of.'

'Fine.'

'Fine.'

'Skittles?' I suggested.

'Fine.'

We played for an hour but we didn't win the Tango or the Celebrations. Daffyd's brother Meredyth (actual name) did, which Nan reckons was a fix. I said you can't fix skittles, they either fall down or they don't, but Nan said Meredyth was a 'ringer', who's been in secret training for months just to win this one contest. Mam said that was a lot of training for some pop and a teeny-tiny chocolate, but Nan said Mam'd be surprised what some people will do to win.

'Or to save their brother a few quid,' said Mam.

And that's when I knew I had to do it.

I have to forget what I said about getting through the week without drawing any attention to myself. I have to forget about slipping into the shadows. I have to be a Butterworth. Be loud and proud.

It's probably all the oestrogen. Or the dog fart. But whatever it is, it's flapping my freak flag, and tomorrow I'm going to let it fly.

10.30PM

If I don't throw up first.

FRIDAY 21ST AUGUST

10AM

It's D-day, i.e. Doom-day. (Not Domesday, which is a book listing all the towns owned by William the Conqueror. Obama Googled it.) By about three o'clock this afternoon I will have finally joined the ranks of the Butterworths i.e. flown my flag of freakiness in front of a hundred strangers, Britney Briggs, and Hywel Hughes off the actual telly. I just have to hope they don't have TV cameras there. Or that my disguise works.

But that's probably the easy bit. First off, I have to persuade Britney.

2.45PM

Like I said, persuading Britney was never going to be easy.

'You're going to do what?' she asked.

'Dress as ... as a girl.'

Britney's mouth was gaping open like she was a giant frog or a Venus fly trap. Then she snorted, which was less frog and more pig. 'What would you want to do that for?'

I'd kind of hoped that would have been obvious. But I guess she's second toughest, not brainiest. 'To ... to help you. So that, you know, you can go on stage. Like a vlogger with your—' I didn't want to say the word 'friend', and I definitely didn't want to say the word 'boyfriend'. I'm not that freakish. Yet.

She was all silent then for a bit, and I couldn't tell if she was thinking about how mental I was or wondering about what crisp flavour to get (she reckons it's an important decision and the wrong choice can ruin your day, like if you have salt and vinegar but it's actually more of a prawn cocktail morning, which sounded mad to me, until I deliberately chose cheese and onion when I really wanted ready salted and I was mardy for a whole hour). And I could feel my stomach swirling about, and not just because I'd had a tin of oxtail soup for breakfast (it was all there was left in the cupboard and Daffyd's didn't open until half nine because he had to clean the peanuts out of the pool). But then she spoke, and it wasn't about snacks.

'You'd do that. For me?'

And her face was painted with happiness and hope and my stomach flipped in what felt like a full somersault because I did that, I made that face happen, and it felt like being a superhero, even without the flame-throwing fingers and invisibility. I nodded. 'We could use a stage name. Like "Double Trouble" or something.' Which I thought was wasn't bad seeing as I'd made it up on the spot.

She shook her head then and I felt a shot of cold rush through me, like having a glass of water tipped on your head (which has happened several times, mostly by Lady, and once by Nan when she thought I was a marauding dwarf), because I thought she was going to say no to the whole thing.

'Not "Double Trouble",' she said. 'How about … "Two True".'

And I could have punched the air, if I didn't think I'd probably fall over doing it. Because that was brilliant, and also, she'd said 'yes'. Not the actual word, but she was going to do it. WE were going to do it.

'It's going to have to be convincing,' she said then, totally getting into it. 'Like, you're going to need a wig.'

'Check.'

'What?'

'Oh, it means "got it". Or rather Mam has. Two of them. One blonde and one made of silver foil.'

'What's that supposed to be?'

'An alien?' I guessed. 'At a disco?'

'Right. Well, nice one. Also an outfit. I can do that. You're skinny enough.'

'Thanks,' I said, my voice faltering.

'I didn't mean it badly,' she said, pulling a face.

'Oh. Right.' Talking to girls was clearly fraught with danger. Worse than trying to wrestle snakes.

'You'll have to do your legs and all.'

'Do what to them?'

'Duh. Shave them? You can't go on stage looking like a flaming gorilla.'

'They're not that hairy,' I protested. Not compared to Nan anyway.

'Do you want to do this proper or not?' Britney asked, hands on her hips like she's Mam with a cob on, or about to do the 'I'm a little teapot' song.

'Proper,' I said, sighing.

'Legs it is then.'

Which is why I'm now in Britney's bedroom, with no leg hair (and only two plasters), and wearing a shoulder-length blonde wig, a silver dress that looks like a fish skin and a bra. Oh yeah, because it turns out you can't be in a girl band without one of those and all.

'I've got nothing to put in it,' I said (the oestrogen still hasn't soaked through thankfully).

'Yes you have,' Britney said, and handed me some cotton wool balls.

'You're more expert than Mam,' I said, stuffing them inside the cups.

'You can learn a lot off the internet,' she said. 'I can also do a fishtail plait, make bath bombs, and say "thank you, you're too kind" in Japanese.'

'Why would you want to do that?' I asked.

'For when I'm big in Japan, innit. For the fans.'

She'd thought of everything, I figured. And as I looked in the mirror, at the girl she'd turned me into, I reckoned she'd do it, whatever she set her mind to.

'We should go,' she said then. 'You know what to do?'

'Just say "shake" a bit and mime the rest, right?'

'Right. Come on then.'

'I'll . . . I'll catch you up,' I said then.

'You are going to show up?' she said, frowning.

I looked at her in her pink sticking-out skirt and crop top, her face shiny with glitter, her hair all styled like she's already a star. 'Totally,' I said. 'For definite.'

'Five minutes, okay?'

'Five. I promise.'

Only now I'm standing in front of the mirror looking at myself, and I'm not sure I want to fly my flag at all. Not even sure I've got one.

This was a mistake. A massive, humungous, gigantic mistake.

What am I doing?

I don't do things like this.

I don't stand out.

I slip into the shadows. I sneak around like Gollum or a house elf.

I don't get up on stage in a bra and wig and sing backing vocals just because some girl in my class wants to be famous.

Do I?

2.55PM

Oh, crikey. I think I do.

SATURDAY 22ND AUGUST

10AM

There's fifteen minutes before we're leaving the jewel of West Wales, so I reckon I've just got time to get it all down.

I didn't write last night. My brain wasn't working properly. Probably the hormones and Jeremy's emissions.

Or possibly the sheer awesomeness of what happened at the contest.

Because it was. Totally and utterly awesome. Like Mam says, with a flake in it and sprinkles.

The weirdest thing is that no one looked at me at all as I snuck into the back of the ballroom. But then the hall was packed with people who looked pretty much the same as me. Okay, so they didn't all have wigs, fake boobs and really tight pants on to hide their willy, but everywhere was a sea of glitter and shiny stuff and massive hair. Even Nan had had hers done, all platinum silvery, which if you ask me only made the sultana face worse, but she seemed happy enough up there dancing to *Who Let the Dogs Out* with Jeremy wandering aimlessly around the stage. Obama had gone for more of a stabbed princess look, with a knife sticking out of her head, but she still had her best dress on, and Lady had done her hair and lips blue, which made her look a bit like she had hypothermia, but I wasn't about to tell her that. I

195

wasn't about to tell her or any of them anything to be honest, I was too busy trying not to be noticed at all, when I felt a hand on my shoulder and heard a voice in ear. 'Nice one, our kid,' it said. 'I knew you'd find the real you one day.'

Mam.

'This isn't the real me,' I said. 'It's . . . a favour for a friend.'

'Whatever,' she said. 'I've never been more proud.'

Given that I got top marks in my SATs, this didn't seem like the best compliment, but it was a Butterworth compliment, and for the first time, that didn't feel all bad.

Until Hywel Hughes called my name.

Well, our name.

'And now,' he announced in an accent that was half-California, half-Cardiff, 'We've got a junior duo who go by the name "Two True", singing *Shake It Off*. Oh, I like that one, I do. Ladies and gentlemen, Two True!'

Britney walked out onto the dance floor then like she was made for it, her smile all massive. And I realised I'd hardly ever seen her smile like that. Mostly she was pulling faces or frowning at her iPhone. And I knew I was doing the right thing. Because she was golden, just sort of shone out there.

Only I wasn't, was I? Because I was down in the crowd and she was up there.

'Two True,' announced Hywel again.

That was all it took. I pushed my way through all the wannabe tap dancers and twirlers and the kid dressed as a lemon (no idea) until I was standing in front of Britney.

And even though I thought I might actually throw up my Crunchy Nut Cornflakes from nerves, I grinned right back at her, to tell her she could do this. WE could do this.

And then she did something amazing. She winked, just as the music started up. And then she started to sing.

I forgot my first 'shake, shake' bit, but the next time I managed it. And more and all. Because I know I was supposed to be miming, but I got this feeling, like Taylor Swift says in the song, and I couldn't stop myself, I just had to sing. Then both of us were out there, doing the hand movements and the hip movements, and shouting 'shake it off!' at the tops of our lungs. And the best bit? The crowd was going mad. And I got it, why she loved it so much. Because it was like she was loved. She had attention then. More than she ever had at home. She was someone.

And so was I.

'And, thank you, Two True!' yelled Hywel above the crowd. 'Up next is ... Obama Butterworth reciting the Leeds United first team line-ups for the years 1974 to 1981. Really? Is that a joke?'

'Not a joke,' I said to Hywel. 'And she's not bad at it either.'

She wasn't bad. But she wasn't good enough to win. And nor was Nan, and nor was Mam with her juggling mandarins (which only caused two facial injuries, and a broken lightbulb). Because guess who got top prize?

Two True.

Or at least, we did for five minutes. And those minutes were amazing – the best minutes of my life EVER. Even better than the time I once got two questions right on *University Challenge*. I was so pleased I hugged Britney, and she was so pleased she let me. But I'd forgotten one thing. That I wasn't supposed to be there. Which would have been fine if I'd kept my hair on. But I didn't, actually or metaphorically.

What happened was that Daffyd and Hywel tried to put tiaras on our heads to crown us both 'Miss Clamshell', only mine wouldn't stick because of the wig, and it was all itchy by then because I was sweating, so I yanked it off and waited for the tiara. Only it didn't come. Instead the crowd did an actual communal gasp. And then a communal 'Ooooh'. And then a voice said, 'That's no Miss Clamshell, that's a mister, Mr.'

'By heck,' said Daffyd. 'So it is. Well, who'd have thought it? A boy with a bra.'

'That's . . . that's not real either,' I admitted. And I pulled out the cotton wool to another gasp and 'ooooh'.

'Cheat!' shouted someone.

'Imposter,' shouted someone else, who sounded suspiciously like Nan.

'Sexist!' shouted someone who sounded definitely like Lady.

'Oh, we're not sexy,' said Daffyd. 'This is family entertainment.'

'Not sex*y*,' said Obama. 'Sex*ist*. Men should be allowed to enter. That's fair. I Googled it.'

'Hear, hear,' said Mr Briggs. Even Britney looked shocked at that. I don't think she thought he'd even show up.

Then Daffyd and Hywel went into a huddle with Daffyd's wife Brenda who was in charge of lights, and there was a lot of whispering and shaking of heads and several 'well I never's. And then Hywel came back, all beaming and said the decision had been made, and that this year's Miss Clamshell was going to Mrs Ffion Jenkins, for playing *She'll be Coming Round the Mountain* on recorder while belly dancing. But that from now on, Miss Clamshell would be called 'Clamshell Caravanner of the Year' and open to everyone. Which even Lady had to concede was a victory for some sort of rights.

Britney wasn't too chuffed though.

'We had that in the bag,' she said. 'And you blew it. And now I'm never going to be famous, am I?'

'Er, yeah you are,' I said.

'What?'

'We're going to be in the *Carmarthen Courier*,' I said. 'Daffyd just told me. They want a photo, with me, you and Hywel.'

'What? No way.'

'What do you mean "no way"?' I said. 'This is what you wanted.'

'Er, no,' she said, like I'm an idiot. 'I'm supposed to be in Florida, remember?'

I am an idiot.

But I'm also Orlando Butterworth. I'm loud and proud. At least for the day. And I wasn't going to let the idiot bit get in the way of that. 'Britney, this is your chance. This is Hywel Hughes we're talking. And an actual newspaper. And . . . and it might get on telly too. And you might get to sing on his show.' And then I said the bigger bit, the really important bit. 'And besides, which holiday was more fun, this one or the fake one you were never going to have?'

Britney looked at me with a face like Jeremy when she needs a poo i.e. sort of sad and desperate all at once. 'Why are you so clever?' she said eventually. 'I hate that.'

And so we had our photo taken, and the man took one on Britney's phone and all so she could remember it (because she says if you don't have a photo of it on your phone, it might as well have never happened).

I don't need a photo though. Because I've got this – my diary.

And besides, I won't hear the end of it when school starts again. Because you know what else we did? We posted the photo to Instagram, just now. 'Me and Orlando rocking Wales' it says under it. 'Our secret summer stardom.'

'Star doom, more like,' I said when I read it. 'Are you sure?'

She chucked a barbecue Wotsit in her mouth, sucked it, and swallowed. 'A hundred and ten per cent,' she said.

'Obama says you can't be a hundred and ten per cent anything,' I said, taking a Wotsit out of the bag and biting it. It tasted perfect, a hundred and ten per cent perfect. The exact right choice for the day. 'But what does Google know?'

Britney took another snack and smiled. 'Not as much as us.'

'Nope. One and hundred and ten per cent brilliant, we are.'

'Marvellous.'

'Magnificent.'

'I'll still ignore you in class, though.'

'Well, obviously.'

'Got a reputation to keep up, innit.'

'Me too,' I said. 'Me too.'

I guess I'll have to find out exactly which reputation it is when I get back. Wild boy or wallflower.

Though it'll be the first if Nan has anything to do with it. Turns out she's in the *Carmarthen Courier* and all. I can't even bring myself to write down why. Let's just say it was classic Butterworth. And that Jeremy won't be needing her fur clipped any time soon.

THE
FOREST
OF
WONDERS

WILLIAM SUTCLIFFE

I

It was one of those mornings when it felt very hard to say yes to anything. Flora refused to get up, she refused to eat her breakfast, she refused to sit at the table, she refused to get dressed, she refused to brush her hair, she refused to clean her teeth, and at one point she even refused a chocolate biscuit, because she wasn't listening to a word anyone was saying to her.

Everyone has mornings like that occasionally. Flora had them more than most. Sometimes it seemed to Flora that a parent or teacher was ALWAYS following her around, telling her what to do, where to go, or to sit still and listen, when what she wanted most of all was to be left alone with the interesting thoughts that bounced around her head when nobody was interrupting her. Ideas and stories were always flickering to life in her imagination, but they were constantly extinguished by some adult turning up and expecting her to behave like a robot.

Flora was very much *not* a robot. The whole point of robots is that they do what they are told, and this was not Flora's way. Flora liked to make her own decisions: she always had and she always would.

On this particular morning she was busy trying to invent a creature that nobody had ever thought of before, but her mum just kept on going on about breakfast, breakfast, breakfast, clothes, clothes, clothes and teeth, teeth, teeth until the half-invented animal slipped away out of her head for ever.

At the moment when Flora's idea finally vanished, she lost her patience and yelled, in her very rudest voice, 'JUST LEAVE ME ALONE!'

The second Flora had said it, she wished she could suck the words back into her mouth and make them disappear. But you can't do that. What is said cannot be unsaid.

Flora looked into her mum's eyes, which suddenly looked so fierce that it seemed like her brain might be on fire.

Flora's mum didn't often get cross. When she did, Flora found that she couldn't really hear what her mum was saying, she just felt swamped by the horrible feeling of being shouted at, and lost track of the words. This often made things worse, but Flora couldn't help it.

On this occasion, Mum wasn't just cross, she was cross

and upset. In fact she was cross and upset and wounded and disappointed, which is the ultimate four-armed bear hug of guilt. As every child knows, when the four-armed guilt bear comes after you, there's nothing you can do except go very quiet and stare at your shoes. (Unless you've refused to put them on, in which case you have to stare at your socks. Unless you've refused to put *those* on.)

After things had calmed down, and Flora had eaten (half a) breakfast, was finally dressed, and Mum had given up on attempting to brush her hair, the morning took a surprising turn.

Mum appeared in the kitchen with a small basket containing a neat bundle wrapped in a red checked cloth. 'I want you to take this to Granny,' she said, handing over the basket.

Granny lived in a magical little cottage in the middle of a magical old forest. I don't mean 'magical little cottage' as in a cute, twee little house. I mean a cottage where strange and seemingly impossible things often took place. And when I say 'magical old forest', I don't mean a scenic rural spot with twisty branches and cosy, dingly dells. I mean a forest where irregular and curious events often occurred. It was known to everyone as the Forest of Wonders.

'Now?' said Flora.

'Yes, off you go.'

These four short words might strike you as a rather ordinary sentence, but they set Flora's heart racing with excitement and terror. You see, Flora often visited her granny, she sometimes even stayed the night, but she had never, not once, been allowed to make the journey through the Forest of Wonders on her own.

'Are you coming with me?' asked Flora.

Suddenly she wasn't feeling quite so noisy and confident. Her   NO-I-DON'T-WANT-ANY-BREAKFAST-IT'S-BORING voice had become high, thin and trembly.

'I can't. I'm busy making this,' said Mum, waving her arm in the direction of a huge pot that was bubbling on the stove.

'What is it?'

'Oh, nothing ... just ... a bit of soup.'

'In a cauldron?'

'Don't be silly! That's not a cauldron! It's just a very large cooking pot. Now off you go.'

Perhaps I should describe Flora's mum to you. She was roughly average height for an adult, not fat or thin, and always wore smart shoes.

That doesn't tell you very much, does it? OK, I'll give you a few extra details. She had a thin, pointy nose, surprisingly bushy eyebrows, and long, straggly black hair. Some people thought she was strikingly beautiful. Others thought she was a bit of a weirdo. These things are a matter of opinion.

Flora, while we're on the subject, looked very like her mother. But smaller. That's kids for you. Small. The whole lot of them. Even tall people are small when they're kids.

Some people thought Flora was beautiful, others thought she was a weirdo, but Flora didn't really care either way. She liked being different. In fact, she sometimes looked at neat-haired, smiley, pretty-dress-wearing girls and felt slightly sorry for them, though she didn't quite know why.

'Go on, you'll be late,' snapped Mum, ushering Flora towards the door. 'Granny's expecting you for lunch.'

'What's in the basket?'

'It's for Granny.'

'What is it?'

Mum kneeled in front of Flora and stared intensely at her daughter. Flora was struck, as she often was, by how her mum had one blue eye and one greeny-grey eye. The blue one was usually on the left, but today it was on the right. 'IT'S FOR GRANNY,' said Mum, in her scary voice, holding Flora by the shoulders. 'IT'S VERY IMPORTANT AND VERY SECRET. YOU MUSN'T LOOK INSIDE. OK?'

'But what is it?'

'It's a Maguffin.'

'What's that?'

'Granny will show you when you get there. You MUSTN'T lose it.' This was in the scary voice again.

'OK.'

'And you mustn't peep.'

'OK.'

'You promise?'

'Promise.'

'And you might need this,' said Mum, hanging a small black purse on a long red ribbon around Flora's neck.

'What's in it?'

'Snacks,' said Mum. 'For an emergency. Now go! Hurry!'

Next thing Flora knew, she was out of the door and running down the path into the Forest of Wonders.

As she entered the forest, two things struck her.

First: the purse around her neck seemed strangely light. If there was a snack inside, it felt like it was probably one crisp.

Second: why would snacks be for an emergency? Snacks were for when you felt peckish. Which is hardly what you'd call an emergency.

Meanwhile, another question nagged away at the back of her mind. What *was* a Maguffin?

There was something odd going on.

2

It was a beautiful summer morning in the Forest of Wonders. Sunlight was twinkling through the branches, bluebells were swaying in a light breeze, and a family of woodpeckers was pecking out the tune of *Yankee Doodle Dandy* on the trunk of an oak tree.

Flora thought this might be a good moment to skip, so skip she did, along the weaving, winding path that led to Granny's house. She whistled along with the pecking from the musical woodpeckers, and soon began to feel peckish herself, which is hardly surprising, since she'd only eaten half a breakfast.

Strangely, the moment Flora thought about sitting down for a rest, and began to look around for a comfy-looking branch, a red toadstool the exact same height as a chair appeared in front of her. She didn't see it pop up out of the ground, but she could have sworn it wasn't there just a moment earlier.

Strange.

It looked comfortable, so down she sat. You don't have to be a toad to use a toadstool as a stool. In fact, toads hate stools. They prefer chairs. It's frogs that like stools.

'Ahhh,' said the toadstool, letting out a contented sigh as Flora sat down.

Flora leapt up.

She stared at the toadstool.

She sat down again.

'Ahhh,' said the toadstool.

This time Flora chose to ignore the sighing fungus and open her snack pack.

Except, as she had suspected, the purse didn't contain a snack at all. It contained a mysterious, bright green webby object, which Flora couldn't identify, and certainly had no intention of eating.

She took it out of the purse, and it sprang into shape. Not just any old shape: this was a pop-up net, the kind you get at the beach for collecting shells.

But she wasn't anywhere near a beach. She was in forest. There was not a single shell for miles around.

Flora gazed thoughtfully at the net, trying (and failing) to think of any object in the whole world of less use to her than this one. She was hungry, and a fishing net was not, by any stretch of the imagination, a snack.

Was it possible that Mum was so cross with her she'd deliberately packed a non-edible snack to teach her a lesson?

No. That wasn't like Mum. But then, sending her off alone into the forest with a mysterious parcel to deliver wasn't like Mum, either.

Strange.

Flora wasn't *starving*. This wasn't what you'd call an emergency. But she really would have fancied something to … hang on a second! What was that in front of her – underneath her – all around her? Had those been there a minute ago? A low bush with rich green leaves was spread all around her like a carpet. It was covered in small blue berries, otherwise known as blueberries.

Did these really grow so close to her home? She'd never found them here before.

Blueberries were Flora's favourite fruit.

She slid off the toadstool, fell to her knees, and began to pick. She picked and ate, ate and picked, until her fingers and tongue were as blue as her jeans.

Then she heard a strange sound. A pop. And another one. And then hundreds more – a symphony of tiny explosions. Not a very good symphony to be honest. It sounded more like twenty over-excited elves being let loose in a drum shop.

She turned her head towards the source of the sound, a seemingly ordinary-looking tree, which, on closer inspection, wasn't ordinary at all. It was covered in fresh, warm popcorn. Flora's favourite snack.

Strange.

Flora picked handful after handful, and ate until she was completely satisfied. Then she ate more, until she felt a bit sick. She wasn't a greedy person – this is what everyone does with popcorn.

I did say satisfied, though one thing was still nagging at her mind. Her hunger may have been satisfied; her curiosity was, at this moment, positively famished. She knew the Forest of Wonders was a place where strange things took place, but she seemed to be in a maze of muddling mysteries, and Flora was the kind of girl who couldn't enjoy a puzzle until she knew the answer. With so many surprising events taking place one on top of the other, she didn't expect everything to be explained at once, but she did think it was reasonable to look for the beginnings of an answer.

And there was one very obvious place to start.

If Flora wanted to know why her mother had sent her off through the forest alone, then it seemed the explanation had to be in the basket she was carrying. If she wanted to know why she'd been given a delivery for her granny, she had to find out what it was she'd been told to deliver.

Her mother, of course, had told her not to look.

She had said, in her most starey-eyed and serious voice, that Flora was not so much as to peek into the basket.

But then who would know?

She was alone in the forest.

Whatever it was in that basket, she could surely have little look, then put it back, and nobody would have any idea she'd done it.

She knew it was naughty. Mum had made her instructions extremely clear. And she knew she was already in trouble. For a moment, Flora wondered if this might be some kind of test.

If she didn't open the parcel, she'd pass the test. That was obvious.

But on the other hand, why *was* she in trouble? She really hadn't done anything so bad. She'd felt frustrated that she kept getting interrupted from her private projects, and what was wrong with showing your frustration now and again?

If she walked on to Granny's house without opening the parcel, she knew that all the crossness between her and her mother would pass. It wasn't much further to go. Easy.

The problem was, now that she'd begun to contemplate the idea of looking in the basket, this thought had become like the itchiest itch she'd ever felt, and not looking had begun to feel like not scratching this world record itch.

She simply couldn't not look.

She couldn't do it.

Flora put the basket on the ground, carefully examined all the folds in the red checked cloth so she could put it back exactly how she found it, and gently, very gently, began to peel it open.

As she undid the first folds, her heart began to pound in her chest. When the cloth fell open, she could hardly believe her eyes.

Curled up in the bottom of the basket was a small furry animal, fast asleep. She had never seen anything like it. It looked a little bit like a beaver, a little bit like a tiny bear with miniature arms, and was the colour of a fox, with long, elegant whiskers, and smooth, curving eyebrows. Its tiny chest was going up down up down quite fast, with every breath. Up close, Flora could hear it giving off a tiny snore. This was the cutest, sweetest (and also the most unusual) little animal that Flora had ever seen.

Then its eyelids flicked open. It had huge, round orange eyes, which at this moment looked startled, afraid and more than a little bonkers.

All of a sudden it leapt from the basket and stood on its hind legs, half-hidden in the blueberry bush, staring at Flora.

'Who are you?' said the creature, in a high, squeaky voice.

'You can talk?' said Flora.

'Why did you wake me up?'

'I ... er ... what *are* you?' asked Flora.

215

'I'm the Maguffin,' said the Maguffin.

'What's that?' asked Flora.

'It's me,' replied the Maguffin. 'I was supposed to be delivered undisturbed to an old woman, and you don't look old. You look young.'

'I'm seven.'

'That would be old for a Maguffin, but for a human that's young, isn't it?'

'I suppose so,' replied Flora.

'So you're not the person who was supposed to wake me up, are you?'

'No. I didn't mean to wake you. I didn't even know you were there, to be honest. I mean – I didn't know you were alive.'

'You thought I was dead?'

'No – I just didn't know what a Maguffin was. I didn't know you were a living thing. I was just taking a little look. If you get back in the basket I'll take you to my granny. She's the person I was supposed to deliver you to.'

'No way,' said the Maguffin. 'There's no way I'm getting back in there.'

'Why not?'

'This is the Forest of Wonders, isn't it?' said the Maguffin, craning its little neck to look up at the canopy.

'Yes,' said Flora.

'Cool! I've always wanted to see the Forest of Wonders! Thanks for the lift. Bye!'

And with that, the Maguffin scurried off into the undergrowth.

'Wait! Wait for me! I mustn't lose you! Stay with me!' yelled Flora.

But it was too late.

The Maguffin was gone.

3

Flora sat down on the toadstool in despair.

'Ahhh!' said the toadstool.

'What shall I do?' sighed Flora.

'Ahhh!' replied the toadstool, who didn't have much of a vocabulary, and was therefore not in a position to answer Flora's question.

'I've lost the Maguffin!' continued Flora. 'Mum told me in her scariest voice not to even look, and now she'll know that I ignored her because I haven't just looked, I've lost him. I'm going to be in such enormous trouble.'

'Yippidy ying ping doo dah day,' said ... something.

Who was that? What was making that ridiculous noise?

'Yippidy ying ping doo dah day,' repeated the voice, which was high and squeaky and reminded Flora of the Maguffin. Which meant that it probably *was* the Maguffin.

Flora leapt off her toadstool and set off towards the sound.

After a few steps, she paused and looked back at the useless fishing net lying on the ground under the toadstool.

217

'Yippidy ying ping doo dah day,' said the Maguffin, from somewhere up ahead.

Flora darted back, grabbed the fishing net, folded it, popped it back in her purse, and set off in pursuit. Every few seconds the same little chirrup emerged from the undergrowth in front of her, but Flora managed to keep up, following every 'Yippidy ying ping doo dah day,' that she heard.

Then a scratching noise skittered up the trunk of an oak tree. A 'Yippidy ying ping,' without the 'doo dah day,' come from high in the foliage of that same tree, before silence returned to the forest.

The Maguffin, if it was the Maguffin, must have climbed the tree, if it was a tree. (Of course it was a tree – what else would it be – a massive daffodil in disguise?)

Flora stared up at the huge, looming branches of the oak. She could see no movement, no Maguffin. It was now so quiet that she could hear the wind rustling the leaves. She had three options:

1. Go home, admit her mistake, and face the consequences.
2. Go on to Granny's house, admit her mistake, face a different kind of consequences, then eat loads of the sweets Granny wasn't supposed to give her but always did.
3. Follow the Maguffin up the tree.

Obviously, it had to be number three.

Flora approached the oak. She liked climbing trees, but this was a huge one, with a thick trunk and no low-hanging branches.

Or rather, it didn't at first seem to have any low-hanging branches, but the closer she got, the more branches the tree seemed to have. Either something had been blocking her view, or this ancient, slow-growing tree was sprouting footholds in front of her eyes.

Strange.

By the time she got to the trunk, a branch was right there, at exactly the height of her stretched-up arm. It looked, now, like a perfect climbing tree. Though, as she pulled herself up off the ground, she did wonder if this whole plan was a wild Maguffin chase (which is like a wild goose chase, but more unpredictable).

'Yippidy ying ping doo dah day,' said a voice high up in the tree. There was definitely something Maguffinish about that sound. Flora couldn't give up now.

Up and up she went.

Up and up and up and up.

And up.

You get the point. She was good at climbing.

Just when she had reached roughly the height where her mum would have screamed, 'WHAT ON EARTH DO YOU THINK YOU'RE DOING, YOU GET DOWN HERE THIS MINUTE!', she heard another 'Yippidy ying ping doo dah day,' but not above her, or below her.

The voice was very near, but muffled. It seemed to be coming from inside the trunk.

Not far in front of her, sharing the same branch, Flora was surprised to see an owl, its proud white face staring aloofly at her through penetrating green eyes.

'Finally,' said the owl, in a nasal, sneering tone, which is an impressive achievement when you remember that owls don't even have a nose.

'I beg your pardon?' replied Flora.

'Bit of a slowcoach, aren't you?' said the owl.

'I thought I did rather well,' said Flora, feeling, and sounding, more than a little wounded.

'*I thought I did rather well,*' mocked the owl. 'Honestly. You people.'

'Us people? Which people?'

'Just ... people. All of you. Can't fly. Can barely see. Crawling around on the ground all the time like overgrown cockroaches. Don't you ever get bored of being a human?'

'No I don't! That's very rude!'

'I like being rude,' said the owl.

'Well, you shouldn't.'

'Why not?'

'Because being rude is ... rude. It's horrible. And mean. And if you behave like that you'll never have any friends.'

'I don't like friends. Friends are annoying and they always turn up expecting food.'

'If you were nicer, maybe you'd have friends who visited to see you, not just to eat.'

'I did have a friend once. Briefly,' mused the owl. 'It was a mouse. We didn't really get on, so I ate him.'

'Well, I'm not trying to be your friend ...'

'Good,' interrupted the owl. 'You look far too chewy.'

'... and I don't want your food, I just want to know if you've seen a Maguffin around here anywhere.'

'A Maguffin?'

'Yes.'

'Do you mean *the* Maguffin? There's only one Maguffin.'

'Really?'

'Yes.'

'Have you seen him?'

'Of course I have.'

'Why of course?'

'Because he's in my house. Hiding.'

Flora noticed that behind the owl was an owl-sized hole in the trunk.

'The Maguffin's in there?'

'Yes. He said he needed a hiding place.'

'And you said yes?'

'No. I said no. But he went in anyway.'

'How do you know he isn't eating your food?'

The owl's neck suddenly swivelled towards his home. 'Oh, my goodness! You're right!' he said, before darting away, shouting, 'Oi! You! What are you up to? Are you

221

eating my food? If you've laid a finger on any of my . . .'

The owl disappeared from view into the tree trunk. A few muffled squawks and squeaks were heard, some white feathers and tufts of orange fir floated out of the entrance, then a startled-looking Maguffin appeared.

'Hi,' said the Maguffin to Flora. 'Long time no see.'

'I . . . I was looking for you. I need to take you to my granny's house,' she replied.

'I'd steer clear of that owl if I were you,' said the Maguffin. 'He's a nutcase.'

'THIEF!' yelled the owl, reappearing on the branch. 'You ate my cheese puffs! I was saving those!'

'I'm off,' said the Maguffin, hopping speedily downwards from branch to branch.

'Wait! Wait for me!' said Flora. 'I mustn't lose you! Please!'

But the Maguffin did not wait. It scurried on down, then disappeared into the undergrowth.

'Typical,' said the owl. 'Never trust a Maguffin.'

'Never trust *the* Maguffin,' corrected Flora.

'Hrmph,' said the owl, shutting his eyes and immediately falling asleep.

Whoever you are visiting, if your host goes to sleep in front of you, that's a pretty clear sign it's time to leave.

4

Flora climbed to the ground where a toadstool seemed to have appeared, which looked exactly like the last toadstool she'd rested on.

Flora sat down to have a think.

'Aaah!' said the toadstool.

Maybe it was the same toadstool. Maybe it was following her around.

Did toadstools do that? Flora wasn't sure. In fact, she didn't really know what a toadstool was. She just knew this one was a good height for sitting on.

Today did not seem to be going well. First there had been that big row with her mother, then she'd been set a simple task in Mum's scariest voice, and Flora had failed, failed, failed.

It was *so* hard to carry around a parcel that someone has told you not to look in without looking in it. Her mother would never understand how hard it was. She had only meant to take a little peek. Now the precious, unique Maguffin was gone.

There wasn't much point carrying on to Granny's house without the parcel. There wasn't much point returning home empty-handed, either. And there wasn't much point just sitting on a toadstool in a forest, brooding. Which meant there wasn't much point in anything.

Flora sniffed, on the brink of tears.

She sniffed again.

And again.

What was that smell?

There was a distinct odour in the air that Flora could only describe as ... Maguffiny.

She got off her toadstool and sniffed the tree trunk, which was giving off the same strong smell – like a mixture of wood smoke, chicken soup and old pyjamas. It was the smell of the Maguffin.

She went down on all fours and circled the trunk. The smell was strongest on one side. She inched forwards. The scent seemed to follow a path.

She sniffed and crawled, crawled and sniffed, moving slowly through the undergrowth, following the route of the Maguffin.

If one of her school friends had turned up at this moment and asked what she was doing, she'd have been really quite embarrassed. But Flora had a strong feeling that nobody she knew was going to find her in the Forest of Wonders.

Then she heard a voice, a mellow and slightly snooty voice, which said, 'What on earth is that?'

She looked up. Right in front of her was an enormous stag, with antlers like two massive hat stands. Next to the stag was a deer with glistening brown eyes and long eyelashes.

'She looks like dog,' said the deer. 'What do you think is wrong with her?'

'Maybe she doesn't know what species she is,' mused the stag.

'She must be very silly,' said the deer.

'Do you mind not talking about me as if I'm not here?' said Flora, standing up on her hind legs. Or, rather, her legs. Now *I'm* forgetting what species she was.

The deer and the stag jumped back, startled.

'That's definitely a human,' said the stag.

'Of course I'm human. I'm following the scent of a Maguffin who I've lost.'

'You've lost a Maguffin?' said the deer. 'But there *is* only one Maguffin.'

'I *know*. That's why I'm following its scent.'

'But humans are terrible at following scents. That's like asking an earthworm to play ping pong.'

'Well, I'm trying my best.'

'The Maguffin went that way,' said the deer.

'Really? Did you see him?'

'No. I can smell him. I can smell everything. I can smell that you've been eating blueberries and popcorn. And your bottom smells faintly of toadstools.'

'Would you help me? Follow the trail?'

'I'll help you,' said the stag. 'If you tell me what you think of my antlers.'

'Great. Thanks.'

'Go on, then,' said the stag. 'You go first.'

'Oh. OK,' said Flora. 'Er ... They're very beautiful.'

'How beautiful?'

'Really beautiful.'

'More beautiful than other antlers?'

'Yes. Definitely.'

'So they're the best antlers you've ever seen?'

'Yes.'

'Do you prefer this side or this side?' the stag asked, turning his head.

'Er ... the first one.'

'You don't like the second one?'

'I like both.'

'But not equally?'

'Er ... yes, equally. Can we go now?'

'But you said you prefer the first one.'

'That was a mistake.'

'What's wrong with this side?'

'Nothing. Let's go.'

'I need to know why you don't like it.'

'I do like it.'

'No, you don't. You said so a minute ago.'

'OH, FORGET IT!' snapped Flora. 'I'LL GO ON MY OWN.'

'*I'll* help you,' said the deer.

'I don't have to tell you you're beautiful?' asked Flora.

'No.'

'Because you are.'

'Thanks. Let's go,' replied the deer, leading the way through the forest, with Flora close behind.

They could hear the stag's voice getting quieter as they

left, saying, 'Do you like my hooves? I've had a buff and polish. Do you like them?'

It was really quite a relief to get away from him. He was exceptionally annoying.

'How far do you think it is to the Maguffin? Is the scent getting stronger?' asked Flora, after a while.

'Bingo,' replied the deer, nodding towards a small brown animal who at that moment was only a few metres in front of them, drinking from a stream.

'There he is!' said Flora. 'You've found him! You're *amazing*! How can I ever thank you?'

'Ooh, I don't suppose you'd scratch my back for me. It's been itchy for about three years.'

'No problem,' said Flora, reaching out to scratch the deer.

'Ooooh!' said the deer. 'Aaaah! Yes! Ooooh! Higher. Lower. Higher. Yes! Aaaahh! Down a bit. Up a bit. Ooooh! Down a bit! YOWZER!'

At the sound of the deer's 'yowzer', the Maguffin looked up, twitched its nose, and dived into the stream.

'I have to go,' said Flora, 'he's getting away.'

'OK. Thanks for the scratch. It was lovely to see you ... I mean meet you. Don't lose heart.'

With that, the deer turned and ambled away. There was something in the deer's voice that reminded Flora of her mother. Which was strange.

Flora set off in pursuit of the Maguffin along the stream, which she soon saw poured into a large, sparkling pond.

And in that pond, she saw something that horrified her. Something that made no sense at all.

The pond was filled with hundreds of splashing, playing, swimming, diving, somersaulting Maguffins.

'LOOK!' shouted Flora after the retreating deer. 'There are hundreds of them! I thought there was only one!'

The deer stopped, glanced briefly at the pond, then gave Flora a thoughtful stare, through eyes that really did look weirdly familiar.

'There *is* only one,' said the deer.

'No, there isn't! Look! How am I going to find the one that's for my granny?'

'There's only one Maguffin,' said the deer, 'but there are thousands of Gamuffins. They're like pests. They get everywhere.'

'But they all look the same!'

'They're very different.'

'How?'

'A Gamuffin has six whiskers. The Maguffin has eight.'

'But ... how am I going to ... I mean ... that's no help! How am I going to find the one animal with two extra whiskers in amongst all those?'

'There is one other thing,' said the deer.

'What's that?'

'Gamuffins hate popcorn. Loathe it.'

'How is that going to help me?'

'The Maguffin loves it. It's his favourite thing. I have

to go. You remember to be careful on your journey, OK?'

'OK,' said Flora, who to be honest barely even heard the deer's strange parting comment. Because Flora's brain was busy thinking about one thing and one thing only. Popcorn.

5

Flora, who was a quick thinker, already had a plan, which began with retracing her steps back to the popcorn tree.

This wasn't straightforward, since there were no steps. She'd crawled most of the way, following the Maguffin's scent, and when you are crawling you don't really notice your surroundings. She could have crawled right past a pink palace made of marshmallows and candy canes and she probably wouldn't have even seen it.

Then she spotted a familiar-looking toadstool up ahead, in what she thought was the right direction. She walked towards it, but however fast she walked, the toadstool never seemed to get any closer. She still felt she was heading in the right direction, though, and she must have been, because soon enough she noticed that the toadstool was directly under the popcorn tree.

And there the toadstool stayed, remaining in just the right spot for Flora to stand on it and pick armfuls of popcorn, most of which she ate. But she did remember to stuff some in her pockets for the Maguffin.

'Thanks for your help,' said Flora, to the toadstool.

The toadstool didn't reply, which perhaps wasn't very surprising given that it didn't have a mouth or a brain.

Flora sat on the toadstool.

'Aaah,' said the toadstool, which ought to have been surprising, but somehow wasn't.

After a short rest and another few handfuls of popcorn, Flora headed back to the Maguffin and Gamuffin-infested pond.

She dropped a piece of popcorn by the water's edge, then another one next to it, then another, laying a trail all the way to a spot next to a large and bushy bush, where she set down all the rest of the popcorn from her pockets (except for a few bits which seemed to fall into her mouth).

Flora hid behind the bush.

Before she did that she opened up her purse and took out the item her mother had given her, which she now realised wasn't a useless beach toy at all, but an extremely useful Maguffin net.

How her mother had known she would end up in this predicament, and had given her the exact tool she needed, was a mystery, but Flora didn't have time to think about that right now. She was on a Maguffin hunt.

Hidden behind the bushy bush, she peeped through a gap in the leafy leaves towards the pondy pond where the Gamuffins and Maguffin were swimming. One of the Gamuffins was practising swallow dives off a nearby rock; another was doing underwater somersaults; a small gang was having piggy-back fights, and only one was still. The still Gamuffin, which Flora quickly realised might be the Maguffin, was perched on a lily pad, sniffing the air, pointing its cute little whiskery nose towards the popcorn trail.

In a flash, it leapt into the water and swam at top speed towards the bank, got out, shook itself dry, and began to gobble up the popcorn. Every piece of fluffy white popcorn the Maguffin ate brought him closer and closer to the bush where Flora was hiding.

Soon he was right there, within reach.

Flora leapt out, brandishing the net, and pounced. The Maguffin jumped away from the popcorn (which is not something you will often see a Maguffin do), but Flora was too fast. The net was over him, pressed into the forest floor. He was trapped.

He jumped and squirmed, wriggled and twisted, writhed, fidgeted, struggled and strained, but there was no way out. The Maguffin net had netted the Maguffin.

'Got you!' said Flora, lifting him off the ground with a deft twist.

'LEAVE ME ALONE!' he yelled, three words which dropped a strange, chilly sensation into Flora's chest.

'I can't. I have to take you to Granny's house.'

'Why won't you leave me alone? I was having fun!'

'You keep running away, but I have to look after you. I promised I'd take you to Granny's house.'

'I don't want to go to Granny's house. Who's Granny?'

'She's my granny. She'll look after us.'

'I don't like her!'

'You've never met her.'

'I don't like houses.'

'It's a cottage, really.'

'I hate cottages.'

'Are you hungry?'

'No! Yes!'

'Which?'

'Both.'

'Why don't I put you in the basket and I'll carry you to . . . somewhere nice . . . and we'll have some food.'

'I hate baskets!'

'Are you tired?'

'No!'

Flora noticed that the Maguffin was doing long, slow blinks, and his head was bobbing up and down as if his neck wasn't strong enough to hold it up.

'I'm just going to pop you in here for a little bit, where you'll be comfy,' she said.

Flora lifted the Maguffin gently out of the net, laid him gently in her basket, and tucked him in.

'I'm not tired!' he yelled, in his tiny, squeaky voice. 'I'm not hungry! I am hungry! I need a wee! I don't need a wee! I'm not tired! I'm not tired! I'm not . . . zzzzzzzzzzzzzzzzzz.'

And just like that, all of a sudden, the Maguffin fell fast asleep.

Flora picked up the basket and set off towards Granny's cottage. Disaster, it seemed, had been averted.

6

By the time Flora arrived she was very tired, very hungry, and very late. Granny, however, didn't seem the least surprised that her granddaughter had taken all morning to cover the short distance from home.

She gave Flora some hot tomato soup, with tomato salad and a tomato sandwich on the side. Granny grew her own vegetables, and whatever was in season, that was what you got. Flora tried never to visit in November, the month of turnips. Only when Flora's soup bowl was empty did Granny ask to see inside the basket.

'Why is it covered with a net?' asked Granny.

'I ... er ... I didn't want whatever is in there to escape.'

'What is in there?'

'It's a ... I mean ... I don't know. I didn't look.'

'Really?' Granny narrowed her eyes.

'Well, maybe I did have one quick peek,' said Flora, 'but that's all.'

'Just a peek?'

'Yes.'

'And ...'

'It's a Maguffin.'

'And ...'

233

'And what?'

'That's all you have to tell me?'

'Well … I did have a slight … accident on the way. It really was just a quick peek, but the Maguffin jumped out. And ran away. And for a while, I thought I'd lost him, but I got him back. So everything's OK. Isn't it?'

'Let's see,' said Granny, carefully lifting the net from the basket and unfolding the red checked fabric.

Flora looked inside. She couldn't believe her eyes.

The basket was empty!

'IT WAS THERE! IT WAS THERE! I PUT HIM BACK IN! I FOUND HIM AND PUT HIM BACK IN! I PROMISE!'

Flora looked up at Granny, and her eyes filled with tears.

Granny said nothing.

'THE NET WAS ON TIGHT. HE CAN'T HAVE ESCAPED!'

Granny still said nothing, which for a moment seemed even scarier than Granny losing her temper.

'I LOOKED AFTER HIM! I DID! I TRIED MY VERY BEST!'

Only now, with Flora beginning to sob, did Granny put her on her knee and give her a hug.

When Granny finally spoke, it was to say something very unexpected.

'I know you did,' she said. 'The thing is, there's no such animal as a Maguffin.'

'But … that's what Mum gave me! To deliver to you!'

'How do you know?' asked Granny.

'Because ... she just did. She gave me the basket, told me it contained a Maguffin, I carried it into the forest, and when I opened it, there was the Maguffin.'

'So how do you know she gave it to you?'

'I just explained!'

'It was there when you opened it. How do you know it was there when she gave it to you?'

'Because I was carrying it. It couldn't have climbed in without me noticing. And Mum told me it was in there. That's how I know what it's called.'

'But you just said it couldn't have climbed out.'

'It couldn't!'

'But it has.'

'Yes.'

'So maybe it climbed in. In the forest.'

'Why would Mum tell me it was in the basket when it wasn't?'

'Maybe she knew what was going to happen.'

'How could she possibly know?'

Granny shrugged. 'There's no such animal as a Maguffin,' she said.

'But I saw it!'

'What else did you see in the forest?'

'I saw ... well ... a lot of strange things.'

'There's no such animal as a Maguffin,' said Granny, placing a reassuring hand on Flora's knee.

'Then what did I see?'

235

'When you spot a Maguffin, you are seeing whatever is in here,' said Granny, moving her reassuring hand from Flora's knee to her heart.

'So what was it?' asked Flora.

'You tell me,' said Granny. 'A little bit of mischief? Some anger, maybe? An urge to run away?'

'I don't understand. The Maguffin was *real*. I saw him. I touched him. I spoke to him.'

'I imagine you've seen lots of interesting things in your dreams, haven't you? Were they all real?'

'No, but ... I was awake. I haven't been asleep. Not for a second. I was on my way here.'

'I know you were.'

'So it *wasn't* a dream.'

'I never said it was.'

'So what *did* you say?'

'I just said the Forest of Wonders is a very strange place. It's a place where whatever is in your heart comes to life. If Mum sent you there on your own, she must think you're ready to deal with that.'

'Deal with what?'

'I don't know. Did the Maguffin want to run off on his own, exploring, or did he want to be safe, with you?'

'He wanted to run off,' said Flora, 'but I think he likes being looked after, too.'

'And you did everything you could to take care of him, didn't you?'

'YES! I really did.'

'Even when he just wanted you to leave him alone?'

'Yes.'

'So does he remind you of anyone?'

A flash of understanding darted across Flora's eyes. 'Do you mean me?' she asked.

'Maybe.'

'So he is real?'

'Of course.'

'But you said there's no such thing as a Maguffin . . .'

'No such *animal* as a Maguffin.'

'Am I the only person who can see him?'

'What do you think?'

'I don't know. Will I see him again?'

'Probably. When he wants to be seen. You've done very well. Now it's time for you to go home.'

Flora looked up at Granny, her brow furrowed with worry.

'What is it?' asked Granny.

'I . . . will you . . . come with me?'

'Are you anxious about going through the forest alone?'

'Yes. I'm tired.'

'Of course I'll come. You never know when you'll meet the Maguffin, and you need to be ready, don't you?'

'Yes.'

'It's not easy looking after a Maguffin, is it?'

'No. But it's worth it.'

'Of course it is. Shall we go?'

'Yes.'

Hand in hand, Flora and Granny walked home through the forest. They saw no sighing toadstools, no popcorn trees, no Maguffins or Gamuffins, and no talking deer.

Flora was relieved to have Granny with her, but as they emerged from the trees and made their way along the path towards home, where Mum as waving from an upstairs window, Flora looked back at the forest and wondered if her Maguffin was in there somewhere.

What was it doing at that moment? Swimming? Climbing a tree? Sleeping? Waiting for her to return?

Flora knew that as soon as she had the chance, she'd go back and find him. And she had a feeling that next time, he'd be pleased to see her.

GHOST TOURS UNLIMITED

DAVID SOLOMONS

Margot sat in the back of the taxi, wedged between her parents, and peered up at Edinburgh Castle atop the crag of Castle Rock. It was wreathed in evening mist, ancient and mysterious.

'*Haar*,' said the driver. For a moment she thought he was choking, but then she realised he was trying to tell her something. 'It's an old Scottish word for mist.'

'*Haar*,' repeated Margot, rolling it around her tongue. She leaned forward, propping her hands on the seat in front. 'Can you teach me some more Scottish words?'

He drummed his fingers thoughtfully on the steering wheel. 'How about … "boggin"? Means dirty or disgustin'. Usage typically, but not exclusively, applied to bodily functions. Ee Gee: "I saw you pick your nose – that's totally *boggin*."'

'Nice,' said Margot, nodding enthusiastically. Maybe being dragged out of bed at the crack of dawn, watching her dad almost burst a blood vessel when it looked like they were going to miss the plane, and having to endure a day enveloped in a constant cloud of her mum's perfume, might be worth it after all. 'Gimme another.'

She felt her mum's hand on her shoulder. 'I don't think that's appropriate. Thank you, driver.' She was gently but firmly guided back into her seat, and when she looked out of the window again, the castle had disappeared in the mist. Sorry, *haar*.

'I have some concealer for *that*,' said her mum, making a circling motion around Margot's forehead.

'It's just a little spot,' she objected. 'Barely noticeable.'

'Well, if you're quite sure, darling.' Her mum said it in the sort of accusing tone reserved for oil companies who've just caused a toxic spill.

Margot gazed out of the window of the taxi as it threaded its way through streets teeming with people. It was her first time in Edinburgh and she was here – like a gazillion other people it seemed – for the world-famous Festival. From what she could see, the city appeared to be one long assault course of fire-breathing, chainsaw-juggling, bagpipe-blowing *artistes* attempting to extract applause and ready money from an endless wave of tourists. It looked like it could be fun, not that she expected any actual fun tonight, not with what her parents had planned. She put the horror out of her mind. Mum drew out the dreaded perfume atomiser and with two sharp squirts gave herself a top-up. Without looking up from his phone, Dad powered down his window, letting in a warm breeze to blow away the biological hazard. Margot had almost forgotten it was summer, what with the lingering mist. And even though it was the height of August, she felt the strangest chill.

The sun was setting when they pulled up outside the hotel. While her parents checked in, Margot checked out the other guests. A cluster of people with long faces and even longer leather coats hung around the reception desk like a colony of bats. In front of an ornate fireplace gathered a group wearing monocles and tweed who looked as though they were set for a day's grouse-shooting. Another peculiar assembly consisted of blank-faced people wearing mobile phone headsets, all blinking in perfect time, as if they were part of some freaky hive mind. As Margot circled the lobby, she picked up snatches of their conversation.

'... Class Four Full-Bodied Apparition ... had it in my sights ...'

'... yeah, the new Spook-Snatcher Mark 2 with the spirit-scope ...'

'... spent the night at Hell's Grange ... definite EVP activity ...'

'... floated straight through the wall at me ... almost caught myself an actual ghoul.'

Who were these people? And what were they talking about?

A large ribbed metal case lay at the feet of one of the bat-people, a man with red hair, a red beard and a hard-to-read expression, since it was currently obscured by a pair of unnecessarily dark sunglasses. A porter bent to pick up the luggage, misjudged its weight, and dropped it. The case crashed down on the marble floor; the lid sprang open and the contents spilled out. Margot gawped. The object on the floor looked like some kind of badly made laser-gun prop from a science-fiction movie. It had a trigger-grip and a long silver barrel emblazoned with the words: *Spectre Detector Collector 9000*. Backing away in surprise, she bumped against a noticeboard. Steadying the wobbling board, she saw what was written across it.

The Balmoral Hotel welcomes the Society for Paranormal, Occult and Otherworldly Capture (S.P.O.O.C.) – Registration – William Wallace Conference Room.

She looked around at the peculiar collection of hotel guests and at last understood who they were. 'Ghost-hunters,' she whispered. And then, unable to contain her incredulity, she added, 'Seriously?'

'Are you excited for tonight, Margot?' asked her mother, having collected the room keys.

Tonight Margot was going to watch two and a half hours of interpretative, underwater sea dance. Without an interval. Which meant two and a half hours watching people waving scarves about pretending to be jellyfish and seaweed fronds while she needed to wee.

'Excited isn't the word,' she mumbled.

*

Margot was more bored than she'd ever been in her entire life. She glanced at her mum in the next seat. Mum dabbed her eyes, clearly overcome by the raw emotional power of the jellyfish thumping across the stage in front of her. Dad was surreptitiously checking his phone. She could tell by the angle of his head of perfectly coiffed hair, which was bent over the screen as he scrolled through his mail. He had the most remarkable hair. She'd never seen it move, not even in a gale. Amazing. She had inherited his hair, but, as her mum continually reminded her, not his sunny disposition. Instead, Margot was a deathly pale girl with long, dark tresses and a long, dark attitude to match. Along with the whole morbid curiosity thing went the standard issue eyeliner, the black clothes (no dresses, *ever*) and army issue boots.

On stage a sea-urchin did a Moonwalk. Margot wriggled uncomfortably. There were still two hours of this to endure. When she'd asked earlier why there was no interval, her mum had given her a two-word answer: 'It's art.' She muttered loudly, 'This show is boggin. Totally boggin.' Mum continued to weep and Dad to check his email.

It used to bother her that her own parents could look through her like she wasn't even there. As far as they were concerned, she might as well be a ghost. Not that she believed in ghosts. Of course not – she was a rational twelve-year-old girl from Basingstoke, for goodness' sake. She wasn't like those S.P.O.O.C. weirdos; she preferred facts. Ideally, they ought to be gloomy, gruesome facts. And when it came to fiction, she only read books with dark endings. A thought began to form. Edinburgh was ancient – it must be brimming with tales of grisly deaths, revolting peasants with pitchforks, maybe even the Black Plague! There had to be some sort of tour that would tell her about the city's dark history. And there *was* an upside to being invisible to her parents.

As a dancing jellyfish went into a pirouette, Margot slipped out of the theatre and into the busy street. She savoured the moment, blissfully free from the horrors of saucepan lid music and wailing seaweed people. But even her parents would notice her absence when the lights went up. She had to be back before the end of the performance, which gave her exactly two hours of freedom. Pulling out her phone, she set a timer, then launched the city guide app she'd downloaded in preparation for the trip. One quick search for 'guided tours' and she was on her way to the street known as the Royal Mile.

According to her guide, the Royal Mile was the spine of the Old Town, an ancient and mysterious route bookended by a royal palace and a royal fortress. It stretched uphill, past tall, crooked buildings towards the castle. Dark alleys jutted off it at irregular intervals, like bottomless chasms ready to swallow anyone who slipped from the well-lit path.

Behind her, a bell chimed and she leaped out of the way to let a bicycle wheel past. It was pedalled by a figure wearing what looked like a monk's habit, but that wasn't the weirdest thing about it. Along its crossbar was a small armoury of knives, axes and wooden stakes. But that wasn't the weirdest thing about it either. No, what was particularly weird was the wicker basket attached to the handlebars, from which hung three severed heads.

The monk was heading towards the castle. She tracked him through the throng and saw him wave to a man dressed in a suit of medieval armour standing by a colourful sign. It sported an illustration of a regal crown and sceptre, and the words: *The Right Royal Tour: Knightly, from 8.30pm.* The man in the armour waved back stiffly.

The monk pedalled on, passing another sign, this one attended by a sallow youth with a bloody dagger through his neck. *Ghostspotting*, read the sign. *Choose Afterlife. 8.30pm daily.* He, too, exchanged friendly waves with the monk. Margot briefly lost sight of him in the crowd. Pushing her way through, she emerged to find the bicycle with its hideous cargo propped against another sign: *Blood and Gore. Meet here. 8.30pm. Bring a sickbag.* The words were written in a dark red script with jagged lettering that promised significant death and anguish.

Half a dozen customers gathered round, waiting for the tour to begin. Margot tried to get the monk's attention, but he was too busy counting their cash to notice. She tugged at his voluminous sleeve, which caused a severed head to fall out of it. On closer inspection she saw now that the head was pâpier-maché. That was a let-down.

The monk pounced on the head, which had started to roll off down the hill, and returned it to his sleeve with a sheepish grin. 'Blood, witchcraft, numinous evil?' he offered, thrusting one of the 'Blood and Gore' leaflets into her hands. 'Ten quid. That's all it will take to open your eyes and dip your toe in the supernatural horrors of the Old Town.' He drew his cowl about his face and lowered his voice to a growl. 'According to experts, Edinburgh is the most haunted city in the world. Death abounds here. Thousands died in agony on the gallows, accused of witchcraft; the Plague took thousands more; war and bad plumbing did for the rest. And their spirits still haunt the dark closes and narrow wynds of this very road.'

'I don't believe in ghosts,' said Margot.

With a huff, the monk tipped back his cowl. 'Look, do you want to go on my tour or not?'

'Not,' decided Margot, pushing the leaflet back at him.

She'd sought an authentic experience, but this was about as authentic as a fairground haunted train. Disappointed, she slouched off down the street. Perhaps this had all been a mistake. She ought to head back to the theatre – if she could remember the way.

She pulled out her phone again and plugged in her earbuds. She was of the opinion that life always worked better with a soundtrack. Without one, you were just some girl walking along some street in a random city, but with the right music filling your head, you were the star of your own movie. The moment called for the new album from State of Rain, tipped to be the most miserable example of Scottish sadcore since their last album. Her finger froze as she reached for the 'Play' button and she stopped in her tracks.

A seven-foot-tall figure in a furry hat and a greatcoat led a party of even more strangely dressed people up towards the castle. She looked around to gauge other people's reactions to the bizarre group. No one else seemed to have noticed them.

The perilously tall figure at the front of the group held aloft a bright yellow flag, which proclaimed in glowing blue letters, *Ghost Tours Unlimited*. As the group passed her, the words vanished and reappeared like a magician's rabbit.

'Scotland's capital city features not one, not two, but three international festivals,' declaimed the guide, punctuating each factoid with a flourish of a hand, 'thirty-one characterful neighbourhoods, two professional football clubs, two hundred and eight CCTV cameras, and an annual rainfall of six hundred and twenty-six millimetres.'

Tedious stuff, she thought, and she was about to turn away when the last of the tourists straggled past. He was a boy about her age, and he was smouldering. Not that he was particularly good-looking, but a thin wisp of smoke appeared to be rising from the top of his head. Curious, Margot tagged along beside him. After ten paces of silence she decided to try her coolest intro. She pulled out her earbuds.

'Hi.'

249

No response. How rude. But then she saw that he too was wearing earbuds plugged into a phone on his hip, and he hadn't heard her. The phone was like no other she had ever seen. It looked as if it had been carved out of a cloud. With an icicle. A shimmering splash screen displayed an unfamiliar logo.

'Appal?' Margot racked her brains, but couldn't remember seeing it anywhere until this moment.

The boy noticed her and removed one earbud. 'What d'you say?'

He was Scottish. A local. For a moment she wondered what he was doing on a tour of Edinburgh, but there were other more pressing questions she wanted answers to first. Why was smoke coming out of his head, for instance? But that seemed a bit too personal, at least to begin with.

'What is that?' She pointed to the phone.

'It's the new AiiiiieeeePhone,' he explained proudly. 'With Enhanced Shriek™ and the pearlescent finish. Just came out last week. I had to queue all night to get my hands on this. I was lucky – there was this ghoul in front of me who—'

'Excuse me?'

'Yeah, this ghoul, she *blah blah blah* ...'

Margot nodded along, but she wasn't listening to the rest of the story. She was stuck on the first part. It must be the accent, she concluded. He was talking about some *girl* in front of him in a line for ... whatever this thing was.

An Appal AiiiieeeePhone. Must be a Scottish brand, she decided, and left it at that.

'I didn't see you in Departures,' said the boy.

'I just flew in this afternoon,' said Margot.

He snorted. '*Flew*. Funny.'

Uh, and what was so funny about *flying* from an airport?

'My parents drag me on this tour every year,' the boy went on. He gestured to a couple in front of them. They were with a girl half Margot's age, listening avidly to the guide. For some reason the boy's dad appeared to be sucking on a lit candle. 'I've done it, like, three hundred times. They like to come back and see what's become of the old country, but it's so-o dull.' He pulled out the other earbud to give her his full attention. 'I'm Tom,' he said, and smiled.

'Margot.'

'So, where you from?' asked Tom. 'No, wait, don't tell me. I'm really good at this.' He rested a finger lightly on his temples and screwed up his eyes in concentration. 'Phantarctica!' He announced with a double click of his fingers. 'It's the accent, and your skin – that particular shade of lifeless white. I'm right, amn't I?' He grinned.

Margot held his excited gaze with a puzzled one of her own.

'Basingstoke,' she said at last. Now it was Tom's turn to look confused. She was about to ask him about the smoke rising from his head when, ahead, the tour guide called a halt. For the first time, she got a proper look at him.

251

He wore a hat pulled down and a greatcoat with the collar pulled up. He had enormous shoes, though from the way he shuffled from one foot to the other it was clear that they were pinching him uncomfortably. The hat was one of those Russian hats with furry earflaps designed to protect the wearer from the extremes of the Siberian cold. But as Margot peered at it, she could have sworn that the earflaps were actually his ears. He caught her inquisitive gaze and looked up from beneath his brim. Most of his face was in shadow, but his eyes flashed the colour of cursed emeralds.

The tourists were just as weird looking. There was an old woman dressed like a queen from a history book, complete with a gold crown and a haughty expression. A livid red scar circled her neck. Next to her was what Margot guessed to be a hen party: three young women in silver spangly tops, tottering in high heels. It must have been some party – two of them were missing arms, and one had a fake axe lodged in her skull. Even Tom's get-up was a bit off. He was wearing jeans and a hoody, but they were made from a material that seemed to absorb the light, like some kind of urban camouflage. Most of the other tourists were clothed in a variety of hoods and hats and high collars that concealed their faces.

'This way. Keep together. Quickly now.' The guide raised his flag and, with a shake, set off smartly along a narrow passage. They passed beneath a pair of winged serpent statuettes on a gate and emerged in a courtyard enclosed on three sides by lofty tenement buildings that cast crooked shadows across the cobblestones. The place was still and quiet. The tourists formed a circle around the guide. He cleared his throat. 'Before we go any further, I'd like to remind you of the rules.' He hoisted a series of fingers as he counted them out. 'One – no walking through walls without the prior authorisation of your guide. Two – no floating or flying at any time. Three – no shrieking.' He directed a meaningful look at a couple in the front row with long, straggly hair and burning red eyes. Contact lenses, Margot assumed. 'That means you, Mr and Mrs Banshee,' said the guide pointedly. They shuffled about and grumblingly muttered their assent. 'Four – absolutely no touching the Living, and no pointing at them and shouting, "Look at the size/colour of that one!"'

Margot listened with increasing amusement, and at this last point she could no longer contain herself. A laugh burst from her lips. The other tourists turned to stare.

'Sorry.' She clamped a hand over her mouth. Tom wasn't laughing. 'Oh, come on,' she appealed to him. 'Sure, it's lame, but it's also kind of funny. I mean, he's talking to us like we're ghosts.'

Not for the first time that evening Tom regarded her strangely. Margot felt the oddest prickling sensation reach all the way from her lower back to the base of her skull. Of course she'd heard the cliché 'spine-tingling' before now, but at that precise moment she felt it in a way she'd never

253

imagined possible. Slowly, she looked from one tourist to the next. The ragged scar round the queen's neck, almost as if her head had been cut off. The spangly-topped girl with the fake axe through her head. What if it wasn't so fake? And the smoke rising out of the top of Tom's head, as if he'd been caught in a fire. Come to think of it, he did look a little crispy round the edges.

Like a stunt driver who's just realised her jet-car isn't going to make it across the ravine, Margot suddenly knew the impossible truth. And simultaneously she and Tom came to the same awful conclusion:

'You ... you ... you're a—'

'You ... you ... you're a—'

'A GHOST!'

'ALIVE!'

'You're ghosts,' Margot stuttered. 'This is a ghost tour. For ghosts.' And then, because her brain was stuck in neutral, added another, 'Ghosts.'

'You can *see* us, you possess the gift,' Tom said, pointing a quivering finger at her. 'You have the Third Eye.'

Margot's hand flew to her forehead. 'It's just a spot.'

'What's going on here?' It was the guide, drawn by the commotion. 'Keep it down or we'll have the Living on top of us before you can say—'

'She's one of them!' wailed Mrs Banshee.

'One of what?'

'ONE OF THE LIVING!'

'You sure?' said the guide. 'Looks dead to me.'

'Hey!' Margot wasn't taking that, not even from a ghost.

As confirmation of Margot's presence in their midst swept through the group, screams of ghostly panic filled the night air. The hen party floated into walls and through them, the queen's head fell off, the banshees ignored rule number three and shrieked the place down.

The guide swiftly unholstered a small, jet-black object the size of a mobile phone. Margot noticed it had the same Appal logo that was emblazoned on Tom's phone.

'Ladies and gentlemen,' the guide said calmly, 'there is no need to panic. The Portal Object Originator has a raft of built-in safety measures – one of which is an actual raft. Fellow spirits, Your Majesty.' He bowed to the headless queen. 'That concludes tonight's tour.' He sank his thumb onto the device's solitary button and, with a reassuring chime, it pulsed into life and a series of lights popped up on the ground, illuminating a path to a newly sprung hole in the wall of the courtyard clearly marked 'Emergency Exit'. Certain perfectly good laws of physics would assert that, were you to make a hole in that particular wall, you would create a view through to the souvenir shop on the other side. However the law responsible for such things was at that moment having its lunch money swiped and being subjected to a wedgie by the bullying invention that was the Appal Industries Mark One Portal Object Originator, for through the hole was – not a shop selling a wide selection of tartan cardigans and shortbread – but an entirely different dimension.

'What ... how ... where ... is that?' Margot gawped. 'Is that ... the afterlife?'

'The arrivals lounge,' corrected Tom.

Their otherworldly screams rending the night air, the ghosts scrambled past, through and over each other for the exit. Less than fifteen seconds later, the hole had closed and Margot was alone once more.

Well, almost.

'Mum? Dad?!' Tom stood in front of the wall. A blue corona, the lingering remains of the ghostly doorway, sparked and vanished. 'Is anybody there?' He stuck his head through the solid wall. 'Hello? Anybody?'

Margot stopped and stared. Everything she'd previously understood about life and death had just been upended, shaken about and poured through a sieve by a boy with a smoking head and a very cool phone. Something deep inside told her that it would take the rest of her life to come to terms with what was happening right now. She couldn't wait that long. After a few deep breaths, she decided to go with it and see where the evening took her.

Tom closed his eyes. And panicked. 'I'm a kid. I've only been dead three hundred years! What am I supposed to do? I agreed to go on the stupid tour this year because I thought I might meet Juan Fantasma. He's famous. He's the best guide in the Netherworld and the face of Ghost Tours Unlimited. You must've seen his new fragrance ad.'

'Uh ...'

'*Fatality* by Tommy Hilfantom. It's in black-and-white and Juan is all bare-chested, up a mountain, with a yak.'

'A yak?'

'Yes, a—' He stopped. 'I shouldn't be talking to you. Ghosts and the Living aren't meant to, y'know, chat. I'm going to be in so much trouble. Unless ...' He hooded his eyes, raised his arms, waggled his fingers, and let out a long, low moan. 'Wooo!'

Margot looked sympathetic. 'Are you trying to scare me away?'

'Wooooo!' Tom continued.

She planted her hands on her hips. 'Because if you are, it's not working.'

'Woooo ... oh,' he finished, disappointed. 'Sorry.'

'No, don't apologise. That's so cool. I just got spooked by a spook!' She was struck by a feeling of unease. 'That's OK, right? Calling you a "spook". It's not, um, politically incorrect, is it?'

Tom ignored her and began to pace up and down. 'This is a disaster. What do I do?'

'Can't you call someone on that?' she said, pointing to his phone.

He raised it above his head, fishing for a signal. 'I can't make inter-dimensional calls. I'm only on a Haunt-As-You-Go contract.' He stopped pacing to stare at her as if she was an exhibit in a glass case. 'I've heard of people like you. Living people who can see us.'

Us. It was still sinking in that he meant ghosts. She realised she might never get another opportunity like this. 'So what's it like ... being a ghost?'

Tom shrugged. 'It's all right. It's not like I was given a choice.'

That raised an awkward question, but she had to know. 'How did you ... pass over?'

'You mean "die"?' he said flatly.

Margot nodded. She didn't like to use the word as she thought it would be impolite to draw attention to his, well, dead-ness.

'My dad was a famous candlemaker.'

'You get those?'

Tom frowned. 'He invented the candle-calendar?' Margot hadn't heard of it. 'Yeah. Never really repaid its research and development costs.' Tom shrugged again. 'Anyway, my family comes from a long line of candlemakers, with one thing in common.' He ran a hand through his hair, momentarily diverting the plume of smoke. 'We all died in fires.'

'I'm sorry.'

'It's OK. It happened years ago. Seventeen-hundred and ten, to be exact. It was my birthday.'

'Oh no!' Somehow, that made it even worse.

'Yeah. Dad was experimenting with a new formula for the candles on my cake. Suddenly, WHOOSH! The cake went up – burned down our hovel, killed the lot of us. My little sister's never really forgiven me – she's convinced she's going to be seven years old for ever.'

There was a strangled cry from the entrance to the close. Alarmed, Tom shrank into the wall so that only his toes poked out.

'It's just a cat,' said Margot.

Tom re-emerged as the scrawny feline swaggered by. It cast a disdainful look at Margot, but turned to Tom and its green eyes flashed with something familiar. Mewing, it tried to wrap itself around his ankles, but to its feline indignation went straight through them.

'I'm going to wait right here,' said Tom, making a decision. 'I'm sure someone will be back to fetch me any second . . . now!' He gazed expectantly at the solid wall, which remained annoyingly solid. 'Now? Or now. How about . . . no—'

A bolt of red lightning fizzed past Tom's right shoulder and smacked into the wall behind him. The stone disintegrated, dust flew up and a charred smell spread through the air.

'Missed!' cursed a voice.

Tom and Margot wheeled around to see two figures charge into the courtyard. The first was a man with red hair, a red beard and a hard-to-read expression, since it was obscured behind a pair of hi-tech glowing goggles. He brandished a familiar weapon. Margot's eyes ran along the words etched in its barrel: *Spectre Detector Collector 9000.*

'Careful, Randall,' said the other figure, a woman wearing a thick duffle-coat, bent under the weight of a huge battery pack strapped to her back. The battery was connected to the Spectre Detector Collector by a thick electrical lead. 'She looks like a Type Three Apparition. Highly dangerous.'

'No' her, ya daft woman,' said the man called Randall. 'She's no' a ghost.' He swung his goggles and weapon to point at Tom. *'He's* the ghost.' Randall planted the butt of the weapon against his shoulder. 'Juice me, Dora.'

'Yes, Randall,' said Dora, throwing a switch.

With a whine of power the SDC 9000 charged up. Randall unleashed another jagged red bolt of lightning. It leaped from the barrel and sliced through the air with a high-energy crackle, cutting deep into Tom's body and lodging there. He wriggled like a fish on a hook. 'I've got one!' yelled Randall. 'Dora, I've finally got one!'

'Don't let him get away, Randall!'

'Initiating spectral capture,' said Randall, rotating a handle on the grip of the weapon. Just as he began to crank the handle there was a blur of ginger hackles and a strangled mew, and something struck him, knocking the weapon out of his hands. It clattered to the ground. The red lightning faded, releasing Tom from its grip.

'Run!' yelled Margot.

She and Tom raced past the ghost-hunters and out of the courtyard. Randall looked to Dora with a mixture of irritation and astonishment. 'Did that wee girly just throw a cat at me?'

'Who ... who was that?' asked Tom, checking over his shoulder as they pounded along the Royal Mile.

'S.P.O.O.C. The Society for Paranormal, Occult and Otherworldly Capture,' said Margot. 'I think it's their annual conference tonight.'

'You're telling me I'm stuck in Edinburgh on the one night of the year when a group of professional ghost-hunters are roaming the city?'

'Would it alarm you unduly if I did?' Margot looked back, and caught a sight of Randall tearing through the crowds, Dora lumbering after him. 'I have a feeling they don't catch a lot of ghosts. They won't give up easily.'

'This way,' shouted Tom. 'I have an idea.' He veered off along a narrow passage, and skipped down a flight of steps. As she followed, Margot's boots rang off the stone steps.

'When I say "jump," you jump, understand?' said Tom.

'Why do I have to—?'

'Jump!'

She jumped.

They landed in a small courtyard and dashed across the uneven cobblestones. 'Lady Stair's Close,' Tom announced in his best tour guide's voice. 'Famous for its twin defensive features ...' He gestured to a turreted corner-house. 'The house built with a spiral staircase that gives a right-handed defending swordsman the advantage over intruders.' They hurtled past it as, behind them, Randall bounded down the steps. 'And please watch out for the second feature . . .'

'Aaaagh!'

' . . . The Trip Stair,' finished Tom with a satisfied grin.

Randall stumbled on the irregular step and flew through the air with all the aerodynamic grace of a brick, before hitting the ground with a bone-crunching thud, his momentum sending him sliding him along until he came to a sudden and painful stop against the door of the corner-house. As he lay there groaning, the cast iron doorknocker fell off, landing with a clunk on his head.

'There are some advantages to taking the same tour three hundred years running,' grinned Tom, as they sprinted back onto the Royal Mile. No sooner had they reached the crowded street than he came to a skidding stop. 'Uh, this S.P.O.O.C. mob you bumped into, how many of them would you say you counted?'

She turned to look where he was staring down the street in horror. A churning mass of figures raced out of the mist towards them. Margot nodded. 'I'd say about *that* many.'

With a yell, they turned tail. The hunters swarmed after them, ghost-detecting goggles glowing, ectoplasmic range-finders probing the darkness for their quarry.

PHREEEEN!

A trigger-happy hunter let fly, and an energy bolt sang past Margot's shoulder. Taking their cue, the rest of the hunters opened fire. Volleys arced across the street like rainbows. Unwitting bystanders *ooh'd* and *aah'd* at the light and sound extravaganza and riffled through their Festival brochures in an attempt to discover which show it was advertising.

They darted beneath an archway, pressing themselves into the shadows, and watched the hunters tear past their hiding-place. 'This isn't going to fool them for long,' she whispered. 'We can't run all night. We need a plan.'

Tom steepled his fingers and raised one eyebrow. 'Double-U, Double-U, Double-U, Dee?'

''Scuse me?'

'What Would Werelock Do?'

'Who?'

'Werelock Holmes?'

Margot shook her head.

'Werelock is a detective by day, vigilante werewolf by night,' explained Tom.

First ghosts, now this, thought Margot. Tonight was one mind-stretching, world-altering revelation after another. 'Werewolves are *real*?'

Tom raised the other eyebrow. 'Don't be ridiculous. It's a TV show.'

'You have TV?' She couldn't keep the amazement from her voice.

'Of course. What d'you think we do all day – hang about old houses floating up and down and going "Wooo"?'

David Solomons

That was precisely what she'd thought ghosts did, but the way he said it, she wasn't going to say so.

'Werelock is an ordinary, mild-mannered ghost detective who can only solve mysteries when he turns into a super-intelligent werewolf during a full moon. It's my favourite show. Though, it's in its seventh season and, if I'm being honest, the stories are becoming a little far-fetched.'

'So, what would Werelock do, then?'

Tom thought for a moment and then dived for his phone. 'Before I left home, I downloaded this.' He touched an icon in the shape of a castle then showed her the device.

She found that if she was very delicate she could hold the AiiiiieeeePhone without her fingers going straight through its ghostly case. When she drew a finger over the screen it barely felt as if she was touching the surface. The title page of the app appeared, and she read it aloud. '"Edinburgh – An A to Dead". A city guide? I have one of these.'

'Not like this one.' Tom tapped a doughnut symbol. A map of the city was instantly overlaid with dozens of similar symbols.

'OK. So I'm guessing these aren't the locations of actual doughnuts,' said Margot.

'The worlds of the Living and the Dead are separated by a curtain,' explained Tom. 'Not a flappy fabric-y sort of curtain, you understand, more of an incorporeal barrier.'

'Yeah, the doughnuts, I get it. Go on.'

264

He indicated the symbols. 'These are points where at some point in the past the curtain was, as it were, pulled back – where our worlds came close enough to glimpse one another. You call these places "haunted". We call them portals. Before Appal invented the Portal Object Originator—'

'That thing your tour guide was using?'

'Exactly. Before the Portal-OO, the only way to cross between worlds was through one of these naturally occurring portals. An old city like Edinburgh has lots of them, so if I can find one that's still active then I should be able to push through from this world back to my own.'

Judging from his app, the portals were scattered about the city, but there was one location around which they clustered like an outbreak of measles. Tonight's final destination felt like fate.

'The castle,' Margot said, stabbing a finger at the map, and then adding a dramatic, 'Dun-dun DUN!' Tom raised his eyebrows in a question, and she shrugged. 'Seemed appropriate.'

It was peak *haar* when they approached the top of Castle Hill. The castle itself was partially obscured. Mist drifted over the ramparts and coiled about the towers.

'I think we lost them,' Margot said, searching the crowds for a sign of their pursuers. 'Let's go.' Before she could take another step, the ground began to shake and the air filled with a terrible din. She felt her whole body vibrate with the sound.

'It's S.P.O.O.C.!' she yelled.

'Uh, no,' said Tom. 'It's the Tattoo.'

Margot was sceptical. 'Tattoos don't make that much noise. My friend Jenna's older sister Jackie got one and she screamed when they first stuck the needle in, but—'

'Not that kind of tattoo,' Tom sighed. 'The Edinburgh Military Tattoo.'

'Nope. No clearer. So what's an Edinburgh Tattoo exactly?'

'Soldiers, marching bands, kilts, and more bagpipes than anyone should ever have to endure.'

'Uh, you know how I said we'd lost them?' Margot began. 'Well, I just found them again.' She pointed back down the hill. The members of S.P.O.O.C. had regrouped and were making their way *en masse* towards their position.

Tom looked at Margot. 'We've got the army on one side and that lot on the other. We're doomed.'

'Yup,' she said with a glint in her eye.

'I've seen that glint before,' said Tom. 'That's exactly the look Werelock has when he comes up with a brilliant plan. But with more facial hair.'

'We've got them exactly where we want them.' She glanced up at the castle and back at Tom. 'Just do exactly what I tell you.'

The hundred or so fully paid-up members of S.P.O.O.C.

marched on Edinburgh Castle. What an annual general meeting this had turned out to be, and the night was far from over! First, fuelled by a rousing keynote address by chairman-for-life Randall McCracken, then tantalised by the sight of a Class *Four* Full Body Apparition on the Royal Mile, briefly outwitted by their prey, and now what appeared to be the same ghostly boy was taunting them on Castle Hill. There he was, registering on every pair of ghost-goggles and Spook-Scopes, waving his arms at them like a drowning swimmer. The cheek! Well, this time he wouldn't get away.

With a tingling battle cry, the ghost-hunters broke into a run and stampeded after the boy. Men and women who had only ever tasted disappointment could suddenly taste … ectoplasm. Nothing would stop them now. They charged onto the long esplanade in front of the castle—

—And came to a crashing halt.

Their battle cry dwindled to a tiny squeak at the sight that met them. Grandstands on three sides formed a vast parade ground illuminated by a row of blazing torches at ground level and floodlights on the ramparts. The floods criss-crossed each other and converged on a battalion of infantry soldiers beating their drums, blowing and squeezing their bagpipes and marching in perfect formation to the bark of a baton-carrying Sergeant Major. Hundreds of hairy knees rose and fell in unison beneath swinging kilts, flags fluttered, flashbulbs popped and a cheer rang out from the audience.

It was about then that the soldiers noticed the intruders, just as Margot had planned.

The members of S.P.O.O.C. liked to think they knew about fear, but no amount of haunted house sleepovers could have prepared them for this. Blood drained from their faces and they turned whiter than a Class Two Spectral Manifestation. A solid wall of soldiers blocked their path. It was like looking up at Mount Everest, if someone had painted it tartan.

Three hundred armed and kilted Scotsmen glowered.

They were not the only ones displeased at S.P.O.O.C.'s unwelcome interruption. The crowds in the grandstands began to boo, even the statues of Robert the Bruce and William 'Braveheart' Wallace, which kept a vigil from either side of the main gate, seemed more stony-faced than usual. Military drums beat, throats filled with roars – and the hunters became the hunted.

'Nice plan,' said Tom admiringly. 'Classic Werelock.'

'That should keep them busy while we find you a portal,' said Margot. Under cover of the rout of S.P.O.O.C, they slipped through the castle gate to begin their search.

'Exactly what does one of these things look like?' Margot asked, as they made their way past the gatehouse. Apart from the doughnut-shaped symbols on the *A to Dead* and a brief glimpse of something blue and glimmering in Riddle's Court, she realised she didn't know what it was they were looking for.

'It's a blue, glimmering doughnut thingy,' said Tom.

Well, that cleared that up.

'Or a pair of tartan curtains hanging in mid-air.'

OK.

'And I have seen one that looked like a running shoe.' Tom tapped a finger thoughtfully against his top lip. 'But that was sponsored.'

'So,' said Margot, 'we're looking for a blue, possibly tartan, doughnut, trainer or window-dressing, perhaps with a logo?'

'Yes.'

Good. Now at least she had a better idea of—

'Except . . . no.'

'No?'

'Mostly, they blend in to their surroundings. All you're likely to see is a shimmer, like a heat-haze. Except it'll feel cold, not hot.'

'An invisible shimmer – are you kidding me?' Margot strode onto a wide terrace bordered on one side by battlements lined with old-fashioned cannons. She stopped in her tracks. 'You mean, like *this*?'

Something glowed amongst the cannons aimed out over the castle approaches. Was that a shimmer? And she definitely felt cold. She held her breath as Tom hurried over.

He studied the evidence and then declared, 'Uh, no. That's an interactive display.'

'Oh.' Margot felt foolish. 'Never mind. According to that map of yours, there are dozens of them around here.'

269

'Margot.'

'Don't worry, we'll find one,' she said, gazing out from the battery across what she could see of the twinkling city through the mist. 'I feel sure of it. Something tells me tonight was meant to be. There's a reason I'm here.'

'Margot,' he repeated.

'I just have to tune in. Hone my sixth sense. Open my Third Eye and—'

'Margot!'

She spun round to see Tom with his arms raised in surrender, standing at the business end of one of the cannons.

'I don't think it's loaded,' she joked.

He didn't laugh. Before she could say another word, from out of the mist strode Randall McCracken, chairman of S.P.O.O.C. The hunched figure of Dora shambled after him, still connected by the electrical umbilical cord. Randall's face was covered as usual by his ghost-goggles. He pushed his Spectre Detector Collector 9000 into the small of Tom's back.

'It's going to take more than the massed pipes and drums of the Scottish army to stop me tonight,' he said with a gap-toothed grin. 'Don't you get it? I've spent my whole life trying to prove ghosts exist. I've put every penny I ever earned into catching someone just like you, *boy*. They called me a madman, said I was unhealthily obsessed.' His shoulders heaved with laughter, and the lenses of his ghost-goggles gave off a silver glow, turning his eyes into blank disks. 'Well, who's the madman now?' Suddenly, he stopped laughing and pointed a quivering finger at Margot. 'And you, don't even think about chuckin' any more cats at me, right.'

Margot held her empty hands up to prove she wasn't concealing a last-ditch tabby. She felt a sudden chill. For a moment she assumed it was the breeze, but then she realised that the *haar* hadn't moved – it lay thick and motionless, much like her dad's hair. And then she saw the true reason for the drop in temperature.

Figures in the mist. A dozen shapes loomed behind Randall and Tom, and for one horrible moment Margot thought that they were more ghost-hunters. But as they drew closer she saw that they were not human. Or, at least, not living.

Ghosts! The oddest mixture of relief and fright swept over her.

A pair of battered leather sandals strode out of the mist. They were attached to the hairiest feet that Margot had ever seen, and she'd watched all the Hobbit films. Legs like tree trunks supported a muscular body clad in leather armour draped with a tartan tunic, beneath which the ghost's broad chest seemed permanently puffed out. His scowling face was daubed with streaks of blue paint. Long, curly hair streamed behind him, as if powered by its own wind-machine. He held a giant sword, point down, planted between his hairy feet. At his back were more warriors with similar blue-striped faces and open-toed footwear.

271

Beside him stood a figure in a suit of gleaming chain mail. Each individual link shone like a jewel, suggesting someone had spent a long time with a packet of cotton wool buds and the silver polish. Over one shoulder he had slung an axe with a curving blade as big as a crescent moon, the sort of weapon that would make a dragon seriously consider booking that holiday he'd been thinking about.

Margot recognised the men at once from their statues that flanked the castle gate. Two of the greatest figures in Scotland's history stood before her, apparently in the midst of a discussion.

'I'm no' saying your monument isn't *nice*,' said William Wallace, 'but you have to admit it's no' a patch on *mine*.'

Robert the Bruce swapped his axe onto the other shoulder. 'I'm not having this conversation again.'

Randall McCracken gawped. If the human jawbone had been capable of separating itself from the rest of the head, as it did in cartoons, by now his jaw would not only have hit the ground, it would have bounced off down the esplanade and be hailing a taxi.

'Randall?' said Dora quietly.

'I see them,' Randall mumbled.

'Aye, well, the only reason anyone's heard of you is because of *that* film,' snapped Robert the Bruce.

William Wallace removed a hand from his sword-hilt, held it up and extended his fingers. 'Five Oscars.' He polished the hand on his tunic.

Robert the Bruce raised his eyes to the heavens. 'You didn't win them! You're not actually in it.'

'Uh, excuse me,' Margot ventured, figuring it was about time someone drew the new arrivals' attention to the pressing situation of, well, if not exactly life and death, at least imminent and dreadful capture. 'Are you here to rescue Tom?'

The question seemed to throw Wallace and the Bruce. They consulted each other in a low mutter.

'Did you bring it?'

'I thought you had it.'

One checked his tunic and the other his armour for whatever 'it' referred to. With a slightly embarrassed look, Robert the Bruce produced a slip of paper and unfolded it, cleared his throat and addressed Tom. 'Tom Caundle?' Tom gave a small, scared nod. The Bruce carefully refolded the paper, tucked it away again, and turned to Margot. 'Yes,' he confirmed.

'You can have the boy!' snarled Randall, swinging his gun away from Tom and levelling it at the other two. 'Now I have a far greater prize.'

'No' bigger than an Oscar, though.'

'Will you give it a rest?'

Robert the Bruce heaved his axe off his shoulder. He seemed to be preparing to engage in battle with Randall, when William Wallace stepped in front of him, saying, 'Leave this to me.'

The Bruce turned to the other ghosts and threw up his hands, mouthing, '*Typical*.'

Wallace marched steadily towards Randall, his hair doing that streaming thing even though there was still no breeze. 'My name is William Maximus Wallace, commander of the Armies of the North, father to a murdered son, husband to a murdered wife . . .'

'Isn't that from *Gladiator*?' said Margot, but no one was listening.

He hoisted his great sword. 'Come ahead if you think you're hard enough.'

Robert the Bruce rolled his eyes. Wallace's supporters banged their swords against their shields and roared. Seemingly undaunted by the jeers or the blue woad, a flint-eyed Randall studied his advancing foe.

'Dora,' he growled. '*Juice me.*'

The battery pack pulsed, the SDC 9000 chimed with a full charge, and Randall squeezed the trigger.

The ghost-catching beam whipped across the terrace like a spitting cobra, and sank its high-energy fangs into William Wallace's arm.

'Gotcha!' said Randall triumphantly.

Never go fishing for sharks if all you've brought is a goldfish net, is *not* an old fisherman's saying, but it ought to be.

In Randall's mind he had caught himself a ghost. However, the ghost in question took the entirely opposite point-of-view.

William Wallace pulled on the line. The smile vanished from Randall's lips as he was lifted off his feet and swung through the air. The cord connecting him to Dora tensed, and she was pulled along too. Wallace whirled the yelling ghost-hunters above his head, spinning them like a cowboy lasso. The battery finally gave out and the lasso blinked from existence. Unfortunately, it cut out just as Dora and Randall swung over the battlements. Untethered, they sailed into the darkness with a dwindling yell.

Margot rushed to the edge of the castle and looked down, squinting through the mist. The ghost-hunters lay groaning on the slope beneath the castle, dazed, but alive. The canopies of a clump of trees had broken their fall.

William Wallace poked his nose over the battlements.

'You've got a good aim,' said Margot, 'landing them right on those trees.'

'Trees?' he grumbled. 'In my day that was a sheer drop.'

Robert the Bruce tapped Tom on the shoulder. 'Right, laddie, time to go home. Portal's just over there – you can't miss it, but it won't be open forever.'

The ghosts turned their backs and began to glide into the mist, picking up the conversation they'd been having when they arrived.

'You should've left those ghost-hunters to me,' complained Robert the Bruce. 'You're always butting in.'

'Relax, Bruce, it's no' a competition,' said William Wallace. 'Sure, I have a major motion picture, but you've got that *great* story about the spider.' He cleared his throat. 'If at first you don't succeed ...'

The rest of his warriors chorused somewhat sarcastically: '... Try, try again.'

There was the sound of ghostly laughter being stifled, and Robert the Bruce muttering to himself. And they were gone.

The *haar* was finally lifting. It had thinned enough for Margot to see across to the other side of the terrace, where tucked in the corner was an empty guard post: a black wooden box just wide and tall enough to shelter a single guard in a bearskin hat. A golden crown insignia shone from the facing under its peaked roof. The air around it shimmered. The portal stood ready.

'I have to go,' said Tom.

It had all happened so quickly. And now it was over. 'Will I see you again?' she said.

'Not sure my parents will let me take the tour any more, not after tonight. They were talking about going on a cruise next year. There's this new liner, the Frightanic ...'

It wasn't fair. They were just getting to know each other. They hadn't had enough time. 'Send me a postcard,' she said. 'Oh wait, I bet you call them something else. Ghostcards! Right?'

Suddenly, Scottish sadcore moped despondently from her pocket. She pulled out her phone. The alarm she'd set before leaving the theatre was going off. She had ten minutes to get back and slip into her seat before her parents noticed she was missing.

'Is that State of Rain?' asked Tom.

She knew that the band were big, but she bet even they didn't know they had fans in the Netherworld.

'From the new album?' he went on excitedly. 'I haven't got it yet.'

Margot made a decision. 'Here,' she said, offering him the phone. 'Take it, please.'

He paused, unsure, then reached for his own phone. They swapped handsets. 'Something to remember tonight,' he said. 'Goodbye, Margot.'

There was nothing else to say. 'Goodbye, Tom.' She closed her eyes and held them tightly shut until the music stopped. When she opened them again, he had gone.

She hurried back down the Royal Mile. The ancient street seemed different somehow. The air felt charged. Or perhaps it was her. She drew out Tom's pearlescent AiiieeePhone and scrolled through his music – the soundtrack to his afterlife. She was about to plug in the earbuds when she passed the entrance to Riddle's Court, where it had all begun just a couple of hours ago. It felt like another life.

'Death abounds here. Thousands died in agony on the gallows, the Plague took thousands more. And their spirits still haunt these dark closes and narrow wynds.'

It was him, the monk whose ghost tour she'd refused

277

earlier that evening. He was running a late tour. Margot carried on walking and his voice faded on the wind.

'Ladies and gentlemen, I give you the most haunted road in the world – Edinburgh's Royal Mile.'

Yeah, she thought, slipping the buds into her ears and pressing 'Play'. You have no idea.

THE NOTHING TO SEE HERE HOTEL

STEVEN BUTLER

None of this would have happened if it hadn't been for my great-great-great grandad, Abraham Banister.

Back in the olden days ... about a hundred years ago ... when everyone wore strange hats and the whole world was in black and white, my gramps went for his usual, morning walk and 'KAPOW!!' changed the future of our family for ever.

According to the boring stories that Dad loves to tell at every family get-together (don't worry, I'll tell it much better than Dad does), Grandad Abe wandered right out to the edge of the beach at the far end of town, and stumbled upon a troll girl – a troll-ette – doing her laundry in the open mouth of a sewer pipe.

Her name was Regurgita Glump, and before anyone could scream 'NO! Wait, Abraham! She's hideous!' the pair had fallen madly in love, run off together and got married in a proper slobber-chopsy, troll ceremony in the sewers under Brighton High Street.

Ha! You weren't expecting that, were you?

So . . .

Fast-forward to a hundred years later, and my family are running the only hotel for retired magical creatures in the whole world.

The Nothing To See Here Hotel.

I'm Frankie. I nearly forgot that part. Frankie Banister. Great-great-great grandson of good old Abraham.

Now you're probably thinking that being a kid who lives in a hotel for magical creatures and has troll blood in his veins sounds BRILLIANT, and I suppose I can see why, but it's not all fairy wishes and sparkly crowns and stuff.

Don't get me wrong. I'm not about to start a story with a load of moaning like Dad would. I love my weird home, and being part troll is pretty cool. It means I can see really well in the dark, which is handy, and my eyes are the colour of shiny, copper pennies (which isn't very handy). Ooh . . . celebrating Drooltide with my trollish relatives is MEGA fun as well. They all come up the loo for a visit and we feast and party for days.

So it's not all bad . . . but it's easy to forget the fun, cool bits after you've been helping Mum clean up when Mr Vernon, The Stink Demon, has been to stay for the weekend, or when you have to spend the whole morning scooping mountains of sardine skeletons out from the bottom of the pool, left behind by Mrs Dunch.

Mrs Dunch is a mermaid, by the way. Berol Dunch. A very old, very wrinkly mermaid, who visits every summer and insists on squeezing into her starfish bikini-top whenever she comes ... BLEURGHH!

Starting to see what I mean?

Things have always been weird in my life. Weird is normal to the Banisters, but it's never weirder than when I'm off school in the summer holidays. That's when the hotel is busiest. When all the other kids in my class are playing on the beach, I'm stuck indoors helping Mum and Dad manage to keep a bunch of magical creatures from wrecking the place.

Sad but true ...

Magical creatures love a bit of chaos. We had a serious drama a few weeks ago, at the start of the summer holidays. A MEGA DRAMA!! THE BIGGEST ONE YET!! Worse than any we'd had before at The Nothing To See Here Hotel. Brace yourself ...

It was a Tuesday. I remember it was a Tuesday because I'd just finished mopping up a spillage on the stairs, and it wasn't the kind of spillage anyone would forget in a hurry.

Lady Leonora Grey has been on holiday from Hampton Court Palace and haunting our staircase all summer.

Ghosts are so weird. They don't need rooms or beds or toilets, so they just rent stairs to wander up and down, moaning to themselves. Some holiday! We've got three ghosts staying in the hotel at the moment. Lady Leonora's got the main staircase near reception, Wailing Norris has got the stairs to the basement, and there's a pair of disembodied legs that run up and down the steps to the back garden, by the pool.

Anyway, if that isn't weird enough, ghosts sometimes just explode bucket-loads of greenish slime called ectoplasm for no reason. It's like a burp or a fart to them, I suppose, and it goes everywhere.

Well, that Tuesday, Lady Leonora was on the upstairs landing, dabbing herself with a ghostly hanky when I got there with the mop and bucket.

'I'm dreadfully sorry, boy,' she chuckled. 'I'm quite sure I don't know what came over me.' If she wasn't completely grey and see-through, I would have sworn she was blushing.

'Don't worry,' I said, trying to smile through gritted teeth. There was slime on everything. It was dripping off the ceiling and the lights, and great strings of gloop were plopping off the door handles into a massive pool on the carpet. It was even running over the edge of the top step. Gross!

'It's not a problem.'

'Oh, you are good, young Francis.'

'Frankie,' I mumbled under my breath. I hate it when

people call me Francis. Mum and Dad only use that name when I'm in trouble. It's their secret weapon.

'What?' Lady Leonora plucked a ghostly hand mirror from mid-air and looked at herself, straightening a lock of hair that had come loose. She wasn't listening. Ghosts never listen. She looked back from her reflection and gasped. 'Ugh! What a mess! This hotel is filthy.' Oh yeah ... they don't have any memory either. When your brain is made from a wisp of smoke, I suppose it would be hard to remember anything for more than a minute or two. 'I really should complain!'

With that, Lady Leonora turned and floated off down the stairs, practising her best moans. I stuck my tongue out at the back of her head, grabbed the mop and started to slop great big globules of ectoplasm into the bucket. When you've lived in a hotel with ghosts on the stairs your whole life, you'd be amazed at how quick you get at cleaning up after them.

I didn't mind really. It's pretty normal for there to be at least one disaster a day at The Nothing To See Here Hotel, and it was only nine o'clock in the morning. That meant we'd got it out of the way nice and early. Once I'd finished mopping, Mum and Dad would probably take pity on me and let me spend the rest of the day watching telly and reading comics in my bedroom.

Ha! How wrong was I?

'FRANCIS!' It was Dad's voice, and it was coming from the kitchen downstairs.

Francis? What had I done now?

'FRANCIS, COME HERE! QUICK!'

I wiped up the last of the mess, left the mop leaning against the wall, and ran down the stairs. Lady Leonora was floating her way back up, screaming and flailing her arms, so I just went straight through her. I love running through ghosts. It feels like ice-cold popping-candy all over your skin.

Heading towards the kitchen, I wracked my brains. What was it this time? Had I left the curtains open in the basement room and turned Ooof the ogre into stone again? Ogres and direct sunlight never go well together. It takes ages to loosen them up again. No . . . no . . . I remember making sure they were closed tight before bed last night.

I ran past the grandfather clock in the hall and smiled at Vlad as I went by its open front. Vlad was a vampire who rented the clock every July. He was hanging upside down where the pendulum should be, humming to himself. 'Good morning, young Francis.'

'FRANKIE!' I yelled over my shoulder.

I got to the kitchen door and stopped. Mum and Dad were standing with their backs to me, looking at something on the table. Both their shoulders were up near their ears, and that's always the first sign that there has been another disaster.

Nancy, the hotel's cook, was on the other side of the table, wringing four of her hands together.

Nancy is a spider. A huge, enormous, GIGANTIC spider. When she stands on her back legs, her head touches the ceiling, and she can easily reach across the whole kitchen to grab the salt and pepper when she is cooking at the stove.

Don't think 'BIG SCARY SPIDER', though, like you'd see in a monster movie. Nancy isn't scary at all. When a giant spider is wearing a flowery apron, fluffy slippers on her four back legs, and sporting a bluish/purplish perm on her head, she soon stops being the stuff of nightmares.

Nancy looked up and saw me in the kitchen doorway.

'Oh, Frankie,' she said. 'We're in a right pickle.'

'What's going on? Mum?' I said. 'Dad?' I headed into the room. Mum turned round and looked at me. Her forehead was all wrinkled with worry.

'Look.' Dad pointed to an open envelope and a letter on the table. Something was really, really wrong. I'd never seen my parents look so stressed. Not even after a coach-load of yetis arrived unannounced last Christmas, and we had to clear out the massive freezer just so they had somewhere to sleep.

I looked down at the piece of paper. There was a fancy emblem at the top and underneath it were the words, BRIGHTON BOARD OF HEALTH: PEST CONTROL.

'We're being inspected, Frankie,' Mum said. She flopped into one of the chairs. 'Someone reported bugs in the food and now a pest control inspector is coming to investigate us.'

'What are we going to do?' blurted Dad. 'We'll be shut down in two seconds. We'll be found out! WE'LL BE RUN OUT OF TOWN LIKE ... LIKE ...'

'Monsters!' Nancy finished Dad's sentence.

My brain started racing. Of all the weird things that went on, nothing like this had EVER happened at The Nothing To See Here Hotel. Who would report bugs in the food? For most of our customers, bugs were the tastiest things in the world and they ordered platefuls of them.

'Who's done this?' I said. 'No one's ever cared about bugs before.'

Mum jumped from her seat, dashed to the window, and yanked on the blind. It shot up, letting in a sudden stream of daylight.

'THERE'S YOUR ANSWER!' she yelled, pointing at the next building along, across the kitchen yard.

In one of the ground floor windows was our meddling, husk of a neighbour, Mrs Flannigan, with a pair of binoculars pressed against her eyes. The old fossil suddenly started flapping when she realised we'd spotted her, and she ducked quickly out of sight. 'SHE'S DONE IT AGAIN!'

Mrs Flannigan runs The Sunny View Hotel next door ... and she HATES us. She always has. Her wrinkly little bonce is filled with jealousy about all our customers arriving, morning, noon and night, even though The Nothing To See Here Hotel has the worst reviews in history.

Oh, I didn't tell you that part either, did I?

To keep humans away and stop them from coming to stay with us, Mum and Dad make sure that we only get TERRIBLE reviews. They type them out every night before bed and send them to the local newspaper, or they use fake names and post angry comments on holiday websites. It's true. If you looked it up, all you'd find about The Nothing To See Here Hotel would be whingey rants saying it was the rudest, most disgusting waste of money on the planet. Dad even has all the 'NO STAR' reviews framed above reception. He's very proud of them.

But it means we're always having to deal with Mrs Flannigan. She never stops spying across the kitchen yard, or trying to get a peek into our windows, and she's always calling the council and complaining 'This hedge is too high ... that coach was noisy and arrived too late ... blah, blah, blah ...' We all know she just wants to get a good look inside and see who all the customers are that flock through our doors. It drives her potty.

'How could you be so stupid?' Mum suddenly snapped at Dad. She was fuming.

Dad looked at the floor and shrugged like I do when I'm being told off.

'What does Mum mean, Dad?' I asked.

'Tell him,' Mum said in her 'Don't Mess With Me' voice.

'I brought the deliveries in while it was still daylight,' Dad mumbled.

'And?' Mum started drumming her fingers on the edge of the counter. I was half-expecting to see smoke coming out of her nostrils like Hoggit, my pet pygmy soot-dragon, who nests in the living room fireplace.

'And I dropped one of the crates ...'

'AND?'

'And it broke ...'

Mum didn't even bother saying '*And?*' again. Instead, she just humphed and stared.

'What was in the crate, Dad?' I said, even though I thought I already knew the answer.

'It was Mrs Venus's beetles ... she'd ordered them specially for Sunday lunch.' Dad looked so miserable that Nancy extended an arm across the table and patted him on the shoulder. 'I tried to scoop them up as quickly as I could, but Flannigan must have seen me do it and ... I was just trying to do something nice for Mrs V.'

I glanced out of the window at Mrs Venus sunning herself amongst the flowerbeds in the back garden. She was sitting in her usual plant trough, scooping up insects from the soil with her long, tendril arms and shovelling them into her spike-toothed mouth.

'When is the inspector coming?' I asked without taking my eyes away from the carnivorous, plant-lady. Mum gasped and hurled herself at the letter on the table.

'I didn't think to check!' she said, snatching the piece of paper and reading it frantically. 'I ... I ... AAAAAAGGGGHHHHH!!!' Mum's face turned red, then white, and then ... she fainted.

In seconds the kitchen filled with people, wandering in from other parts of the hotel to see what all the fuss was about.

'Is it playtime?' Gladys the werepoodle yelled as she bounded from the hallway with a ball in her mouth. She sniffed at Mum for a moment, then started barking furiously as a floorboard lifted up and a gaggle of grubby, potato-sized dust pooks clambered out, complaining about the noise.

'What's all this hollerin'?' came another gravelly voice, as Ooof clomped up the basement stairs. 'Someone startin' a rumpus?'

Next came the Molar sisters (Dentina, Gingiva and Fluora), hobbling in from the conservatory. 'Whath going on, darlingth?' they said in unison. It was nearly always impossible to understand what they were saying because they were all missing so many teeth.

I bet you didn't know that tooth fairies eat nothing but sugar lumps, did you? Ha ha! They have the worst dental hygiene in the whole of the magical world.

Nancy helped Mum off the floor and sat her at the table. Then she quickly spun a blanket out of web and wrapped it around Mum's shoulders. Everybody stood back and gawped.

'What is it, love?' Nancy said, smiling nervously.

Mum opened one eye, then the other. She blinked at us as if it was the first time she'd ever seen magical creatures before.

'What does it say?' Dad poured a cup of tea from the pot by the stove and handed it to Mum. 'When is the inspector coming?'

Mum's bottom lip trembled, and for a split second I thought she was either going to burst out crying or vomit.

'Whath goin' on?' the Molar sisters hissed again. They each stuck out a boney finger and prodded Mum on the arm. 'Tell uth, Mitheth Bannithster.'

'The inspector is coming t ... t ... t ...' Mum's right eye started twitching and it looked like she might faint again.

'I think she'th gone off 'er rocker!' said the Molar sisters, blinking through their oversized spectacles. 'Bonkerth ath a bonker!'

'THE INSPECTOR IS COMING TODAY!!'

It didn't take long to arrange a hotel meeting with all our guests. They crowded into the living room, shrieking and grumbling, wanting to know what was going on.

'Ladies and gentlemen, settle down,' Dad yelled over the squabbling. 'SETTLE DOWN!'

It's at times like that meeting, I remember just how weird my family's life is. Seeing our customers huddled around the living room sofas reminded me of a scene from my *Ministry of Mutants* comic books.

Mum shuffled me over to two chairs against the far wall. We sat together. Hoggit trotted towards us, puffing out a thin wisp of smoke, and flopped across my lap. His black scales were hot and I could feel the gentle rumble of fire coming from inside his belly.

'Will this take long?' said Gladys. She was perched on the arm of the sofa and had almost completely turned back into a human. The only trace of poodle left on her was a pair of white pom-pom ears that hung on either side of her face. 'I'm getting my paws massaged at twelve o'clock.'

'What's all this about then?' came a voice. For a moment no one could figure out where it came from, until a man's toupee wig glided into the room.

'Ah, Alf ... it's nice to see you ... or not ... please take a seat,' Dad said, trailing off into a mumble.

Alf had been in a science laboratory accident when he was young and has been invisible ever since. Even though it's impossible to see him, he's still super embarrassed about going bald in his old age and he insists on wearing a toupee. He has loads of the things in different styles and colours that he keeps in a suitcase under his bed. No one really understands why, but it makes it easy to spot him as he dodders about the hotel.

'I'm afraid we have some bad news,' Dad said. 'We received a letter this morning and ...'

'WE'RE ALL GOING TO DIE!' wailed Wailing Norris.

'No, Norris,' Dad snapped back. 'If you let me finish, I'll explain ... and ... well ... you're already dead.'

'Aren't we all?' Vlad chuckled from behind his massive

sunglasses and sombrero sun hat that he always wore outside the grandfather clock.

'I KNEW IT!' Norris bellowed.

'Oh, be quiet, you blithering idiots,' said Lady Leonora. She plucked a ghostly fan out of the air and flapped it in front of her face dramatically.

Dad took a deep breath.

'As I was saying ... we received a letter and ... well ... we're going to be inspected ... today ...'

'By a dentitht?' the Molar sisters asked. 'Oooooh, lovely.'

'No, not a dentist,' Dad said.

'BY A VET!?!?' Gladys suddenly turned back into a poodle and dived behind the sofa, whimpering to herself.

'No, not a vet either,' Dad's face was getting all blotchy. That always happened when he was nervous. 'We're being inspected by a health inspector. A human ...' Dad lifted up the letter and glanced at it for a second. 'Mr Croakum,' Dad read. 'He'll be expecting the hotel to be spotless, and checking the kitchen is stocked with only fresh, human food and ... and ... he doesn't know that magical creatures stay here, and if he sees even the slightest clue that any of you aren't normal, everyday people, he'll scream and run away and will close down the hotel for ever.'

Everyone was silent for a moment until ...

'An outsider? Here?' the dust pooks squeaked. 'It's madness!'

'What if his first name is JACK!?!?' bellowed Ooof. He

swung a few practice swings of his club ... just in case.

The ghost legs jumped from the sofa and started running laps around the rug.

'This is TERRIBLE,' said Mrs Dunch. She was sloshing about in the inflatable paddling pool that Dad had blown up for her in the middle of the room. Her tail kept slapping water over the carpet, and every time she moved, all the other guests gasped, bracing themselves in case her tiny starfish bikini-top snapped and sprung open.

'Everyone, please calm down,' Dad yelled over the commotion.

'Unless!' Mrs Dunch threw her arms in the air, and pulled a face like she'd just had the most amazing idea in the history of amazing ideas.

Everyone froze and stared at the wobbly, old mermaid. She looked like a grape that had been left in the sun for too long.

'Unless ...'

'Unless what?' said Dad.

'Unless I just drown him.' Berol Dunch smiled as sweetly as if she'd just announced she was going to bake the health inspector a cake.

'Oooh! Thath a good idea,' the Molar sisters agreed, clapping their hands.

'NO!' Dad nearly fell backwards with shock. 'We're not killing anyone, Mrs Dunch!'

'I'll squish him!' said Ooof.

295

Steven Butler

'I'll suck his blood!' Vlad cried.

'I don't mind eating him,' Mrs Venus said. She was sitting in a wheelbarrow that Mum had hauled in from the garden, leaving a line of mud right down the hallway. 'I've never tasted health inspector before.' She gnashed her flytrap mouth hungrily, and her tendril arms shivered with excitement.

'NO! NO! NO!' Dad looked at Mum in desperation. She walked to Dad's side and blew the loudest whistle you'd ever heard. Mum was great at whistling. Dad says it's because she's always full of hot air. Ha ha!

'Ladies and gentlemen,' Mum said. She was using her 'Don't Mess With Me' voice again. 'We have two hours to make this place pass for a human hotel. TWO HOURS! If we don't, it will be closed forever and you'll have nowhere to stay on your summer holidays.'

Nobody spoke. I think they were even holding their breath.

'Me, Frankie and Mr Banister can't do it alone. We haven't got enough time or enough hands. We need your help.'

'HELP!' Lady Leonora gasped. 'You mean us … do … chores?'

'What about my paw massage?' Gladys said, coming out from behind the sofa. She was now a bizarre mix of poodle and granny. Her face and hands were human but the rest of her was covered in curly, white fur with a pom-pom tail.

'Ooof tired …' grumbled Ooof.

296

'I'm meant to be working on my tan,' came Invisible Alf's voice as his toupee floated towards the door.

That was it. I nudged Hoggit onto the seat next to me and ran to Mum and Dad, as everyone started shuffling away.

'There won't be anyone to mop up your ghost-glop when we're closed down, Lady Leonora!' I shouted. The she-ghost stopped in the doorway and turned around slowly.

'There won't be bowlfuls of sugar, or paw massages, or fresh compost and bucketfuls of beetles, if the hotel is gone.'

Nancy joined Mum and Dad from the corner of the room.

'There'll be no more sardine-head-sundaes,' she said, looking at Mrs Dunch, who had wriggled out of her paddling pool and was making a break for it on her elbows.

'I can't rustle up any washing-machine-lint omelettes if I don't have a kitchen to cook in.'

The dust pooks looked horrified.

'NO LINT OMELETTES!?!?' they screamed.

We stared at our customers. Our customers stared at us.

'If we get away with this,' Dad said, 'I'll let you each order one very special dish for next Sunday lunch. Anything you want . . .'

'Seaweed pancakes?' said Mrs Dunch.

'Scab flakes!' said Vlad.

'Fudgey-caramel-brittle-bites, with extra thweetner?' the

Molar sisters cackled. Fluora coughed and a tooth flew out and rattled across the floor.

'Cockroaches!' said Mrs Venus, rocking so wildly she nearly uprooted herself from the wheelbarrow.

'Anything,' Dad said. 'But . . .'

The cheering stopped. All eyes were on us.

'You have to help . . .'

Well what do you think happened? Magical creatures are all just as greedy as they're weird. There was no way they'd pass up on the chance to scoff themselves silly. Everyone agreed to help out and before we knew it, the hotel was in full swing. There was SO much to do.

Don't get me wrong and think that The Nothing To See Here Hotel is a scruffy, dirty place. It's just that magical creatures don't really care about cleaning, or dusting, or wallpaper patterns, or cushions, or flowery bed spreads. Most of them never sleep, and they seem to spend all of their time looking for food, gossiping, or making even more mess.

Mum and Dad locked the crates of bugs, bags of scabs and buckets of fish heads from the kitchen fridge in the cold basement, out of sight. Ooof wasn't too happy about it, but Mum put him and Vlad in charge of swapping all the magical books on the reading room shelves with boring, humany-type stories, and they were far too busy to complain. I was in the living room helping Nancy, and every now and then I could hear Vlad reading the human titles out loud, and Ooof grumbling from across the hall.

'Fishing for beginners?' Vlad read.

'Humans are weird, weird, weird!' Ooof moaned.

'We'll have this done in a jiffy,' Nancy said as she clattered about on the living room ceiling. From the floor, I yanked down the tattered curtains at every window, and in no time, she had spun a beautiful, new pair of curtains in its place. Her hands moved so quickly, they were a total blur.

Gladys was galloping about, picking up stray objects that looked like they didn't belong in a human hotel, and burying them in the garden.

Mrs Dunch was back in the pool scooping out the stinking remains of her massive, fishy breakfast onto the patio, whilst Mrs Venus held the hose in her toothy grin and washed the bits of sardine heads and tails away into the bushes.

In the kitchen, the dust pooks were up on the counter, crowding around the sink. As a team they dunked and rinsed the dirty plates, and Lady Leonora and Wailing Norris did their best to dry them with a ghostly breeze. Ghosts are brilliant at making breezes, in case you didn't know, but they kept getting distracted and wandering off.

The Molar sisters had unpacked their magic wands for the special occasion and they cackled happily with one another. Every time the ghosts finished drying a stack of washing-up, the sisters would flick their wands and the plates and dishes flew out of the kitchen door, hurtled down the hall, and arranged themselves neatly on the tables in the dining room. Knives and forks and glasses jumped from the drawers and cupboards, following the plates until every place was set for dinner.

The only person who managed to get out of helping was Alf. He must have slipped his toupee off in all the rumpus, and the last we saw of him was a few footprints crossing the freshly mopped floor in the hall.

'That ungrateful weasel,' Mum snapped when she realised he'd done a runner. 'I should have known not to trust someone who walks around naked all day, except for a ratty wig.'

We were just about to head back to the kitchen when ...

DIIINNNGGG DOOONNNGGG!

'The door!' Dad half-yelped, half-whispered as he ran out of the living room, dragging the vacuum cleaner behind him. 'He's here! Mr Croakum!!'

Everyone came darting from all directions and huddled around Mum and Dad. We watched in silence as a silhouette appeared in the frosted glass of the front door. It belonged to a short, round man carrying a cane and a briefcase.

'Here goes,' Mum said, heaving a deep breath. She took a step towards the door and stopped. 'What are we doing?' Mum turned to us with an expression of shock spreading across her face. 'Quick, everyone, back to your rooms. Disguise yourself ... AND ACT NATURAL!'

There was panic for a second as magical creature jostled with magical creature.

'Move!'

'Out of my way!'

'Mind my tail!'

THUD THUD THUD THUD THUD …

'Right,' Mum said, once Vlad had dived into the grandfather clock and closed it, and the last of the dust pooks had waddled to a low air vent on the wall and clambered through. 'Shall we?'

She grasped the handle of the front door, and opened it.

'Mrs Banister, I presume?' Mr Croakum said. He was even shorter and rounder than his silhouette in the window made him look. He was like a bread roll in a suit. He peered over the top of his glasses and squinted, glaring past Mum, at me and Dad in the hallway.

'Yes,' said Mum. 'Please come in.'

'If I must,' he replied and walked slowly past her, eyeing the reception with a look of disgust. His cane tick-tapped sharply on the floorboards as he went, making him sound like he was clockwork. 'I've heard some very disturbing reports, Mr and Mrs Banister. Very disturbing indeed.' With that he swung his briefcase onto the nearest dresser and pulled out a clipboard. Attached to the front of it was a piece of paper with a list on it. 'Now then, what's first?' he said, tapping his pen on the first item of the list.

Mum glanced nervously at me and Dad. *Here we go,* I thought to myself, and I crossed my fingers for good luck.

301

'Bedrooms,' said Mr Croakum. 'I want to inspect one of your rooms.'

We all had the same idea at once ... Invisible Alf's room!

Alf was by far the tidiest of the customers at The Nothing To See Here Hotel, and since he'd slunk off without helping, it was the least he deserved to have Mr Croakum poking about in his things.

Dad led the way up the stairs and unlocked the door to Alf's room.

'I'm sure you'll find it's all very clean and ...'

Dad opened the door and gasped as seven mini balls of hair waddled out of Alf's room and darted about on the carpet between our feet.

'What the—?' Mr Croakum jumped back. 'Rats!'

For a second I couldn't figure out what I was looking at, as each hairy shape jostled about, cooing to itself. Then I spotted that each one was a different colour and style from the last. THE DUST POOKS! When Dad had told everyone to disguise themselves, they must have shimmied up the inside of the walls and raided Alf's wig collection.

Here's a tip for you: never trust a dust pook to make the right decision. Their heads are full of lint and belly button fluff. I nearly laughed out loud when one of the pooks winked at me and gave me a tiny thumbs-up. They actually thought they looked like humans.

'RATS!' Mr Croakum said again, scribbling furiously on his clip board.

'No. .. no . . . not rats,' Mum blurted. You could practically hear the cogs whirring inside her brain. 'They're Guinea pigs.'

'Guinea pigs?'

'Yes,' I said. 'They're my pets. I was playing in here earlier and forgot to put them away in their hutch. Sorry.'

Croakum glared at me through his spectacles.

'They're very clean,' said Dad. 'Aren't they, son?'

I nodded. 'Actually they're a special breed of extra-clean Guinea pigs. That's why Mum and Dad let me have so many.'

We watched as the dust pooks formed a chai, disappeared along the upstairs landing and bobbed round the corner.

'Interesting,' mumbled Mr Croakum. I could tell he was searching our faces for signs of lying, but the Banisters were experts at bluffing to other humans and we smiled like everything was completely normal.

'As you can see,' said Dad, pushing Alf's door open wide, 'everything is neat, clean and well ordered.'

The short, fat health inspector poked his head into the room and looked almost angry at how tidy it was. 'Yes,' he said, scowling. 'I see . . .'

If there's one thing I learned on that Tuesday lunchtime back at the start of the summer holidays, it's that no matter how weird we think magical creatures are . . . they think we're weirder.

Every time we came across one of the customers trying to pass as a human, the day got that little bit crazier and Mr Croakum got a lot more bad-tempered.

Downstairs in the hall we ran into Ooof wearing flippers, one of Mum's dresses and an enormous straw hat. After having to pick Croakum up off the floor when he fell down with shock, Dad somehow managed to convince him that the ogre was our distant cousin Hildegard from Switzerland.

'It's that brisk Alpine air,' Mum said, dusting off Mr Croakum's jacket and hurrying Ooof away in the direction of the basement. 'They grow up big and strong in the mountains.'

Okay . . . let's get on with it. I did promise I'd tell it better than Dad, after all.

I would love say it all went brilliantly. I'd also love to say that we completely fooled Mr Croakum and we passed the health inspection . . . but we didn't.

The more he explored the hotel, the further away our chances of ever managing to trick Croakum got.

I'm not even joking! If finding Vlad hanging upside down in the grandfather clock wasn't enough to make him suspect something, then stumbling upon Mrs Dunch sitting in the flooded bathroom, wrapped up like an Egyptian mummy in soggy towels probably did it. To make matters worse, when Mr Croakum opened the bathroom door and a sea of bathwater and bubbles washed out around his feet, Mrs Dunch cheered and invited him to join her in the tub.

'I thought that was the most human-ish thing to do!' she told us later on.

We tried MEGA HARD to make up excuses. Dad told Croakum that Vlad was a clock repairman, and Mum said Mrs Dunch was just really, really friendly. But it was no good. Every strange thing that happened was noted on Croakum's clipboard. We'd barely seen half the hotel before he'd practically run out of space to write on the paper.

But it wasn't until he sat in the dining room for lunch, that it all fell through. Yep . . . we were foiled by a sandwich.

'I'll have the deluxe afternoon tea,' Croakum said.

'Coming right up, Your Royal Highneth.' Dentina Molar was dressed in one of Dad's work suits with a bowtie made from a stained, old dish cloth. The sleeves of the jacket hung way past her short arms and she flapped them about as she toddled back to the kitchen. 'OOOOH! It'th gonna be deliciouth!'

You're probably wondering what on earth Dentina Molar was doing, serving a suspicious health inspector. Think about it . . . Nancy usually took all the orders for mealtimes. How do you think things would go if a gigantic spider calmly walked up to the table, smiled and said, 'How would you like your squashed-fly-fritters served? With or without frogspawn mayo?'

We had no choice. The minute Croakum arrived, poor Nancy had to scuttle off to the attic and hide herself away with a good book for the afternoon.

It was all down to the Molars.

Mum and Dad tried to keep our health inspector friend talking, to distract him from the sound of cackling and smashing plates coming from the kitchen, but it wasn't working.

'So, Mr Croakum ... do you inspect many hotels?'

CRAAAAAAAAAAASSSSSHHHHHH!!!

'It really is a lovely day, don't you think?'

THUUUUUUUUUUUUUUUUUUDD!!!

It took nearly an hour before the three Molar sisters appeared again, pushing the tea trolley. They were so short, they could barely see where they were going.

'Your deluxth afternoon tea,' Gingiva said, smiling a rotten, gappy smile.

'Jutht you wait,' beamed Fluora. 'We took exthra care!'

We all stared at the top of the tea trolley. WHAT HAD THE MOLAR SISTERS DONE?

Heaped in the washing up bowl from the sink was a mountain of soggy-looking sandwiches. There was a teapot with an old sock dangling out of the lid and a pile of toothpaste tubes with a dollops of jam on top were arranged on a doily.

'What would you like to try firtht?' Dentina asked. She was holding a dainty pair of silver tongs and she snapped them together, grinning.

Mr Croakum stared at us on the other side of the table with a look as if to say: *This is a joke!* We stared back at him and held our breath.

'How about a thandwich?' said Dentina. She grabbed a sandwich with her tongs and slapped it onto Croakum's plate. 'Lovely!'

Croakum slowly picked up the soggy bread and eyed it suspiciously. 'Ummmmmm ...' he said. He slowly raised it to his mouth, took a bite out of the corner and chewed.

'BLEEEUUURGGGHHH!' Croakum spat the blob of sandwich across the room and dropped the other half. The two slices of bread fell open on the tablecloth and I could see that they had been filled with sugar lumps. SUGAR LUMPS!?!?

'THAT'S DISGUSTING!' he coughed.

'How rude,' said the Molar sisters in unison. 'We'll have you know them thandwicheth are yummy!'

'That's it!' Mr Croakum yelled, his face getting redder and redder. 'What's going on here?'

'I don't know what you mean?' Mum said. 'Didn't you like the ...'

'Don't try to fool me, Mrs Banister. Something strange is going on and I'm going to get to the bottom of it.'

With that he hopped off his chair, barged past the Molar sisters, and ran into the kitchen.

'Quick!' Dad said, and raced off after the little man.

*

In the kitchen we found Mr Croakum yanking open cupboard after cupboard and hurling their contents on the floor. Dog treats, cockroaches, huge lumps of seaweed. You name it . . . it was now splattering over the tiles.

'WHAT IS WRONG WITH YOU PEOPLE?' Croakum screamed. 'ARE YOU INSANE?' He spun around so fast, he let go of his walking stick and it flew through the air.

'Hooooowwwwllll!' Gladys ran into the room from the conservatory in human-form. She leaped off the ground and came to land as a white, curly poodle with a walking stick in its mouth.

Croakum gasped. His eyes were the size of dinner plates. 'I . . . I . . . I . . .'

We had been rumbled.

'Monsters!' Croakum looked like he'd seen a ghost. Well . . . actually he had . . . at that moment Lady Leonora and Wailing Norris floated through the wall.

What were we going to do? We couldn't let him escape now that he knew our secret. The Nothing To See Here Hotel would be closed down in seconds.

Vlad, Ooof and Nancy came in from the hall and blocked his exit. The dusk pooks crowded around his ankles, armed with teaspoons and Mrs Venus poked her head through the kitchen window.

'Now listen here,' Dad said, stepping closer to the gawping man. 'We can talk about this.'

'Magical . . .' Croakum stammered. His eyes were darting

about like the inside of a pinball machine. 'Magical creatures!'

'Yes,' said Mum. 'There are magical creatures here. You've found us out. But ...'

'MAGICAL CREATURES!'

'I know,' Dad said. 'But if you give us a second, we can explain and ...'

Mr Croakum screamed. His face was doing something strange. What started off as a look of total shock, twisted into ... well ... unless I was going crazy ... he was smiling!

'Why didn't you say so?' Croakum threw back his head and laughed.

'That's done it,' Nancy said. 'He's gone crackers.' She walked up behind him and steadied the laughing man's shoulders with her four hands.

'Magical creatures ... here!?!?'

'Please don't tell anyone,' I said. 'This is our home. I know it looks scary but ...'

'Scary?' Croakum stopped laughing and stared at me. 'Scary? It's not scary, boy ... it's ... it's ... TERRIFIC!' He opened his mouth and his tongue shot out and stretched almost the whole length of the kitchen. It slapped stickily onto a fat cockroach crawling up the wall then snapped back between his teeth. Croakum chewed it slowly. 'Delicious!'

Ha! I bet you didn't see that coming, did you? Neither did I, if I'm honest.

Turns out that Mr Croakum had been keeping his secret

his whole life and had no idea there were other people like him in the world. I've never seen anyone as happy as that froggy-health-inspector was in our kitchen. It took a lot of coaxing to stop him from hopping about all over the walls.

At first Croakum wanted to give The Nothing To See Here Hotel a shining report and five stars, but Dad managed to convince him to give us an unimpressive, one star review and offered him a permanent room.

Croakum leaped at the chance. He resigned from his job that day, and has been staying with us ever since. He's even having a little romance with Mrs Venus. I know … bleeuuurgh! They sit out in the mud patch together, eating insects and giggling.

So what started as a MEGA DRAMA turned out to be a pretty standard afternoon for us. Weird is our normal, after all.

At least one disaster every day.

And … we even got it out of the way by dinnertime.